W9-BNX-723

continued . . .

The More the Terrier

"Johnston's heroine's compassion for her four-legged friends and their owners make her a likable heroine. Readers who enjoy a mystery heavy on this subject matter will enjoy Johnston's latest."   —*RT Book Reviews*

"[A] first-class whodunit . . . Well written . . . Johnston, an animal lover and advocate, is using her writing not only to give readers a great mystery but also as a platform for animal issues and awareness, and I find that commendable."
                                        —*Debbie's Book Ba*

"[A] great story . . . Enjoy!"   —*Once Upon a Romance*

Beaglemania

"Gutsy Lauren Vancouver easily wins over the hearts of animals in need—as well as readers . . . [Vancouver is] an ardent advocate for homeless pets."
                    —Rebecca M. Hale, *New York Times* bestselling
                                        author of *How to Tail a Cat*

"Animal lovers will delight in a new series filled with rescued dogs and cats needing loving homes. Lauren Vancouver is a determined heroine who will solve the intriguing mystery at her private shelter."
          —Leann Sweeney, author of the Cats in Trouble Mysteries

"Lauren Vancouver is a likable, efficient amateur sleuth, passionate about her work and smart about how she goes about her investigation."   —*Mysterious Reviews*

Teacup Turbulence

LINDA O. JOHNSTON

BERKLEY PRIME CRIME, NEW YORK

THE BERKLEY PUBLISHING GROUP
Published by the Penguin Group
Penguin Group (USA) LLC
375 Hudson Street, New York, New York 10014

USA • Canada • UK • Ireland • Australia • New Zealand • India • South Africa • China

penguin.com

A Penguin Random House Company

TEACUP TURBULENCE

A Berkley Prime Crime Book / published by arrangement with the author

Berkley Prime Crime Books are published by The Berkley Publishing Group.
BERKLEY® PRIME CRIME and the PRIME CRIME logo
are trademarks of Penguin Group (USA) LLC.

For information, address: The Berkley Publishing Group,
a division of Penguin Group (USA) LLC,
375 Hudson Street, New York, New York 10014.

ISBN: 978-0-425-25997-9

PUBLISHING HISTORY
Berkley Prime Crime mass-market edition / January 2014

PRINTED IN THE UNITED STATES OF AMERICA

10 9 8 7 6 5 4 3 2 1

Cover art by Jennifer Taylor, Paper Dog Studio.
Cover design by Rita Frangie.
Interior text design by Laura K. Corless.

Teacup Turbulence *is dedicated to all of the amazing people in pet rescue, and most especially those with vision and enthusiasm enough to determine where a particular type of pet is most likely to find a new home fast—and then figure out a way to get him or her there!*

Plus, I've done it before, but I particularly want to thank my wonderful editor, Michelle Vega of Berkley Prime Crime, as well as my fantastic agent, Paige Wheeler of Folio Literary Management. I love working with both of you!

And once again, it's nothing new, but I dedicate this book to my amazing husband, Fred, who's my anchor as my mind flits around creating and writing. I additionally thank my adorable dogs, Lexie and Mystie, just for being there, and for giving me orders . . . and love.

Acknowledgments

As with all my Pet Rescue Mysteries, *Teacup Turbulence* is fiction, but it's themed around something that's real—in this case, pet rescuers who are dedicated to the idea of moving homeless animals to a place where they're more likely to get adopted fast. Many of them are affiliated with groups that fly pets from one place to another, as in *Teacup Turbulence*. Others drive them long distances for the same purpose.

I want to particularly thank Hanoch Kohl for his information about this kind of flying, which he and others do in their spare time for Wings of Rescue.

Chapter 1

"But I was here first!" The senior lady with frizzy yellow hair stood in front of me on the crowded sidewalk. She placed her hands on her hips and looked up with her lower lip jutting belligerently.

I tried to smile, in case this woman was a better potential dog adopter than she initially seemed. "That never matters in pet adoptions. What's important is finding the right home for each of our wards."

That's my job. My passion. I'm Lauren Vancouver, director of administration of HotRescues, a wonderful shelter in L.A.'s San Fernando Valley.

"Well, I'd give the best home to Marvin," the woman said. "I'm sure of it." Now she sounded almost desperate.

We both turned to look at the long row of temporary wire enclosures that ran along the HotPets storefront behind us. Most contained dogs of all breeds and sizes. Farther away were crates that held cats.

I was happy to see lots of people staring into the fenced areas and crates, talking to the HotRescues staff and volunteers who'd come to help at this mobile adoption event, and petting leashed dogs brought out at an interested person's request. An occasional round of barks hid the happy exclamations of potential adopters.

The closest pen held the miniature pinscher Marvin—along with some medium-sized terriers and a French bulldog mix.

Next to me on the other side, Naya Fayler regarded me with a worried expression. "I don't want to cause you any trouble, Lauren," Naya said. "But I really love Marvin."

I'd gathered that. It was why I'd accompanied her and her husband Tom out here so quickly. I had sensed a pending adoption.

"And in fact, we were here first," Naya continued. "I filled out the application to adopt Marvin before we went inside to the party."

Naya appeared to be fiftyish, with short chestnut hair framing her face. Laugh lines crinkled at the edges of her blue eyes, but her skin was otherwise smooth and flawless, possibly the result of an excellent makeup job. She wore a dressy white tunic top over a long black skirt.

Tom stood talking with Bev, a senior, experienced HotRescues volunteer who had come along to help at this mobile setup. Tom's hair had receded from his forehead a bit, and what was left was salt-and-pepper and short. He had wide cheeks and a broad smile revealing slightly yellowed teeth. He was the manager of the new subsidiary, HotPets Bling, and I had just met him and Naya at the party taking place in the store's back room to celebrate the HotPets empire's fifteenth anniversary.

Dante DeFrancisco, the company's owner, was also Hot-

Rescues' generous benefactor. After he'd introduced me to Naya and Tom, they'd told us about their immediate bonding with Marvin, and that's when I'd accompanied them outside.

Not that I generally liked to okay a same-day adoption. But Dante had vouched for them. And they clearly were animal lovers.

Bev had handed me the Faylers' adoption application that they'd filled out before. I, too, was dressed up, in a shimmering blue shirtwaist dress and low heels—very different from my usual HotRescues knit shirt, jeans, and athletic shoes.

I skimmed over the form, very aware of the still emotional woman at my other side. I had an idea how to handle her but needed to deal with this first.

Everything on the application seemed in order. The Faylers owned their home, had no other pets right now—they'd lost an aging dog a month before—and were empty nesters.

As I was, sort of. My daughter and son were away in college, although Kevin's school, Claremont McKenna College, wasn't too far from L.A.

I noticed something of particular interest. "You used to run your own pet-grooming chain?" I asked.

"That's right," Tom said, joining us. "But we sold out a few years back—nice profit, too, I might add. I already knew Dante from the pet industry, and he offered me a job with HotPets."

And under hobbies . . . "You fly a plane?" I'd seen all kinds of hobbies listed on our application, but this was the first time I'd seen that the potential adopters were pilots.

"Yes—it helped us visit our grooming shops all over the western U.S. before. Now we just do it for fun."

All seemed fine. In fact, it was better than a lot of applications I reviewed and approved.

That was a relief, since I would have had a difficult time vetoing an adoption by an executive of HotPets.

But that woman remained at my side, eagerly awaiting my decision on Marvin. I motioned for her to join me, and we meandered toward the parking lot at the far side of the walkway.

"I'm really sorry," I lied. I'm seldom sorry about anything, and finding a great home for one of my shelter dogs was not something I ever regretted. "But there are extenuating circumstances beyond who saw Marvin first." I didn't need to explain that the Faylers had seen him first anyway. "Have you looked at any other dogs here?"

She shook her head sadly. "I just really liked him."

"Well, let's go see who else might fit even better with you."

I nodded at Bev as I started leading the woman through the crowd and along the line of temporary pens. I mouthed the words "Okay" and "Marvin" and nodded toward the Faylers. Bev knew me well enough to understand that I'd approved the adoption. She'd have questions, but she could notify a staff member to start the paperwork.

"Now, let's see," I said to the lady. "I'm Lauren, by the way."

"I'm Georgia."

"What are you looking for in a dog, Georgia?"

"Tiny," she said. "And cute. Just like the ones in those HotPets Bling ads."

She gestured toward the small digital sign in the Hot-Pets window, which looked like a miniature of the large billboards now set up in many areas within L.A. Notwithstanding how controversial these bright, illuminated signs were around here, Dante—wealthy and smart entrepreneur that he is—had negotiated the city council's permission to post a lot of them in commercial areas.

The ads also ran on TV, all featuring adorable teacup-sized

dogs—Pomeranians, Pekingese, Maltese, Chihuahuas, and more—that wore the new decorative HotPets Bling collars with attractive, unique, and fun designs set into them using rhinestones and other faux jewels—all attached, of course, in a way that they couldn't be chewed off and swallowed by the animals wearing them. The actual collars were made in all sizes, though, so one could be bought to fit any dog.

Right now, there was a little Yorkie on the ad wearing a bright pink collar inset with designs of dog bones topped with halos, all in shiny gems. I had to admit the dog and his adornment were extremely cute.

Sure, a lot of other dog collars existed that were decorated in fun ways, including sparkling designs, but these were really special, like everything from HotPets.

The Bling ads had gone viral here in Southern California. Dante was using this as a test market, and so far it had been a huge success. I was delighted for him.

What was less delightful was how the ad campaign had caused a run on teacup-sized dogs. There used to be an overabundance of small dogs in this area, but now they were being adopted from HotRescues almost as soon as we saved them from the high-kill shelters and made them available. The same was true for every other local shelter, even the public ones.

Lots of lives were being saved that way, and I was delighted.

But the popularity of the tiniest dogs made them harder for interested adopters to find. No wonder Georgia had tried to glom immediately onto small min-pin Marvin.

"Marvin is a cute pup," I told her. "But I'd like to introduce you to someone else." I hurried her toward the far end of the enclosures—as fast as possible in the crowd.

Unsurprisingly, one of the volunteers, Ricki, already held the dog I had in mind in her arms, showing her off to a young couple with a child.

Not necessarily a good match anyway, I thought.

"Sorry, Ricki," I said. "I want to introduce Mimi to Georgia." I gestured toward the woman beside me as I took the little Yorkie from Ricki's arms. "Why don't you show Frenchy to these nice people?" That was the French bull mix—small, but not as small as Mimi, and given up by a household that had kids. Seemed a better fit.

"Mimi?" Georgia said, reaching over to pat the little Yorkie. "Oh, she's perfect! Can I take her home?"

"I'll have a volunteer come here and let you play with her," I said. "Then you can fill out an application. We'll need to check some things out, but if all goes well you may be able to pick Mimi up at HotRescues tomorrow."

Unless someone else with better credentials put in an application on her. In that event, all would not go well for Georgia.

What mattered was the care and future of the dogs.

"That's wonderful!" she said. I showed her to one of the sturdy card tables we'd brought along to make it easier for people to fill out applications, and handed Georgia one. She started to work on it immediately.

I was finally able to check on the Faylers' adoption of Marvin—almost complete, fortunately. Because Tom worked for the HotPets empire, I decided to waive the usual nominal fee we charge for adoptions.

"No way!" Naya exclaimed. "Paying that amount is the least we can do. In fact, I'd love to come volunteer at HotRescues someday. Could I do that?"

"Sure." I explained the process, which consists of an application and a visit to HotRescues for a tour and orientation.

"Great. Tom will do it, too, won't you, dear?"

"Do I have a choice?" Tom said, aiming a fond smile at her.

I checked over their paperwork quickly, accepted their payment via credit card, and then we were done.

I rose and walked to the nearest fenced-in area, where I bent over to pick up Marvin, who was small and warm and lovable. When I put him near my face, he licked my nose. "Gonna miss you, guy, but you're going to have a really great life now."

I assumed that was true, with obvious pet lovers like the Faylers. But even so, I'd check to be sure.

I clipped one of our standard leashes on the ordinary collar we always provided with adoptions. "Looks like Marvin needs one of the HotPets Bling collars," I said.

"Count on it," Tom responded. "In fact, let's go back to the party."

We passed through the large HotPets store, probably one of the best and busiest in the chain. Why not? It's in Beverly Hills.

In moments, we were back in its vast stock room, where I picked up a flute of champagne from a table near the door.

The place had been reorganized for the party. All the huge crates and other containers holding items sold at the store that weren't on shelves had been stacked along the edges of the room and draped with metallic fabrics to feign elegance.

The center was filled with partygoers. Songs with animal themes played around us, although the volume on "Hound Dog" and the rest was low enough not to ruin the crowd's ability to chat.

I quickly rejoined the group of friends I'd brought along: Matt Kingston of Los Angeles Animal Services, the really great animal-loving man I'm dating; my good friend, veterinarian Carlie Stellan, who also has a weekly TV show on the Longevity Vision Channel; and her boyfriend Liam Deale, who works at a local TV station.

"How'd it go?" Carlie asked.

"Very well, I'm delighted to say."

"Glad to hear it." Our host, Dante, had joined us.

So had his lady friend, Kendra Ballantyne, an attorney and pet-sitter. She wore a lovely sapphire-colored gown, much dressier than I'd ever seen her in before. Of course I'd mostly seen her dressed for one or the other of her careers.

"Lauren, I'd like you to meet more of my staff." Dante was a good-looking man even when not dressed up in an elegant suit as he was today. His wavy hair was dark and immaculately styled, his expression as pleased as I'd ever seen it as he waved the people accompanying him toward me. "This is the store manager, Marie Ellis, and I think you've already met my new administrative assistant, Sheila Sheltron."

"Hi, Lauren." Marie was the first to approach. "I'm happy to meet you." Her voice was high but not shrill, and it seemed to peal with sincerity. "I've already met the adorable dogs and cats you have out front for adoption. Thanks so much for bringing them." Her grin was huge, and her grip, as we shook hands, was firm and quick. If personality helped to sell pet supplies and food, I wasn't surprised that she ran this huge Beverly Hills store.

"Glad to meet you, too, Marie." I'd held other HotRescues mobile adoptions at HotPets stores, but this was my first one here—and I had a feeling it wouldn't be the last.

"Hi, Lauren." Sheila moved around Marie to face me. I had met Dante's assistant before, since I visited the HotPets headquarters often to keep Dante updated on how things were going at HotRescues. She'd worked there for a few months now. Sheila was a tall, slim woman. She wore a soft gray dress that looked tailored and professional, but her black stiletto shoes yelled out for attention.

"Hi," I said. "Did you help to arrange this party?" I didn't wait for her proud smile and nod before adding, "I thought so. It's wonderful. And," I said to Dante, "happy birthday to HotPets, and many, many more."

He laughed. "You'd better be right. Ah, look who's here."

Tom and Naya joined us. Naya was, unsurprisingly, hugging little Marvin. "He's ours now!" she exclaimed with glee.

"He needs a Bling collar." A guy I didn't know had joined us.

"Of course," Naya said. "Lauren, have you met Chris?"

I hadn't, but I was quickly introduced to Chris Mandrea.

"Are you also with the HotPets Bling subsidiary?" I asked.

"He's not only 'with' the company," Naya said, "he's crucial to it. He designs all the collars and other things that will eventually be released and sold."

I was a bit surprised that Naya was the one to sing his praises rather than her husband. Tom was the manager of the new subsidiary, not her. But it was great to see Naya's enthusiasm.

"Yep, I'm the heart of Bling." Chris's grin was implike in his long and narrow face. He wore a shining lilac shirt tucked into jeans, which, though not as dressy as the outfits most of us wore, still looked sufficiently partyish.

As Dante, Kendra at his side, went off to play host some more, I talked with the Faylers and Chris about HotPets Bling. They were clearly proud of the new products— justifiably, it sounded.

But after a few minutes, Tom said, "I think we have to get ready for . . ."

"For the big secret?" Naya asked, holding Marvin against her cheek. The sweet little min-pin licked her nose.

"What secret?" I asked.

"You'll see," Chris said, and the three of them walked off.

I glanced around. My invitees were now off on their own, drinking more champagne and eating hors d'oeuvres displayed on a table in the center of the room. I joined them, still wondering what the big secret was.

I considered mentioning it to my friends, but there wasn't time. Nearly as soon as I rejoined them, Matt handed me another glass. "The servers said Dante is about to make a presentation and we should all be prepared to celebrate."

I wasn't about to resist more champagne. And my curiosity had definitely been piqued.

Tom Fayler joined Dante in the middle of the crowd, while Naya continued to hold Marvin. "May we have everyone's attention?" Tom called.

Conversations were loud enough that those of us who heard started clapping to encourage silence. Soon, the crowd was quiet.

"I want to thank you all for coming to our celebration," Dante said. "And right now, I want to add to it. We have something special for all the women who are here."

Chris walked up to Dante and Tom holding a large box.

"This is both to add to our celebration—and to promote our new venture," Dante said. He gestured first to Kendra. "Got a little present for you." When she joined him, he pulled something out of the box and went behind her. With flair, he put the item around her neck and fastened it.

It was a light blue necklace that resembled a sparkling dog collar—a HotPets Bling collar.

"Thank you," she said. Judging by her conspiratorial grin, she'd known this was coming.

All of Dante's staff helped to distribute the necklaces contained in the box. I received one identical to Kendra's—highly appropriate, I thought, since the knit shirts all HotRescues staff members wore, including me, were also blue. Not that I was likely to wear this necklace around our shelter. At least not all the time.

But I really did like it. It was artificial leather containing faux jewels set in the same designs as those in the smaller Bling dog collars—this time, several grinning pooches.

Once all the necklaces had been given out, I decided it was time to make a spectacle of myself. I hurried to Dante's side.

"Thank you," I said, loudly enough for the whole crowd to hear. "I'd like to make a toast." I held up my champagne flute and waited while the crowd had time to figure out what I was doing and hold up their own glasses. "Here's to Dante DeFrancisco, to HotPets, and HotRescues. And, today especially, here's to HotPets Bling. I hope that the new products do as well on the market as I'm sure we all believe they will. In fact, I wish them all the success and popularity that we can imagine. May HotPets Bling become the best-known dog collars in the country!"

Chapter 2

"That's quite a necklace," Nina said.

I had just walked into the HotRescues welcome room from our parking lot. My number one assistant, Nina Guzman, had remained behind to oversee any visitors to the shelter that day, along with the volunteers who had stayed behind to help. We'd brought with us only a fraction of our pets available for adoption, and there were plenty remaining behind who also deserved good homes.

Plus, since it was a weekend, a lot of visitors typically came by to check out our animals. I'd called Nina on my way back, and she'd confirmed we'd been busy that day.

"Like it?" I asked, fingering it. I intended to change clothes right away, but I knew the necklace looked good with my dress. I hadn't had an opportunity to look in a mirror, but I figured the blue of the collar must set off my green eyes, at least somewhat. It would certainly contrast nicely with my dark hair, which I kept short so that I didn't need to fuss with it while working.

"I sure do. It wouldn't be an example of HotPets Bling, would it?" She grinned. No one was more aware of the relationship between HotRescues and HotPets than Nina, and she of course knew where I had been.

"What makes you think that?" I said, kneeling as Zoey, my beloved Border collie–Australian shepherd mix, barreled out from behind the welcome desk, which was covered in faux leopard-print veneer. In my absence, she'd hung out there with Nina. "Hi, girl," I said as I hugged her.

"Just a guess. Don't suppose you've got any extra, do you?"

"Well, I just happen to have . . ." I reached into my tote bag and pulled out a necklace in white for Nina and a dog collar in black, both with the requisite Bling faux jewels in the same cute patterns I'd seen before.

Nina stood and ran around the welcome desk almost as fast as Zoey had. She hugged me, too, as I handed her the necklace. "You're the best, Lauren."

"Of course." I buckled Zoey's new collar on without removing her old one with its identification information attached.

Nina had come a long way since I'd hired her. She still got frazzled now and then, but nothing like the way she had at first, while she was still recuperating from an abusive marriage.

Now, her former angst had disappeared from her face, ironing out its earlier wrinkles, which had seemed out of place on someone in her midthirties. Her eyes remained large and waiflike, still framed by the bangs of her long brown hair. She was a real animal lover and sometimes volunteered at the L.A. public shelters.

She glanced around. "Want me to go help bring things inside?" She knew the drill. After a mobile event, we had to bring back not only the pets—except for the rare few I allowed to go home on the spot—but also all the fencing, crates, and other equipment.

"That would be great," I said. "Give me a minute to change clothes first, though."

I hurried down the hall to my office, where I closed the door behind Zoey and myself and took off my good shoes. I then carefully removed the necklace and hid it at the bottom of one of my desk drawers. At last, I pulled off my dressy outfit and replaced it on the hanger where my HotRescues uniform—the blue staff shirt and jeans—had hung. I put them on, and then my athletic shoes. Now I felt more comfortable.

Dressing up that way reminded me of how I'd worn suits and other professional attire recently while observing some of the filming of *Sheba's Story*, about the saving of some stray poodles. The director had been murdered then, and I'd gotten involved with finding out who'd done it.

Never again. Nor had I encouraged the head of the movie studio, who'd hinted about doing a film on how I'd helped to find the killer.

Finally, I returned to the front, Zoey at my heels. Nina was still behind the desk.

"Cinderella back from the ball," she commented, looking at me in my usual clothes.

"Guess so," I said. I didn't make any comments about princes, even though Matt was as good-looking as a prince any day. "Anyhow, if you're ready to go help, I'd appreciate it."

"Sure." But, standing, she hesitated. "First, how'd we do?"

I told her briefly how well the event had gone—not only

the party, but the mobile adoption, too. "We brought back several applications I'll need to follow up on. I did allow one immediate adoption—little Marvin went home with the manager of the HotPets Bling subsidiary and his wife."

"How about Mimi? Did you get many applications on her?"

"One, and I discouraged any more, since the lady's information looked good. She'll be in tomorrow to follow up."

"Mimi's our last toy dog," she said, as if she needed to remind me. "And I doubt we'll be able to rescue any from the public shelters."

"Me, too," I agreed. "Matt's still on notice to tell me if any tiny dogs are brought in to Animal Services that need rescuing, and I may also hear about them as a New Hope Partner"—New Hope is a program of L.A. Animal Services where private shelter members are officially informed when pets become available for them to take in—"but lately they're adopted as fast as any here."

Nina looked down at the HotPets Bling necklace that remained in her hands. "Thanks to these things." Her voice sounded wry. "Maybe I should give mine back."

"Won't make a difference, and in some ways it's great to know that at least one class of dogs is safe, even in the high-kill shelters in this area."

"But not everywhere," Nina reminded me.

"No, not everywhere." I let my voice drift off as I pondered the irony. "Anyway, why don't you go around back and help for a while? Zoey and I will take charge up here."

"Fine." I watched as Nina's slim body, clad almost identically to mine, headed down the hall past my office and out the door into the kennel area.

"Come here, Zoey." I slid around the counter and sat at the desk behind it, carefully saving everything on the computer screen, including Nina's e-mail. My dog settled by my feet.

Then I began a computer search.

I'd gotten an idea while talking to Nina about how rare teacup dogs were in the L.A. area these days. We might not have enough to adopt out, but surely other areas of the country had some that were in need of saving and rehoming.

All I had to do was find them and get them here.

Yeah, as if either was easy.

But I found that the first part actually was.

As a long-time private-shelter manager, I'd developed a list of Web sites for other rescue organizations all over the U.S. There were even some online groups where we traded information.

I began with the places I referred to most, where I knew the administrators, or at least had heard enough to respect them.

Nothing on their sites. I sent a group e-mail out explaining our predicament in Southern California.

To my surprise, I got responses nearly immediately. *Check out what's going on in Janus County, Missouri, near Springfield*, was the gist of all of them.

I Googled the public shelters in that area and got links to a bunch of media sites and the articles and newscasts they'd published.

There had been a gigantic puppy-mill rescue nearby. The dogs had been bred in huge numbers and horrible conditions, and local authorities had finally shut them down, rescuing those that remained alive.

For now.

There weren't enough private shelters or fosterers in the area to take them all in. Some help had come from larger cities nearby, but they hadn't been able to accommodate them all. If they weren't rescued some other way, a lot of those poor little dogs would wind up being killed.

There were too many teacup dogs there. Not enough here. The answer was obvious—and yet how could I get a large quantity of endangered dogs from Missouri to California?

First things first, though. I checked online to learn who was in charge of the rescue. Unsurprisingly, that was a nearby public shelter. I looked up the person in charge— Director Juliet Ansiger—and sent an e-mail explaining who I was and letting her know that I, and probably others in Southern California, were in the market for a lot of small dogs. I didn't go into detail, but I mentioned that a recent ad campaign showing teacup dogs had ramped up their local popularity.

I spent a while editing what I'd said, making sure it made sense, and then I hit the send button.

And waited. Not that I just sat there. In fact, a family of four with two teenage daughters came to check out the dogs available for adoption here. I chatted with the Clertons and was glad to hear they were most interested in a midsize dog.

We had plenty.

I couldn't leave the front desk until Nina returned, so I used the phone system to send out a general page for someone to come up front to accompany some visitors into the dog areas. The person who showed up first was Mamie Spelling, my former mentor. I'd lost track of her for a while, and the now senior citizen had unfortnately become a hoarder. I'd helped to rescue the animals in her possession—and later had also helped to clear her of a murder charge.

The once-confused lady was now much more alert, and she volunteered at HotRescues often.

"Hi, Lauren," she said, coming down the hall from the door to the kennel area. She was in her late sixties, short, with curly red hair. "Can I help?"

"Sure," I said. "Please introduce these nice people to a few of our medium-sized dogs." I rattled off the names of some I thought would be most appropriate—shepherd mixes and Labs and more—and sent them on their way.

I returned to the computer. There were a lot of possibilities, if Ms. Ansiger was okay with the idea of HotRescues helping, but no answer jumped out at me.

A pet airline existed, but it would undoubtedly be prohibitively expensive to rent an entire plane. Even so, I could check with Dante to see if he'd be willing to foot the bill.

The Best Friends Animal Society's Los Angeles group had begun a system called Pup My Ride, where people drove rescue pets from one area to another. That was a possibility, but even if it could be worked out, it might take a while.

There were also several organizations that flew rescued animals from places where there were few adopters to those where people craved that size or type of pet. That might be the best possibility, but I needed more information.

I decided to call Matt to see if he had any ideas, but I got his voice mail.

Next, I called Carlie. With her veterinary practice and TV show, she was usually a font of knowledge.

Fortunately, I reached her at her hospital in between patients. "I've heard a lot about those rescue organizations where volunteers fly from place to place," she told me. "It's often done in a relay. I haven't featured any on my show yet, so I can't tell you offhand which are the best."

"If they work, that sounds like a perfect solution," I said. But just then Mamie returned, so I told Carlie I'd call her back later. The Clertons wanted to put an application in to adopt Albert, a gray miniature poodle mix who'd been around HotRescues for a while.

He was one of those who was a mystery dog to me. I'd no idea why a smart and friendly pup like him was still here.

But now he might finally get a new home—provided that I approved the Clertons.

They had to complete the application, but I chatted with the father and kids while the mother worked on it. Their situation sounded fine. They had no other pets at the moment, so we didn't have to check for compatibility.

We talked animals and lifestyle and their home— owned by them, so no lease issues. All the while, as I conversed with them, my mind also swirled around the small dogs needing to be rescued and the possibility of one of those organizations with pilots helping out.

Pilots. That jabbed something in my mind.

The Faylers were pilots, and they liked animals. Plus, they'd offered to volunteer at HotRescues.

Maybe we could solicit their help. But I'd see if there was an established way first.

At last the application was complete. I went over it with the Clertons. All looked in order. I preferred when our part-time shrink, Dr. Mona Harvey, could work on an adoption, but she wasn't around today. I'd use my own judgment.

Still, I never wanted buyers' remorse to unravel one of my adoptions. "Why don't you think about it overnight?" I said. "I'll need to check out a few things, but it looks good to me. I'll call you, but you'll probably be able to come back for Albert tomorrow."

"Really?" squealed the teenage girl. Her brother beamed. So did the parents.

"See you tomorrow, then, Lauren—unless you tell us otherwise." That was the mother.

I had a feeling that Albert would be going to his brand-new home first thing tomorrow morning.

Mamie had been sitting nearby, watching and listening. "I introduced those people to their new best friend," she said after they'd left. Her smile was enormous, and I didn't shy away from giving her a hug.

"Yes, you did," I said.

Nina returned to the welcome room just then, looking tired.

It was pretty late, almost time for her to go home. But when Mamie left, I couldn't help sharing with my second-in-command not only that Albert would probably be going home tomorrow, but that I'd learned about some teacup dogs in dire need of being rescued—and my dilemma about how to go about it.

"Have you contacted Airborne Adoptions?" she asked right away.

"What's that?"

It turned out to be a charitable organization that did exactly what Carlie and I had been discussing: flying animals in need from one area to another, where they would be welcomed.

"I've read a lot about this group," Nina said. "Others, too, but this one seems to be rising in popularity—and success. They do flights in relays. They've even taken small dogs to Canada, since it sounds like they don't have enough small dogs there."

"That's great!" I said.

And I knew what I'd be doing when my staff and volunteers left for the evening.

I only hoped I got a positive response from Director Juliet Ansiger.

Chapter 3

Next time I checked my e-mail, only a few minutes after the last time, a message was finally waiting from Juliet Ansiger. She sounded thrilled about my inquiry and, yes, a lot of teacup-sized dogs were still available and definitely in need of rescuing.

I quickly sent her my phone number and heard my ringtone almost immediately. It was seven o'clock here, so it had to be nine o'clock where Juliet was.

"Hello?" I tensed my other arm on my desk. I really wanted this conversation to go perfectly. I intended to save as many of those little rescues as I could.

Zoey must have sensed my concern, since she stood up from where she'd been curled up on the floor and put her head on my lap as I sat on my desk chair. I petted her comfortingly.

"Lauren? This is Juliet. I'm so glad to hear from you. Tell me a little about your shelter."

I quickly extolled the many virtues of HotRescues, although I didn't mention how generous Dante was. I didn't want her contacting him for a donation, although I'd request funds for this major rescue if I needed them. I was protective of him—partly because I wanted to make sure he'd always be there for HotRescues and the animals we saved.

I did explain why HotRescues and a lot of other private shelters in Los Angeles might be able to find many small dogs new homes, thanks to the charming HotPets Bling ads.

"That sounds really promising. But you're all the way on the West Coast. We need to find a way to get our dogs to you."

"I'm working on that," I told her, and then suggested a relay via Airborne Adoptions.

"That's one I've heard really good things about."

"Great. If you have any other ideas, please feel free to look into them. Meantime, I'll move forward on my end and will definitely keep in touch."

"Wonderful. Oh, Lauren, I really hope this works. There are so many—and they're so adorable. And in danger."

"I'll do everything I can to help them, Juliet." I said good-bye and hung up.

Meanwhile, I'd stopped petting Zoey and was using my free hand to do another computer search. I found the home page for Airborne Adoptions. They were headquartered in the DC area. I doubted I'd reach anything but an answering machine at this hour.

I had to try, though. Lots of little dogs' lives were at stake.

Unsurprisingly, I got a recorded voice that asked me to leave a message. I did, explaining briefly who I was and what I wanted.

Then I said they could call me back as early as six AM L.A. time tomorrow.

Which they did. I was lying in bed at my home in the gated Porter Ranch community with Zoey at my feet, when my phone rang. I glanced at the time.

Six o'clock on the dot.

"Hi, Lauren?" said the voice as I grumbled hello. I'd been awake, but just barely.

"Yes?" I tried to sound livelier. "Who's calling?"

"Mike Relfer from Airborne Adoptions."

I was definitely awake now. "Yes, Mike. I take it you got my message."

"I sure did. I've heard about all those small dogs rescued from that puppy mill. In fact, some of my pilots in the area contacted me and offered to fly them somewhere, but I always put out feelers before contacting the rescue organization with possession of the animals so I can suggest where we can take them. This time, we had a lot of concerned rescuers but no takers."

"Well, you've got takers now."

"We have a problem, though. Most of our pilots are located in the east, or even the middle of the country. Usually, depending on distance, we do air runs as relays, with a pilot team dropping the animals off at one airport, to be picked up by another and taken elsewhere. That can happen a couple of times more. That way, no one has to make a very long run—a good thing, since most volunteers are doing this on their own. Sometimes they get a contribution of gasoline, but not much more. Thing is, we don't currently have any volunteers who can fly the animals any farther west than Las Vegas."

I hesitated for only an instant. "I'm not certain yet, but I may be able to find someone."

"Really?" Mike sounded excited. "Do you think they'd be interested in joining our network for future rescues, too?"

I laughed. "Let's take things one at a time. I'll ask if they can help this once, and then we'll see about more."

I promised to get back to him as soon as I had any news, positive or negative.

When I hung up, I looked at the phone. Only six fifteen. Dante would be awake, but it was too early to call him. And I'd want his okay before asking the Faylers to help.

I showered, dressed, fed Zoey, and prepared to head to HotRescues.

By then it was seven o'clock. And this was a quasi emergency.

Sitting at my small kitchen table with a newly brewed cup of coffee in a mug in front of me, I called Dante.

I didn't have to say much before he caught on. "Of course you should contact Tom. Sounds like a good fit, and knowing him, he'd probably be delighted to help not only in this rescue, but in others as well. Naya, too. Let me know how it goes."

"Is it okay to call this early? I apologize, by the way."

"No need. This is important. And knowing Tom, he's probably already at the office." He gave me Tom's contact numbers.

I hung up and stood, pouring some more coffee into my mug to warm what was already there. When Zoey danced a little circle in front of me, I let her into my fenced backyard, watching her even as I pushed in the number for Tom Fayler's office phone.

Tom answered so fast that it seemed he could have been waiting for the call.

As it turned out, he was.

"Hi, Lauren," he said, almost before I'd identified myself. "I just got a text message from Dante. If you're calling to find out if Naya and I would fly out to pick up some of those small rescue dogs, the answer's a definite yes!"

Chapter 4

"We need to get on our way," Tom said.

"Sounds good." I stood on the tarmac at Van Nuys Airport with Naya and him, beside their small plane—a Cessna, they'd told me.

It was nearly twenty-four hours since I'd spoken with Airborne Adoptions for the first time to put this air rescue together.

Yesterday had been extremely busy, both helping with the logistics of this long-distance rescue and performing my regular duties at HotRescues. For one thing, several adoptions had resulted from the mobile event at the Beverly Hills HotPets. I'd approved the new homes for both Mimi, the Yorkie, and Frenchy, the French bulldog mix.

But staying at the forefront of my mind and heart was what was about to happen today, starting now.

Well, not really now. Some of it had already been happening farther east.

A noisy plane took off, but I refrained from holding my ears. When I could hear again, Naya assured me, "We'll stay in touch, Lauren." Wearing a lot less makeup than at the HotPets party, she appeared more matronly. But some youthfulness came through, thanks to her black T-shirt with the HotPets Bling logo on the front, a representation of a dog collar with glittering rhinestones set into the shape of—what else?—a dog collar.

Her apparel made all the more sense when she told me that the managers of a couple of Vegas HotPets stores were meeting them and acquiring a box each of the HotPets Bling collars to introduce in a fairly low-key way at their shops.

A big rollout, complete with the ads and hype we'd seen here in L.A., would follow. No doubt it would be a success there as well.

"I'll be waiting to hear from you," I said to encourage her to make good on her promise.

Beside her, Tom was a little dressier in a button-down shirt, although it wasn't tucked into his jeans. He wore tennis shoes and a huge smile on his round face. The HotPets Bling manager obviously loved to fly.

They'd already shown me around their plane. It seated four comfortably, although the two backseats were where they had piled the boxes filled with collars.

The area behind the seats was stacked with crates from HotPets, in which they could enclose the small dogs they were about to pick up. HotPets—rather, Dante—had also paid for the gasoline for their trip. No surprise.

I knew nothing about planes, large or small. Flying was not one of my favorite pastimes, although I took commercial flights when I needed to on vacations, usually with my kids—but since both were in college, our vacations together were on hold.

Occasionally, too, I went on trips related to pet rescue, primarily going to conferences about saving animals and meeting administrators of shelters from other areas.

I'd never ridden on a private plane. Didn't think I wanted to. But of course I would if animals' lives were at stake.

Fortunately, I didn't have to, at least not now. These people were doing it all. And I couldn't express to them enough how much I appreciated it.

"Thanks again," I called as they climbed the steps into the plane. "From me, and from all those little dogs whose lives you're about to save."

"Just seeing them safely here will be thanks enough," Naya hollered barely audibly over the engine of a landing plane. The meetings in Vegas, too? I wondered cynically.

Heck. They, and Dante, deserved any additional benefits they could derive from this generous expedition.

The plane door closed behind her.

I got a call from Naya a few hours later.

I was in the kennel area of HotRescues helping to clean an enclosure where a setter mix named Mabel had shredded not one, but three fluffy toys.

With us for a little more than a week, she had just been released for possible adoption after a vet visit and our standard quarantine. The toys she'd been given before were chewy ones, not stuffed animals.

No more stuffed animals for her.

I wriggled out of Mabel's enclosure as my phone rang in my pocket. Mabel wanted to follow, and I had to make sure she didn't. I'd come back and lavish some hugs on her later.

I glanced at the caller ID. The number wasn't familiar, but I had a good idea who it was. I hadn't programmed the

Faylers' numbers into my phone yet, but this was around when I'd hoped to hear from them.

"Hi, Lauren, it's Naya," confirmed a female voice that sounded somewhat grim. Had something gone wrong?

"Hi. Where are you? Do you have the dogs with you?"

Her laugh also sounded more brusque than humor-filled. "We're about to take off from Vegas. We do have some dogs with us, though there are fewer than we'd originally thought. Apparently the Missouri shelter found a sanctuary that took the rest in—temporarily, at least—to keep them safe. Our bringing these guys to L.A. is a bit of an experiment."

"Experiment?" Something didn't sound right about this.

"I'll tell you more when we're there." Obviously, she couldn't talk right now. Because of timing—or because someone was with her? "We need to see how quickly you can rehome these guys, for one thing."

"If they're as cute as I assume they are, that'll happen fast."

This time, when she spoke, her voice sounded genuinely excited. "Cute? You just hold on. We're about to show you the epitome of cute. Well, except for our little Marvin, of course. We left him with our daughter for the day. We'll see you in about an hour. Will you be at the airport?"

"Count on it."

With only a dozen little dogs and their crates expected, I aimed the HotRescues van toward the airport rather than having my shelter's handyman, Pete Engersol, drive it while I caravanned after it in my Venza.

Why only a dozen? Sure, that was a lot, but quite a few more had been saved from that puppy mill. I realized that

the people from the shelter where they'd first been taken
didn't know me except for my initial phone conversations
with Juliet Ansiger. Even so, my having the dogs, keeping
them safe, and finding them new homes as fast as I could
would be a lot better than whatever had been done with
them.

Don't get me wrong. Sanctuaries are wonderful places,
and many take extraordinary care of animals in their
charge. But those animals are usually ones that can't otherwise be rehomed easily—like some of the senior and dis-
abled animals at Save Them All Sanctuary, one of my
favorites.

But at least all those puppy-mill dogs had apparently
been taken to a place where their lives weren't in danger.
Unless you counted danger as including failure to get a
new, loving home.

That was where I could really help.

But for this first load, I, or at least HotRescues, was
apparently on trial. Considering what the HotPets Bling ad
campaign had done to help adopt out huge numbers of teacup pets in the last month or so, I'd no doubt that I'd find
this first dozen dogs homes within a week or two. Three at
the most.

Meantime, I'd negotiate to get another bunch here for
rehoming as soon as possible.

It was the middle of the day on a Monday. Traffic on the
short drive from Granada Hills to Van Nuys Airport was
sparse, so I got there fairly quickly and parked the van. I
got out and waited beside it, watching the not-too-distant
runways for a small plane resembling the one the Faylers
had introduced me to.

It arrived about fifteen minutes after I did.

I did get to see and hear two other small planes land

first, but their shapes and darker colors were different from the beige-and-blue one I sought.

When I spotted the Faylers' plane, I stayed where I was, watching it land and then taxi to the same spot where I'd gotten my tour. I waited until it, and its propellers, came to a complete stop.

Maybe only a dozen dogs to start with was a good thing in some ways. I pulled a bunch of leashes from behind my seat. The dogs would all need to be walked before being put back into crates for transportation to Carlie's animal hospital for their first checkups here, our standard procedure.

I knew that the Faylers would help me walk the dogs. Three people, twelve dogs, maybe two at a time . . . It shouldn't take too long.

But when I got to the plane and walked around to the side where the door was open, I was surprised to see a woman standing there talking to the Faylers. The runway and tarmac were fairly isolated, and I hadn't seen anyone walk up to the plane.

Had she ridden with them?

It turned out that, unfortunately, she had.

She spotted me walking toward them nearly immediately and stared. My first impression was that her expression was accusatory.

Accusing me of what? I wondered.

"Hi. Are you Lauren Vancouver?" she asked.

"Yes, that's Lauren," Naya told her. Naya held a tiny, black toy poodle in her arms, snuggling it against her cheek. I felt sure that little guy would find a new home in no time. I wanted to hug him myself.

"She's the administrator of HotRescues," Tom said, "the really great shelter we've been talking about. The one that's affiliated with HotPets." He was holding a little gray Chihuahua mix. Another easy one to find a home for—especially when she licked Tom's cheek.

The woman didn't even glance at Naya, who was beside her. She had no dog in her possession. "I'm Teresa Kantrim." She didn't hold her hand out but merely stared at me with deep blue eyes that looked as hard as the fake sapphires on the Bling collars.

"Hello, Teresa," I said, then glanced quizzically toward the Faylers.

Tom responded. "Teresa is a staff member at the Janus County, Missouri, shelter that rescued all those little teacup dogs from the puppy mill. She's very concerned about them and considers our bringing this dozen here an experiment."

I felt my body stiffen, as if this woman had insulted me. I told myself she didn't know me, and it was a good thing she cared that much about the animals. But I didn't believe it.

Even so, I said, "I'm delighted to meet someone who cares that much about rescue animals. Welcome, Teresa." As I've said, I'm prone to lying when necessary. I didn't yet find this lady welcome, but maybe she'd change my mind. "Right now, I want to see all our new temporary residents. Do they have names?"

"Not yet," Tom said.

"Can we give them the names of gems like the faux ones in the HotPets Bling collars?" Naya asked.

"Great idea!" I enthused. "Really appropriate. Can you help me get them out, walk them, then put them in the van? I need to take them to The Fittest Pet Veterinary Hospital for an initial exam before bringing them to HotRescues." That information was for all of them. I doubted that the

Faylers knew our protocol, even though Tom worked for
Dante.

"Where is that vet located?" Teresa asked. "I'll want to
check them out."

Of course you do. I again reassured myself that this
woman must really care about the animals or she wouldn't
be acting so domineering and nasty.

"Not far from here—Northridge. Do you know this area
at all?" *And do you have your own transportation?* I really
didn't want to offer her a ride.

"Please give me the address," she said. "I brought the
address of your shelter. I'll want to check it out, although
I'll only be here for a few days."

And where are you staying? Another question I didn't ask.

She answered it anyway—both questions, in fact. "My
cousin is supposed to pick me up here any minute. I'm
staying with her."

"Great." I said that rather distractedly, since Tom had
begun bringing the small crates from the plane. Naya was
holding both of the dogs I'd seen them with before, and she
deposited them in one of the first two crates Tom carried
down the steps.

"These two got to ride on our laps," she said with a
smile. I didn't meet Teresa's glance but figured she hadn't
been holding a dog, though that would have been safer than
having them in the pilots' arms.

But the Faylers were experienced flyers. They must
know their capabilities.

"How fun," I said. "Bet they enjoyed that." Then I asked
Tom, "Can I help?"

We formed a line, with Tom the one who entered the
plane for the crates.

Since I was younger than either of the Faylers, I toted the crates down the steps, handing them one by one to Naya, who put them on the ground.

Teresa looked younger than my own mid-forties, but she just stood there watching. Another reason for me not to become immediately fond of her.

As we worked, I looked inside each crate, talking softly to the dogs, who mostly appeared scared. A few whined. No wonder. They'd been through a lot already and didn't understand that things were about to get a lot better for them.

I told them so, though, and hoped my soft tone was reassuring.

Eventually, all the crates were out of the plane, and then we did another relay to the HotRescues van, all the while watching, hearing, and smelling the bustle of more small planes taking off and landing near us, people getting in and out, a lot of activity.

I insisted on removing the dogs from the crates and giving them short walks on the leashes I'd brought. I also passed out poop bags. While walking dogs myself I wasn't able to keep track of those being walked by others, but I hoped they'd all produced.

Even Teresa walked a few dogs. Maybe she really did care about them, and it was just people she had no interest in getting along with.

Soon, we were done and put the restless pups back into crates, which we then organized in the van. Teresa had talked on her phone a couple of times, and as we loaded the last crate another car pulled up.

"That's my cousin," Teresa said. "Did you write down the vet's address?"

I did, though I wasn't thrilled that I was likely to see Teresa again shortly. But I'd be cordial, for the dogs' sakes.

"You're heading there right now?"

"That's right. This is Elsa, my cousin," she said as a large, smiling woman who looked to be in her midtwenties joined us. Turning to Elsa, she said, "We need to go to a vet now."

"Okay," Elsa said. Maybe she was used to being told what to do. Or maybe she truly was fond of her cousin.

"Are you going there, too?" Teresa demanded of Naya and Tom.

"Nope," Tom said. "We've done what we promised, flew all those guys here." He gestured toward the still open back of the van and the crates inside. Some dogs barked restlessly, mostly in shrill, little-dog voices.

"Thanks again," I said to the Faylers.

"I will see you again, won't I?" Teresa demanded, facing Tom and Naya. "I need to talk more about the dogs. Other things, too."

Like what? She didn't say, but she earned a glare from Naya.

Naya's voice was soft, though, as she said, "I'm sure we'll run into each other while you're around. At least we will if you really want to help Lauren find these dogs good homes."

"I mostly want to make sure she does a good job of it," Teresa said. She had toted a carry-on bag from the plane. "I've heard a lot of weird things about how animals are treated in L.A."

"Weird?" I demanded. "What's weird is how these poor guys were treated before. Now, they'll be just fine. You can stay here as long as you want to assure yourself of that.

And to make sure you understand how well we'll do with rehoming the others you left behind."

"I intend to stay as long as necessary," Teresa said. "There's a lot around here I want to learn more about." She glared at Naya first, then Tom, as she said that.

I wondered what she wasn't saying.

Chapter 5

I knew the staff at The Fittest Pet Veterinary Hospital well, since it was where we always brought the HotRescues animals. I called Carlie as my van and its wonderful contents neared the veterinary facility.

As a result, several vet techs and others were waiting outside in the back parking lot of the pink stucco building.

"They're so adorable!" gushed Sher, a tech dressed in the standard turquoise scrubs that they all wore. She grabbed two crates from the back. "Do these two have names?"

"None do yet," I told her. "But my staff's working on it." I'd called Nina and told her Naya's suggestion about using the names of jewels, and she'd promised to come up with a list that could work.

Sher grinned. "I'll be eager to hear them." She strode toward the clinic's back entrance.

Everyone who'd come out to meet us got a crate to handle. I did, too.

The hospital's structure formed a one-story circle around a courtyard, where the animals could be taken out for walks or games if they were well enough. I knew I'd like the place even if the chief vet wasn't my closest friend.

I followed the gang into one of the largest treatment rooms, where they all put the crates down and looked expectantly toward Carlie in the middle. She looked very professional in her white jacket over dark slacks. She was a pretty lady—a good thing, since she was also a TV star. She had a weekly show called *Pet Fitness* on the Longevity Vision Channel, and it was all about saving animals, either healthwise or as rescues.

"I want to see them, Lauren. Door closed, and let them out, everyone!"

I'd already confirmed with Juliet Ansiger, and had informed Carlie, that all the rescued dogs had been checked over by a vet who helped out at the Missouri shelter, and they were all reportedly healthy. We'd need to confirm that, but at least none had anything contagious, so letting them loose together should be fine.

I watched as Carlie's violet eyes flashed while, one by one, the crate doors were opened and a pack of tiny canines started dashing about the room. Chihuahuas and Pekes and Poms and Malteses and more, they evaded the legs of the examination table in the middle and seemed eager to jump up on every one of the techs in the place. And me. And Carlie.

I wasn't immune from the gaiety that pervaded the room. I knelt and hugged them one at a time, receiving leaps and tongue kisses, and being ordered, by a couple of them rolling over, to give them tummy rubs. Of course I complied, followed by more hugs.

"Okay," Carlie finally said with a laugh. "Let's get down to business."

With the techs' help, Carlie started checking each little guy or gal after putting them one by one on the table. She looked in ears, noses, and mouths, stretched legs, scanned bodies as if for fleas and injuries and obvious skin issues.

She then had the techs check temperatures.

My phone rang. It was Nina.

"Got names?" I asked her. "I've got dogs."

"I sure do."

I grabbed pen and paper from Carlie's counter. "Go ahead."

Nina read me a dozen names of gems in alphabetical order. I jotted them down.

I'd need to figure which name went best with each of the cute dogs. But that could wait.

The names worked well, though, considering the situation:

Amethyst, Aquamarine, Diamond, Emerald, Garnet, Lapis, Onyx, Opal, Rhinestone, Ruby, Sapphire, and Topaz.

When I hung up, I read the list to Carlie. "Great names," she said. "Sounds like they came up with them after reading the newspaper."

"What?" I asked in confusion, then realized what she was talking about. There had been an armed robbery in L.A.'s downtown jewelry district a couple of weeks ago, and the news had been full of it until another shooting had occurred in a local park and the media had glommed on to that instead. I'd paid little attention and had no idea what kinds of jewels had been stolen. A dozen different kinds?

After a while, the last dog had been checked over—a sweet, yellowish Yorkie whom I thought would soon be Topaz. "Okay, gang," Carlie said to the techs. "Next, take them into the lab and draw blood and collect stool for tests. When you're done, bring them into the holding room and put each into one of the crates along the wall." She looked at me. "We'll get the results soon and let you know, but I'd contacted the vet you mentioned to me and he's sent the records online. We're just confirming that they're as healthy as they look."

I grinned. I also gave each pup a reassuring stroke with my fingers through the mesh fronts of the crates as the dogs were taken out of the room and down the inside hallway.

"Unless we find something I don't anticipate, they'll all be ready to be picked up in a few days," Carlie said. "Then you'll keep them in your usual one-week quarantine?"

I nodded. "But I can still publicize their upcoming availability."

"You sure can."

We walked down the outer hallway. Carlie stopped outside another examination room. "We'll talk soon. Oh, and I've numbered and described them in their records so far, but I'll want their names as soon as you've assigned them. We'll need that for the records once we microchip them, too." And then she went inside.

I headed for the reception area to start payment of our bill. A dozen new dogs being given preliminary exams. This was another of those times when I felt so glad that Dante paid our expenses.

Inside the reception area, I stopped. Teresa Kantrim stood there with her cousin Elsa. She looked at me and glared. "They wouldn't let me come in to see how things were going."

"Sorry," I lied. "But there were so many dogs and veterinary staff there that I can understand." I shot a glance toward the reception area, where the person behind the desk—probably a newbie, since I hadn't met her before—looked at me gratefully. "Once their tests are complete and they're in the room where they'll stay for observation for the next couple of days, maybe you'll be allowed to see them then."

I didn't look at the receptionist but figured I could ask Carlie for the favor, just to attempt to keep the peace.

The woman did seem to care about the dogs, and she'd been among those who'd rescued them. I didn't understand her attitude, but she'd come a long distance.

And I hoped she'd go back there soon, before I had to see much more of her.

I wasn't that fortunate, though. Teresa showed up at Hot-Rescues not only later that afternoon, after I'd returned, but for the next four days. I'd picked the dogs up from Carlie's by the end of that time, but they were still in quarantine before we would adopt them out.

Today, it wasn't her cousin Elsa who came in with her but a man named Mark Black, apparently her boyfriend, who'd driven all the way from Missouri to take Teresa back home when she was ready. He was skinny, with a large brow and red plaid shirt. He was nice enough to introduce himself to me when I came into the welcome room to greet them. Maybe he didn't have the same nasty attitude as his girlfriend.

I was curious about why any guy would be interested in a woman as grumpy as Teresa. Or maybe that was only the way she acted in La-La Land, as she continually referred to Los Angeles.

"Are you in animal rescue, too?" I asked him.

"No, though I'm supportive of it. I'm a real estate agent. Could I take a tour of HotRescues? I've heard a lot about it."

None of it good, I figured. Even so, I said, "Sure."

"Would you mind showing me around?"

I traded glances with Nina, who sat, as usual, at the welcome desk. Would Teresa come with us? Otherwise, Nina would be stuck with her. As would Zoey, who was asleep under the counter.

But Nina gave a brief nod, as if recognizing the onus I might be foisting on her. I'd owe her.

"Sure," I said again. "I'm always happy to show off my shelter."

We walked down the hall toward the door to the kennel area. I glanced back, but Teresa wasn't following. She'd been heading toward the table under the window when we left, a magazine in her hand. Maybe she wouldn't bother Nina after all.

I started the usual spiel I gave when providing tours. "This is our older kennel area. We try to keep it full because it's usually the first place people who may be interested in adoptions see. We'd love for them to bond with one of our dogs right away." I started to explain our recent remodeling, but Mark interrupted.

"Will we get to see the little dogs in quarantine?"

"You can look through a window at them, but otherwise, no. No one except our staff can be in contact with them, and they know our sanitation protocol."

"Okay." He hesitated in front of the kennel that held Hale, a terrier mix who was one of our old-timers at HotRescues. I wasn't sure why he hadn't been adopted yet. He was a lovable dog. But other than the current teacup craze, I seldom understood why some dogs were adopted fast and others took awhile.

Of course, all our animals could stay here, with love and excellent treatment, as long as they needed to.

"Nice dog," Mark commented. Then he stopped walking

and looked at me. "I gather, from talking to Teresa, that she's still not happy about this situation."

"Apparently not," I said, "although I'm not sure why."

"She hasn't told you?" He proceeded to explain that she'd been planning to open her own shelter near her home and had thought the puppy-mill rescue was an omen, that she was destined to found a rescue organization. "But the manager of the public shelter where the little dogs were brought was thrilled when you got in contact, since HotRescues has such a wonderful reputation in the shelter community, even nationally." He, though, looked less than thrilled. In fact, he was scowling. "Everyone's heard of HotPets, and most have heard about HotRescues' affiliation with it."

"I see," I said thoughtfully.

Was he resentful of HotRescues' great reputation? Its funding? Or was he only displaying his girlfriend's resentment?

"You know, there's a lot involved with running a pet shelter," I continued. Maybe I could educate him a little. "Has Teresa worked at hers long? She might not realize—" I broke off to wave at Mamie, who was walking a little sheltie mix. She waved back and smiled.

"Oh, Teresa's smart. Plus, I've got some accounting experience, and I've already discussed funding issues with her. I'm not sure how it went, since she hasn't talked to me about it, but she apparently called Dante DeFrancisco and visited him yesterday, before I got here."

"Really?" I felt shocked, not only that Dante had seen her, but that he hadn't informed me about it. Or maybe it had gone so badly that he hadn't thought it worth mentioning. As far as I knew, he had no intention of funding other pet-rescue organizations.

"Yes, and—" He was looking behind me, and as he shut up I figured I knew who he'd seen.

Sure enough, Teresa was there. "I'd like to go see the little dogs in quarantine now," she said. The chilly look she shot at Mark suggested that she knew he'd been talking about her.

I didn't have to repeat my litany of not getting close to the dogs in quarantine to her. She'd heard it before.

But there was one thing I could tell her that she probably wasn't aware of—unless she'd gotten the information from another source we apparently both knew.

"The little ones are doing well," I said as we walked around the loop at the back of the shelter, beyond the first kennel area and all the volunteers who were inside enclosures helping to socialize the dogs. "That means their quarantine will be over in a few days. In fact, next weekend we're going to throw a party right here to help celebrate their availability for adoption."

"And we're invited?" Mark asked hopefully.

"Everyone's invited," I said, glancing at Teresa. She didn't look impressed.

And if I'd known the results of that party, I would never have held it at all.

Chapter 6

I'm usually not one for throwing parties, but this was definitely a special occasion.

The little dogs were finally out of quarantine.

I could have let them out yesterday, which was Friday, about a week after we'd brought them to HotRescues. But it's easier to get attendance at a Saturday event, so I'd apologized to the little gem-named puppies and waited until today.

Sort of. In actuality, I'd let our kennel staff and volunteers take them out to play starting yesterday. No sense penalizing the little guys for timing that was my responsibility, not theirs.

Now, though, I was the HotRescues chief greeter as people came in through the usual public entrance, our welcome area. It was a small room, so to keep it from getting jammed up I greeted attendees quickly, then pointed them to the hallway with the door to the kennel area.

"So glad to see you here," I said to Naya and Tom Fayler as they came in the door.

"Couldn't resist," Tom said. "Or at least Naya couldn't." Tom was dressed in what I assumed to be his business casual. I'd only seen him in button-down shirts, and this afternoon the blue one he wore was tucked into nice slacks instead of loose over jeans like his outfit on flying day. But he'd not lost his broad smile nor his loving glances at his spouse.

Naya was also in a shirt and slacks today. She had dolled herself up with makeup for the event and looked quite pretty. "Thanks so much for inviting us, Lauren," she said, giving me a quick hug.

"No," I said, "thank *you*, since without you I wouldn't have all those adorable little dogs whose freedom and availability we're about to celebrate."

"Where are they now?" Naya asked.

"Yes, where are they?" That frigid tone came from behind the Faylers. Teresa Kantrim walked around them, her boyfriend, Mark Black, edging around to stay with her.

"We're going to have a ceremony soon showing their release from quarantine." I tried to smile, but Teresa's scowl didn't invite one in her direction. Instead, I aimed it at Mark.

"Welcome," I said. I'd have preferred not inviting either to the party, but if I wanted to have any hope of being able to rehome the rest of the teacup dogs still left in her area, I'd had no choice.

"Thanks," said Mark. His large brow was furrowed, which only called attention to the narrowness of his face. At least it seemed to fit his thin body. Like his girlfriend, he wasn't dressed to party. Jeans are accepted everywhere, but his Chicago Bears T-shirt looked grubby.

Teresa wore an animal rescue T-shirt, at least, one that

depicted two happy dogs smiling at each other. Too bad she couldn't mirror their expressions.

More people were coming through the door. I needed to clear out this space. "You've been here before," I said to Teresa. "How about if you show the Faylers down that hall and into the kennel area."

Of course I'd given her a tour of HotRescues to show off our wonderful facilities—where the dogs she had followed cross-country would be housed till adopted.

She hadn't seemed impressed. Oh, well.

"Sure," she said now. "I'd be glad to show the Faylers something they don't already know. Maybe then they'll start telling the truth about what they do know." With that, she turned her back, gestured for Mark to follow, then started walking down the hall.

I looked toward Tom. "What was that about?" I asked quietly.

"Damned if I know. But I think maybe someone should keep an eye on that kook." He took Naya's hand and they followed Teresa and Mark.

I was shaking my head in astonishment when our next guests arrived. Dante and Kendra. I'd also invited their dogs to this special event. Dante had his German shepherd Wagner on a leash, and Kendra had brought Lexie, her cute tricolor Cavalier King Charles spaniel.

"Welcome," I said. "I'll be holding the ceremony soon outside the quarantine building. You know the way."

They were followed by some of the HotPets staff, including Chris Mandrea, the HotPets Bling designer, and Sheila Sheltron, Dante's administrative assistant. Sheila had brought her boyfriend, a football-player-broad and tall guy named Vince, who smiled a lot but looked uncomfortable in the crowd.

The women, including Kendra, were wearing Bling necklaces like the ones distributed at the anniversary party—and like the one I, too, wore over my HotRescues T-shirt that I'd dressed up by wearing a frilly shirt on top and a swingy black skirt beneath.

I greeted them all, delighted at our turnout. Since this was Saturday, we also had a rush of potential adopters, and I invited them all in for the party, too.

And of course a lot of our staff and volunteers were also there, including our part-timers like Margo Yardley, our groomer, and Gavin Mamo, our trainer, as well as Dr. Mona, our pet-adoption shrink.

Plus, to my surprise and pleasure, two people originally from Missouri who now lived in L.A.—and who'd been contacted by Juliet Ansiger—were there, too: Rhoda and Stu Krieg.

"We're real pet lovers," Rhoda said, "and we heard from Juliet about that really special cross-country rescue you did." She was a slight young woman, with buckteeth and black short hair with a single highlighted silver streak, who smiled and shook my hand. "One thing, though." She frowned.

"What's that?" I asked, though I suspected I didn't really want to hear it.

"We—" began Stu, who was about the same height as the woman I presumed was his wife. But he was interrupted by Teresa, who suddenly joined us.

"What are you doing here?" she demanded. "Did Juliet tell you I was here? I thought I'd never have to see you again once you moved away, but here you are."

"Yes," Stu said with a grin that somehow looked malicious on an otherwise bland face. "Here we are. And I have a good idea what your ulterior motive is for being here. But you aren't staying, are you?"

"Of course not," Teresa spat. "Especially because you're here."

Before I could ask what that was all about, Teresa stormed off.

"What a witch," Rhoda said, and then she and Stu, too, walked away—in the opposite direction, leaving me shaking my head.

"Everything okay here, Lauren?" asked Nina, who had bucked the crowd going down the hallway from the kennel. Our staff and a lot of volunteers were already in the back schmoozing with and entertaining our guests.

"Fine," I assured her, wishing I believed it. Well, heck, I did believe it. Those strangers had nothing to do with anything around here. "It's almost time for our ceremony, isn't it?"

"That's why I came up here. I'd love to hear you, but someone needs to be here since people are still arriving."

As if she'd needed to be introduced, Carlie walked in just then. Liam was with her, and the TV executive carried a camera. "It's okay if we take videos, isn't it, Lauren?" Carlie asked.

"Are they likely to show up on *Pet Fitness* or on KVKV?" That's the TV station where Liam works. I was never quite certain of his function there, but he sometimes appeared on camera as well as working behind the scenes.

"Only if you okay it," Liam assured me. The guy acted like a know-it-all sometimes, and I wasn't always sure he was right for Carlie, but lately he'd been on his best behavior.

"Which I'll probably do. The more publicity those cute little dogs get, the sooner they'll get adopted—and the easier it'll be for me to get more from that puppy-mill rescue. So," I finished, "take all the pictures you want."

Leaving Nina in charge, I walked down the hall with Carlie and Liam.

"How are my little friends?" Carlie asked. She'd dressed up as if she knew she would be on camera—which of course she would. Liam would get her in some of the shots, I felt sure.

"Doing very well, thanks to you," I said.

"I didn't do anything but examine and watch them," she said. "They were fortunately already healthy."

I looked at Liam. He wore a suit today, as if he planned on getting in the picture, too. Or maybe just so he could look like the TV big shot he was. The shows he got involved with tended to be sensational or gossipy stories, but he was one cute announcer, with wavy hair and a hard-to-resist come-hither smile.

Apparently Carlie didn't resist.

"Hey, Lauren." I turned toward the voice behind me, not even attempting to hide the grin on my face.

Matt had made it. He hadn't been sure he could when I'd invited him. L.A. Animal Services personnel could be on call twenty-four/seven, and he knew of a training session that would be carried out today. He wore his brown logo T-shirt over green slacks, as he did a lot of the time on the job.

He caught up with me and gave me a quick kiss. "I take it you haven't done the big release yet, right?"

"Right. You're just in time."

There were a lot of people in our kennel area now, including Dr. Mona, Margo, Gavin Mamo, Security Director Brooke Pernall, and handyman Pete. Then there were a bunch of volunteers, most of whom spread out when they visited, always at times most convenient to them.

But it seemed that a lot of them wanted to attend this fun event.

There were kennels on both sides of the path at the beginning of our shelter area. A building on the right contained a kitchen and security area downstairs, and the apartment where our security staff slept overnight upstairs. Our large shed, full of animal food and other supplies, lined the back of the shelter, and the path formed a U there. Around the bend was the newest part of our facilities. It contained more kennels for medium to large dogs, plus several buildings. One was a cat house. Another was a place for smaller dogs, where our new little temporary residents would be housed.

And then there was the building we used for quarantining new arrivals and the ill.

I led the way through the crowd, with Matt, Carlie, and Liam in my wake. Some of the dogs in the kennels were barking, which at this point couldn't be helped. I did order people to keep their fingers out of the enclosures, though. None of our dogs were particularly aggressive, but with all the extra tension caused by the crowd, one might just decide to nip a guest or two.

I had to stop briefly and say hi to a lot of our guests, so it took a while to get around the corner and to the building that was my goal.

But soon, I was inside. With the help of Pete and some of our volunteers, I leashed up the teacup pups and we brought them outside. I'd already asked other volunteers to work on clearing an area near the door, and they had succeeded.

Holding the leashes of two of the little guys—all of them wearing HotPets Bling collars in addition to their own—I yelled out to get everyone's attention.

"Hi, everyone. Thanks for coming." I waited for a moment

for the roar of conversations to soften to a soft buzz. "Now's
the time we've all been waiting for, or at least these guys
have. I'd like all of you to welcome to HotRescues our special newest rescues"—I glanced at my notes—"Amethyst,
Aquamarine, Diamond, Emerald, Garnet, Lapis, Onyx,
Opal, Rhinestone, Ruby, Sapphire, and Topaz." If anyone
asked which was which, I could tell from my notes, which
contained breed and coloration, and I did know most of
them by heart. Because I really cared about them. "Okay,
pups, you're free from quarantine and ready to find new
forever homes. Welcome to HotRescues, and let's celebrate. Let the party begin!"

Which it did. With my supervision, the staff and volunteers
first paraded the little guys around the podium area, all of
them adorable and prancing proudly on their leashes: three
Pomeranians, two Yorkies, a shih tzu, a miniature poodle, a
silky terrier, a Maltese, a Pekingese, and two Chihuahuas.

Then my human gang moved the new temporary residents
into kennels on the first floor of the small-dog building. There
were offices upstairs, but no one was in them now. I didn't
want the little dogs to be frightened by all the people—if they
weren't already—from my little ceremony. I had staff and
volunteers stationed at the door to let only a few people in at
a time to see the dogs up close and personal.

Otherwise, we were all here to party.

I circulated through the crowd. We had drinks and food,
nothing as elegant as there'd been at Dante's party, but it
was still good stuff.

I kept my eyes and ears open. Most of the HotPets corporate staff hung out together, and their conversations
seemed to focus on the new Bling line and what would

come next. They all seemed jazzed about it, so I assumed that the dog collars were continuing to sell well.

I noticed that Teresa was being her usual brittle and nasty self. She joined that group for a while, apparently to goad the Faylers, even as she seemed to swig one drink after another.

And they weren't the only people she was nasty to. She seemed to argue with nearly everyone she met, including the other HotPets folks, my staff and volunteers, our would-be adopters, and even Dante.

I wished I could just throw her out. But I gritted my teeth and tried to ignore her.

Later, in hindsight, I wished I'd given her the boot.

But that was only after the party had ended, and I'd said good-bye to a whole bunch of people, including Dante, Kendra, and their dogs. Matt left, too, to head to one of the public shelters for an after-hours meeting, and Carlie and Liam also said good night.

By then, it was past our hours for being open. With everyone else gone, our staff and volunteers got down to work to feed our poor residents, who were understandably nervous after our event.

While the animals were eating and our staff and volunteers were cleaning our regular areas, I went inside the quarantine building to start cleaning it as well.

That was when I found Teresa Kantrim.

Or rather, her body.

She was lying on the floor and, judging by her position, she was dead.

Chapter 7

I couldn't be certain she was gone, though, no matter what she looked like. "Teresa?" I called, hurrying quickly to where she lay on the concrete floor. Her limbs were splayed, and her complexion was gray. I knelt to feel her neck for a pulse.

Nothing.

I yanked my phone from my pocket and called our security chief, Brooke, quickly telling her to call 911 and then come to the quarantine building.

Then, just in case, I started doing CPR on Teresa.

No response to chest compressions. I didn't really want to try breathing into her mouth, but in case that would help I repositioned her with her head back, held her nostrils shut, and opened her lips.

But when I got closer, I smelled something. Nuts? I wasn't sure, but I hesitated putting my mouth on hers.

Brooke shoved in the door just then and ran into the room. "What the hell?" She bent beside me and repeated my attempts to find a pulse as I again started chest compressions.

"I didn't want . . . Smell her breath."

Brooke did. "Hell, was she poisoned? It smells like almonds—and I've always heard that's the scent of cyanide. You okay doing that?"

Continuing the chest compressions, I nodded, my own breathing now somewhat irregular and short. "For now. But I think it's too late. Did you call 911?"

"Yeah, on the way here. Let me take over. You can go let the cops in."

Unfortunately, Brooke's guy Antonio Bautrel, an LAPD detective, had been on duty that day and hadn't made it to our party. I told Brooke to call him first, and then I'd gladly let her continue CPR on the woman I believed by then was already a corpse.

Brooke pulled out her phone and pushed one button. I wasn't surprised that Antonio was programmed in. I kept up my strenuous attempts to revive Teresa as I listened to Brooke give a brief description. She waited for a few seconds with the phone at her ear, then pushed a button again. "He's coming, too."

We traded places. I watched her for a few seconds. She was the pro when it came to saving lives and handling security matters. I'd done some training on reviving animals, but not people. I was glad to see I'd been doing things right.

Even so, Brooke had no better luck than I had.

Teresa was gone.

Later that night, the coroner came and took Teresa after she was pronounced dead by the EMTs. A crime scene team from the Scientific Investigation Division was at work as well.

Even after the cops arrived, I remained scared for our guests and my HotRescues personnel. Even more scared for the animals. Were they all okay? If something had been laced with poison, the danger might not be limited to Teresa.

Still, while Brooke and I had struggled to help Teresa, staff and volunteers had done as they were supposed to: feed the animals and clean their enclosures.

No one else had found anyone—canine, feline, or human— who was anything but fine.

I'd asked everyone if they'd seen anything unusual. No one had.

I would have time to talk with them—more than I'd wanted. I knew the drill, and Antonio, arriving about half an hour after Brooke's call, confirmed that no one was to leave until their information had been collected and they'd been questioned by the police.

This time, as people congregated in the walkways between kennels and buildings, the mood was a lot less exuberant.

The dogs whose kennels faced those areas must have sensed something. When one barked, a whole bark-fest ensued. Each ended quickly but it wasn't long till the next. And instead of our usual interactions initiated by people from the path outside the kennels, it was the dogs who looked out hopefully, noses to the glass doors or mesh gates as they wagged their tails.

I let Brooke show the crime scene investigators where to go, including leading them to rooms to conduct their interviews.

This unfortunately wasn't the first time there'd been a murder at HotRescues. But I fervently hoped it would be the last.

I made a few calls as I waited, including to Tracy and

Kevin. My kids at college always worried about me, and I wanted to let them know what had happened as well as that I was okay. This situation would undoubtedly make the news, and they'd told me more than once when they had seen or heard something about HotRescues or me in the media.

I was glad that Antonio decided to interrogate me himself. He'd be gentle, at least.

I'd left Zoey in my office during the party so I wouldn't have to worry about her getting loose. I walked her again now, and then we returned to my office. She stayed close beside me, as if she knew something was wrong.

Antonio joined us there, sitting across from my desk. "Tell me everything you can remember about this afternoon," Antonio said, "moment by moment." He was dressed like a detective that day, although he had removed his suit jacket and tie. Despite our being friends, his tense demeanor combined with his official-looking white shirt and black trousers were a bit intimidating. The furrow of his jutting brow and his penetrating gaze intensified my unease. He wasn't a handsome man but his looks were—well, arresting, in more ways than one.

I described my preparations for the party with the help of mostly staff—Nina and Pete—and with some assistance by volunteers. "I made it a point to be in the welcome area, though, when people began to arrive. Some were here because they have relationships with HotRescues and came to celebrate, but we had some visitors today, too—people who didn't know this was anything besides a normal Saturday, when they're welcome to check out our animals to see who's available for adoption. I can give you copies of the forms some completed—the ones who wanted to adopt and therefore filled out applications."

"That'll help."

I went to the welcome area, extracted the applications from the file, and made copies for Antonio. Then we returned to my office.

Seated on the couch across from my desk this time, I started recounting to the best of my recollection the people I knew who'd been here and the order in which they'd arrived.

And then I stopped and stared at him.

"I almost forgot," I said. "Maybe the most important person of all. Teresa didn't come here by herself. Her boyfriend was with her."

"Where is he now?" Antonio asked. He sat on the other side of the sofa, both recording what I said and making notes on a pad of paper.

"That's just it. I don't know. I didn't pay attention to him much, even when he was with Teresa. The other day, he tried to explain her to me, why she acted so unfriendly—jealousy, I guess, since she had hopes of starting her own shelter in the area where all those little dogs were saved. He was with her when she arrived here today. But when I kept seeing her wander around the place—and, most especially, hanging out with the HotPets staff and giving them a hard time . . . Well, I think he stayed with her part of the time, but he sort of blended into the crowd. I didn't see him when I set our staff and volunteers to their end-of-day duties, nor when I left Teresa's . . . body."

Antonio looked at me quizzically with his intense brown eyes. "Do you have any reason to believe he killed her?"

"That would make more sense than anyone else here, wouldn't it?"

"Would it?"

I wilted a little. "I'm not actually sure. He loved her, I

assume. He drove all the way across country to be with her, to drive her back home when she was ready. He—you know, she has a cousin here named Elsa. That's who she stayed with before Mark arrived. Mark Black. That's her boyfriend. I don't know Elsa's last name. Maybe they both were staying with Elsa. I don't know."

"We'll look into it." He paused. "Thanks, Lauren. I'll try to get our SID folks out of here as soon as possible."

"At least the crime scene is our quarantine building—and it's empty now."

"Oh, right. Your reason for the party was to celebrate the release of the little dogs into the regular adoption areas, right? I think that's what Brooke told me."

"Yes." I sighed. "I'd already figured they could get adopted fast, since teacup-sized dogs are really popular around here at the moment. And now—well, they may go even faster when news about the murder goes public and that attracts nosy people to check the place out. People addicted to gossip and paparazzi like animals, too."

"Maybe. Meantime, I'd suggest you call your security company and have them put an additional detail on the premises tonight."

I did that, of course.

EverySecurity, the company that also took care of the HotPets stores, had missed seeing the first murder months ago, which had taken place outside here at night, despite their security cameras mounted nearby. There were none in the quarantine building, though. And since then, Every-Security had been a lot more attentive. I felt sure it was because they were concerned more about losing Dante's business than the security of our animals.

But we also had someone sleep here each night—Brooke or one of her private contract staff. Tonight, she had designated herself as the person who'd be here. Fortunately, Antonio decided to remain with her.

And me? Well, I had Zoey at my side as I took my final walk of the night through HotRescues, staying as far as possible from the crime scene investigation. I even brought Zoey into the cat house but commanded her to stay by the door.

The cats seemed their usual selves, some friendly and some aloof, but all wonderful potential pets. I was glad that today's activities hadn't affected them.

Then we went into the building where our newest little rescues were now housed. Zoey again just sat by the door as I went from one kennel to the next, patting and hugging the small guys and girls and assuring them that they were so adorable that they were sure to get new homes soon.

I didn't mention what had happened to the woman who'd accompanied them across the country.

Eventually, it was time for us to leave.

But I felt unnerved. Uneasy. Not afraid to be by myself . . . yet not wanting to be, either.

I said good night to Brooke and Antonio.

And then, returning to the welcome area, I called Matt. Again. I'd already phoned him to let him know what had happened.

His workday was over. He and his dog, Rex, would meet Zoey and me at our house.

Chapter 8

Preparing to leave, I went through my usual routine of shutting down my computer and checking to make sure that everything in the entry building, from the welcome room to my office and the door to the kennel area, was in order. Then I grabbed my purse and snapped a leash on Zoey. "Time to go, girl."

I felt exhausted. Way too much excitement for one day—both the good stuff, celebrating the little dogs' graduation from quarantine to adoptability, to the really terrible stuff, another apparent murder at HotRescues. My place. The shelter where the only thing that should matter was saving and rehoming animals.

And certainly no one, pet or human, should die here.

But that was what people would hear now about HotRescues. As I'd figured, the death of Teresa Kantrim was already in the news. Liam had called me to confirm it, and he would only add to the hype.

At least he would put a positive spin on the shelter where the death had occurred. Who knew what the other news types would do?

And maybe it hadn't been murder. An odor near Teresa's mouth didn't mean she'd been poisoned. Maybe she'd just had a heart attack, or some other health issue had felled her. The situation was sad no matter how she died, of course, but at least a health issue wouldn't reflect badly on HotRescues.

I checked the door after we walked through it to be sure it was locked. Then Zoey dragged me along with her leash toward our car in the parking lot. She had a lot more energy than I did.

Plus, we were going home, where she would have all my attention for a few hours, even when we slept.

The side parking lot was nearly empty. I'd gathered that the authorities had parked in the alley behind our storage building. I reached into my pocket for my key and pressed the remote button to unlock the Venza's door.

That was when Zoey darted from in front of me, barking and pulling even harder on her lead. I pivoted to look at what she was lunging toward.

Mark Black emerged from the shadows beneath one of the parking-lot lights.

I held Zoey back from leaping on him. At the same time, I hurriedly opened the car door and pulled Zoey even harder, wanting her to jump inside before me.

If Teresa had been murdered, the person likely to be the number one suspect was right here, and we were alone with him.

But Zoey was intent on reaching Mark. She'd stopped barking, but she continued to pull on her leash. "Come, Zoey," I commanded, yanking in a tug strong enough to get her attention but not hard enough to hurt her.

She stopped for a moment, and I pulled again.

She finally started to obey. But it was too late.

Mark was right in front of me. His back was to the light, so his face was in shadow. All I could see was the silhouette of his tall, thin form.

"She's dead," his voice rasped.

I moved slightly, positioning my purse so I could reach for my phone. I didn't have anything I could use as a weapon if he attacked.

Nothing besides Zoey, and I was scared that he'd harm her, too.

"Yes," I managed to say brusquely, edging backward. Maybe I could turn enough to encourage Zoey to jump inside the car. I'd follow quickly and lock the door behind me, and—

"It's my fault," he said with a sob, his words slurred. He sounded drunk, and although he stood still, his body swayed. Was this a murder confession? I wasn't recording it.

And the fact that he was telling me wasn't good. Maybe he intended to kill me, too.

I wouldn't let him. I carefully dug down in my purse, still seeking my phone. At the same time, I kept moving slowly toward my car. If I kept talking, maybe he wouldn't pay attention to what else I did. "Would you like to tell me what happened, Mark?"

"Do you know where she is now?" he responded.

"The authorities took her away. Some police are still here. Would you like to tell *them* what happened?"

"No, I just want to know . . . did she suffer?"

I'd no way of knowing. She'd looked more or less at peace when I found her, but who knew what she'd gone through?

"That's something the police will be able to tell you

better than I can," I said gently. "Let's go back inside and I'll take you to them."

"It all went wrong," he said, folding onto the ground. "She was drinking too much. We argued, and I told her she was acting like an ass, that no one would want to listen to her. She was fighting with everyone, including me. I wanted to show her I didn't care, so I walked away. One of the volunteers was leaving then—Pam—and I invited her out for a drink. We left. And then Pam left me at the bar because all I could do was talk about Teresa."

Pam. She was a relatively new volunteer, young and enthusiastic and pretty.

Would she provide this man an alibi for murder? Of course, he hadn't said when they'd left or what he'd done after Pam walked out.

"That's when you came back here?" I prompted. "And you got Teresa alone to talk to her and make up, right?"

He suddenly stood again, towering over me even as he swayed again. "Are you implying that I killed her?" Even in the shadows, I couldn't help seeing how he clenched his fists at his side. I smelled alcohol on his breath, despite the distance.

Zoey must have sensed his anger, too. She started growling, low in her throat. I wanted to hug her for trying to protect me, but I was as much afraid for her as I was for myself.

I hid what I felt as I spoke in a businesslike tone. "I'm only asking what happened. I found her, and she was gone. I know you're in pain, and I'd like to understand how things went between you. I'm not accusing you or anyone else. That's up to the police, assuming they determine she didn't just die of natural causes. And so far, I haven't heard otherwise." Despite what I might suspect.

"I blame you for what happened, Lauren. She shouldn't

have come here. She shouldn't have had to worry about those little dogs. She wanted to save them herself, and you stopped that. And she told me there was something else going on. Something—"

He'd been moving closer to me as he spoke. I was near enough to get into the car, maybe even slam him with the door, but I couldn't be sure what Zoey would do.

I wouldn't let her be hurt, no matter what.

But before I had to make a decision, I heard the building door burst open and footsteps running toward us. I didn't dare take my eyes off Mark, so I just stood there ready to hit him with my purse or gouge his eyes or whatever it took to protect Zoey and me, but I waited.

Good thing I did. "Mark Black?" growled the angry voice of Antonio Bautrel. In moments, he had put himself in front of Zoey and me, facing Mark. He flashed his police badge. "Come with me, please. We have some questions for you."

"Matt was frantic when he called," Brooke told me a few minutes later as I sat with her at the front table in the welcome area. "You'd better phone him right away and let him know you're okay."

I did so, promising I'd still meet him at my house, but not for another hour. He offered to come pick Zoey and me up, but I figured I'd be all right now.

I was sure that Brooke and Antonio would accompany me to my car this time, though. Thank heavens for them and their quick reaction.

I'd managed to push the button on my phone that called the last number I'd connected to. That had been Matt. He'd overheard some of what was going on and called Brooke immediately.

That was why Antonio had rushed outside to help me—and to bring in a major suspect in Teresa Kantrim's death.

Even though it wasn't yet established for sure that she'd been murdered, that was the assumption everyone had made.

I wasn't the only one who'd smelled burnt almonds around her face. The coroner would be conducting tests.

I heard the door open at the end of the hall toward the kennel area, and Zoey, who'd been lying on the floor beside me, stood at attention. Antonio soon appeared.

"Did you get a confession?" Brooke asked immediately. I, too, waited for the answer.

"The guy's smart enough not to talk right now. He asked for a lawyer. But so far, he's denied harming his girlfriend. I've left him with the detective assigned to this case, and I suspect he'll stay in custody at least overnight."

I nodded. Mark was certainly the most likely killer, if it was determined that Teresa had been murdered.

On the other hand, she'd not made a lot of friends on her short visit to L.A. Little dogs? Maybe. People? No, I'd consider those I'd seen her with anything but buddies.

But who else would have had a motive to kill her?

This time I'd surely be able to leave it to the police to find out. No one I cared about was likely to be named a person of interest, let alone a suspect.

Or so I believed as Zoey, Brooke, Antonio, and I walked to my car. I called Matt again, confirmed we were on our way home, and he promised he'd be waiting at the entrance to my gated community.

I drove home carefully but quickly.

Chapter 9

Though it was late, my gated community was safe, and the streets were well lighted.

Rex and Zoey deserved attention and a nice, leisurely walk. Or so I'd insisted to Matt as soon as we got inside my home.

He'd waited at the outside gate for me as promised and followed me down the road. I'd hurried all four of us out the door almost immediately after we got inside my house.

I knew what to expect from Matt, and I figured he'd be more patient if the neighbors might hear or observe what he did.

He was a kind guy. And concerned. He kept telling me to stay far away from danger and other kinds of trouble.

If only that had been possible . . .

"Okay, I think I've waited long enough," he said when we were on the sidewalk only a few feet from my house. "Tell me everything that happened."

I stopped and looked up at him. Matt was a good-looking man, with short, dark hair, toast-colored eyes, and a killer smile. Not that I'd ever mention the latter to him.

He'd told me often that I was around killers too much. And he was right. But each time, I'd really had no choice.

"That's exactly it," I told him. "Things just seemed to happen. I didn't go looking for any of it. I know I promised I'd tell you if I ever got involved with trying to solve a murder again. I don't want to try to solve this one. But it happened at HotRescues."

"And you found the body." It wasn't a question. I hadn't mentioned that when he'd been listening on the phone to my conversation with Mark, but I'd let him know when he and I had actually talked. Plus, if he hadn't believed it, he could have heard it on the news.

"Yes." I sent him a rueful look, then decided standing here discussing it wasn't a good idea. I turned and pulled slightly on Zoey's leash.

Rex and she had been sniffing at the same area on a tree trunk—low enough that I figured some male dog had probably lifted his leg there. Rex was a smart black Lab mix, and he and Zoey got along like best friends. That was a good thing, since Matt and I hung out a lot together and we both loved our dogs. That meant the dogs, too, hung out a lot together—sometimes overnight in one home or the other.

Zoey and I started walking along the sidewalk, and Matt and Rex joined us. Matt had actually found Zoey, a rescue dog he'd brought to meet me. Of course we had fallen for each other. Zoey and I, I mean . . . although the same held true with Matt and me. Or so I believed most of the time.

"So, are you going to tell me?" Matt said.

"As long as you don't act judgmental."

"Lauren," he said in a tone I couldn't quite interpret.

Suddenly he was right in front of me, his hands on my upper arms. "In case you don't get it yet, I really care about you. And you keep getting into situations where you could be hurt. I know you don't always choose to. Well, I don't always choose to have to worry about you, but I do."

I felt the dogs' leashes around my legs as I framed a response in which I wouldn't sound overly irritated. And then I saw the expectation in Matt's gaze, where he obviously knew I was about to scold him.

Instead, I reached up and drew his head down. Right there on the street, I gave him a big kiss.

"I know you worry," I said a little breathlessly when it ended. "I appreciate it. But I still have to deal with things as they happen. I'll tell you what I can, when I learn it. You don't need to protect me. Honest."

His laugh was rueful. "Yeah, I do. Or at least I feel like I do." He put his free arm around me and we started walking again, still holding our dogs' leashes as they, too, walked side by side.

I love this neighborhood. The houses are upscale suburban, mostly in earth tones, with sloped roofs and protruding entrances. The four-lane street has parking allowed along each curb, but not many cars lined it since people tend to park in their two-car garages or on their short driveways.

I also like my neighbors—and fortunately didn't see any outside just now. Nor did any stare out their windows, at least not obviously.

"So . . . ?" Matt said into my ear. "Tell me." He wanted more detail than the little bit I'd already informed him about.

I couldn't help shuddering as I told him how I'd found Teresa in the quarantine building, on the floor, not breathing. How I'd tried CPR, called Brooke and told her to call 911, and so forth.

"But she was dead?" he asked gently.

"Yes. The EMTs confirmed what I had already figured."

"And you didn't see anyone around there. Had you seen her go into the quarantine building, or anyone else?"

"You know how things were at the party. Fun but chaotic. Frankly, I watched the dogs in the outer kennels a lot more than I watched people. And I, of course, checked on our cats, and on the small dogs—now that we had some again—in their inside kennel building." I stopped walking for a moment. "You sound as if you're trying to help solve the murder—assuming that was how she died."

"Maybe because I understand that you're already involved, whether I like it or not. So—never mind the police. Do you have any suspects?"

"Her boyfriend, Mark, is the obvious one."

"And you accused him, so he attacked you?"

"No. It wasn't like that at all." I related to Matt the strange interlude in the parking lot, ending with his eavesdropping over the phone and the arrival of Antonio. "I'm sure the police will want to talk to our volunteer Pam. I do, too. She might provide Mark with an alibi, but I can't imagine who else around here would have hated Teresa enough to kill her."

Or maybe I just didn't want anyone I knew to be involved. Not this time.

"One question I'm sure you don't want to hear, but do you think this is going to prevent you from rescuing the other little dogs?"

He was right. I didn't want to hear it.

But I had already been considering it.

Our dogs had stopped to both relieve themselves on a neighbor's drought-tolerant landscaping near the sidewalk—fortunately not too near the closest cacti. I pulled a couple of biodegradable poop bags out of my pocket and handed one to Matt, although I felt pretty certain he had his own. I was able to delay my response until we were done cleaning up our respective dogs' eliminations.

I still held Zoey's sealed bag in my hand as we started walking again, and I held out my hand to take Rex's. My neighborhood; my access to garbage cans. But it was time to start heading home anyway.

"I've considered whether the head of the rescue organization in charge of saving those little teacup dogs will assume that L.A. isn't the right place to send the others, and I intend to make sure that those we have are adopted out as fast as I'd originally planned. In fact, the notoriety might even speed the process—but before you say anything, don't worry. I won't mention that to anyone else, and even if it does, I totally revile the fact that there was a murder connected to the situation."

"I figured," Matt said. "But you're right. Don't repeat that anywhere. People may take it wrong."

We were at the walkway through my own yard of low-maintenance plants that included cacti and hedges that didn't need a lot of moisture.

"Come on in," I told Matt. "I'll serve drinks all around—water for the dogs and beer for us. Assuming you're okay with that."

He stopped and smiled down at me. "Sounds great to me—as long as that beer is a nightcap."

I smiled back, glad that, after all that had gone on that day, I wouldn't be alone that night.

Chapter 10

There are times I'm thrilled to have HotRescues in the news. That's when we do a special event or are otherwise singled out for a particularly touching rescue, or even an adoption of a pet to a star or someone else well known.

But the next morning was one of those times I would have done nearly anything to keep HotRescues from being the subject of media gnomes' attention.

In my kitchen, I kept a supply of the healthful kind of cereal Matt liked to eat for breakfast as well as the equally healthful dog food Rex ate, in addition to Zoey's and my equivalents. Matt and I walked and fed our dogs first, then sat down at my small kitchen table with our food and mugs of the coffee I'd brewed, and I turned on the television on the counter.

And braced myself. Last night, Liam had confirmed that the murder at HotRescues had made the news. I knew it would only be worse this morning, and it was.

"That ridiculous hype is as bad as I figured," I grumbled to Matt as I used the remote control to switch from one local newscast to the next.

"Deaths are newsworthy no matter where they occur," he said, though he didn't have to remind me of that. "And since this one is suspicious in nature, a possible murder, that makes it even more sensational."

"Yeah," I said. "I know." I took a sip of coffee, wishing that it were later in the day and I was drinking something alcoholic instead.

While waiting for my cop interrogation last night, and after calling my kids, I'd also called Dante to tell him what had happened. Kendra and he and their dogs had left the party fairly early, and I wanted to make sure he had a heads-up about the situation. He'd been kind and even sympathetic when I'd told him I had found Teresa's body.

To the extent I could, I would minimize publicity about my shelter's affiliation with HotPets. That was irrelevant to what had happened. But HotPets is a big company, and Dante's wealth, and the fact he funds HotRescues as well as a sanctuary for wildlife called HotWildlife, have always been thrown out for the world to hear about when anything supposedly newsworthy touches any of the organizations.

A murder at one was definitely newsworthy. But I also knew Dante had a public relations staff for HotPets that would put as positive a spin as possible on the affiliation.

No reason for HotPets to be associated with the murder. It was too bad that HotRescues was associated with it.

This morning, Matt had dressed in his Animal Services uniform: a khaki shirt with green slacks and a jacket decorated with patches and badges that showed he was an officer with people reporting to him within the city department.

We'd spent the night in each other's arms. I'd needed

just the comfort, but I knew he would have made our time together even more enjoyable had I even hinted at interest.

That could wait until another night. At least I felt sure there would be more ahead of us.

As long as I listened to him, and kept him informed if I felt compelled to put myself into harm's way.

He pulled his phone out of his pocket and looked at it. "I need to get to work, Lauren."

"Any problems?"

"No, but it's time for me to start dealing with the usual, and I need to take Rex home first." He rinsed his dishes and placed them in the dishwasher, nice guy that he is. Then he returned to where I was just rising. "Are you going to be okay?"

"Of course." And I would be. I always find a way to deal with issues. But I knew this wouldn't be my favorite day.

Then I castigated myself. My day would involve handling all I had to. But Teresa Kantrim, however I felt about her, was dead. She would never be okay again.

I took a deep breath. Matt must have recognized the change in my mood, and took me into his arms. "Call me if you need a friendly ear. And let's plan on dinner tonight."

"We'll talk later," I said, not wanting to commit to any plans. "But thanks."

We kissed each other good-bye, and I saw him to the door. I kept it open, watching Rex and him get into his car.

Then I sighed again. "Okay, Zoey." My dog, beside me, nuzzled my hand. "We'd better get ready to go, too."

I was surprised to see Antonio Bautrel's car still in the HotRescues parking lot. Though he sometimes stays with Brooke when she's the security person on overnight duty, he usually leaves early in the morning.

I wondered if the crime scene investigation team was still present. I hadn't driven past the alley behind HotRescues where they'd parked, so I wasn't sure.

Zoey and I went inside, and I locked the welcome area's door behind us. It was still too early for potential adopters to arrive, and staff and volunteers entered through the back door, where Pete Engersol let them in. Although . . .

"Come on, Zoey." I motioned for her to follow as I hurried down the hall. I shut her in my office for now, then headed toward the door to the kennel area. I had to make sure that all was relatively normal, and that even if there were still investigators present, our staff and volunteers could get inside as usual.

The dogs in the nearest kennels greeted me with barks. I saw that some had bowls inside their enclosures, which meant they'd already been served breakfast. Plus, their kennels were clean. It didn't appear that I'd need to help out this morning.

As I passed the building on the right, the door opened. Antonio and Brooke emerged. Neither was dressed up as they'd been last night. Brooke wore her black security shirt and dark slacks, and Antonio had on a gray T-shirt and jeans.

"Good morning," I called, then stopped. Brooke would know if there'd been any issues about our usual people getting inside. "Is everything okay in the kennel area?"

"It's pretty much back to normal," she told me. "There's still crime scene tape around the entrances to the quarantine building, but no one's still around, at least not right now."

"And everyone who needs to can get inside through the back?" I asked.

"Yes."

I noticed that Antonio's craggy features seemed even more pinched than usual.

"Is everything else okay?" I looked directly at him.

"Let's all walk through the grounds." That made me feel positive there was something he knew that I didn't want to hear—but that I should hear anyway.

I glanced at Brooke. She was watching my face, her expression sympathetic.

"What?" I asked.

"The investigation . . ." Antonio looked at me. "It's going in a direction I didn't anticipate. If you want me to tell you more, you need to promise this won't go any farther. You can't tell anyone. The suspect or suspects will have a sense of what's happening soon, but word's not to get out yet."

I froze. We were near the end of the first walkway, toward the area outside the large storage building. Some of our volunteers were diverging, heading for the kennels. They were going to pick up empty bowls and start taking dogs for walks.

All as usual.

But things weren't all as usual here at HotRescues. And since I knew I wasn't going to like what Antonio had to say, my mind started racing around who he was hinting at as a suspect.

Me? I'd found Teresa's body.

Mark, her boyfriend? Despite his claimed alibi in Pam, he still seemed most likely to me. But Antonio wouldn't be considering breaching his obligation of silence if it were Mark.

A lot of people had been around yesterday. I had no idea how anyone could have slipped inside the quarantine building without being noticed, but Teresa apparently had.

And so had her killer.

Was one of our staff members or volunteers the prime suspect? But why? They hadn't known Teresa. If the woman had been abusing any of our residents, then maybe there'd have been a reason to confront her, yet surely they'd have told me about it.

Others present had been potential adopters. Were any of them suspects, or were the people who had relocated from Missouri?

But for Antonio to act like this, his main suspect had to be someone I knew.

Teresa hadn't exactly been friendly toward anybody who'd been here. But she'd only been particularly nasty to a couple.

I suddenly began quivering. I thought I knew what Antonio was going to say. But there were still too many people around for him to say it.

"Hey," I said as brightly as I could. "I need to go check on the little teacup pups. Want to come with me?"

They were inside the building around the corner of our facility. I could easily chase out any people inside.

Which I did. A few of our volunteers, some of the younger ones, were inside the kennel areas socializing the small dogs. I thanked them, then asked them to go walk some of the midsize dogs and come back later.

When they were gone, I turned to Antonio. Brooke's gaze at me remained sympathetic.

"Okay," Antonio said. "Here it is. There are two persons of interest involved here, one more than the other."

"But they are a couple," I said, "aren't they?"

"How did you know that?"

"I guessed. I don't believe they had anything to do with it, but I'll bet I know who you're talking about."

Antonio pursed his lips, and the way he looked at me appeared sympathetic and admiring.

"I'll bet you do, too," he said. "It's—"

"Naya and Tom Fayler," I finished.

Chapter 11

After sharing his information, Antonio left. I didn't. Instead, I entered the kennels and sat on the hard, recently cleaned cement floor with the first set of little dogs—Amethyst, a black Pomeranian, and Lapis, the black-trimmed reddish silky terrier.

We'd tried to have the dogs' gem names fit their appearances somewhat, but that didn't really work, considering the actual coloration of some of the jewels. For example, amethysts are generally purple, and lapis lazuli is blue—neither colors of dogs' coats. But I still thought those were cute names for our new little charges. And of course, whoever adopted them could change their names anyway.

For now, all I wanted to do was hug them and give them attention—as much for me as for them. I let each of these two jump onto my lap, lick my face, demand to be petted, try to distract me.

I didn't let them know they didn't fully succeed.

I felt frustrated. I had learned something important but couldn't say anything. Like warn the Faylers.

Warn Dante.

I hated that.

I suspected, though, that if Antonio had been able to find out that the Faylers were major suspects, they might already know. They'd at least have been questioned by the police. Had they been careful with their answers? Had they hired a lawyer?

Had one or both of them killed Teresa Kantrim?

Yes, I now wondered that, too. The police might not always zero in immediately on the right person, but they were certainly accurate most of the time.

I'd seen Teresa goad the Faylers without understanding why. Had they argued on the flight here from Las Vegas? It sounded that way. But if so, about what? Was it serious enough for one or both of them to have killed Teresa?

Maybe I could get that answer, at least, from the Faylers. Assuming that I would be able to talk to them.

That they weren't under arrest.

"Good morning, Lauren."

I jumped, startled at the voice from outside the kennel. My motion scared the two little dogs, and they leaped off me. But not to be deterred from their quest for attention, both hurried to the front gate and wagged bodies and tails at Angie Shayde, our veterinary technician. She smiled back at them, her cherubic face lighting up beneath her wavy hair as she observed the excited dogs. She wore a bright, new turquoise lab jacket over her jeans.

"They're so cute!"

"So you're back from vacation." I rose to my feet. It was time for me to move on anyway. To visit more dogs—and to move my train of thought onto something I could act on right away.

"Yes, I got back last night, and—" She hesitated. The distress on her face told me what she wasn't saying.

I gave the two dogs each a good-bye pat, then maneuvered my way backward out of the enclosure, and Angie helped to make sure that neither of my recent companions escaped. Then I turned around.

"And what?" I finally prompted Angie, even though I didn't particularly want to talk about it. But even if I couldn't tell our staff and volunteers much about the situation, I wanted to ease their minds as much as I could— even if I had to make things up as I went along.

"I heard about what happened here last night, Lauren," she told me. "It's all over the news. I don't know the people who the media's saying are the persons of interest in that woman's death, and—did you know her?"

"I'd met her." I nodded toward the row of highly occupied kennels near us. "She accompanied all these guys from the puppy-mill rescue in Missouri." I paused outside the next kennel door. "So . . . are the media saying that the woman didn't die of natural causes?" I wasn't sure enough time had passed for an official decision.

Angie tilted her head quizzically. "Honestly? I don't know. But though the reporters I heard said the cause of death is still under investigation, the speculation is that she was poisoned. Toxicology reports are still pending."

"I see." So the media jackals were making premature assumptions—maybe. But I still wanted to know all they were saying. I'd find out by tuning in on the computer in my office soon, but Angie might be able to give some info now. "Who do the media claim are persons of interest if the death is ruled a homicide? Any names?" Did they already know about the Faylers? If so, I wouldn't be forbidden from talking about it, too.

"They weren't specific, though they said it may be some people who work for HotPets and reminded viewers that it's the company owned by the founder of HotRescues, where the body was found. They promised more information when they get it."

Of course they did.

The nearest little dogs, Ruby, a red Pomeranian, and Topaz, the yellow Yorkie—this time both with appropriate color names—started yapping.

Angie knelt and put her fingers through the fencing. "These guys are all so cute."

"They sure are."

A page sounded from the welcome room. "We need a few volunteers to accompany some visitors." Nina's voice resonated. I glanced at my watch. Time had passed quickly. It was not only time for her to be there, but also the hour when people could start coming to look at animals for adoption.

The day had officially begun.

While I usually greeted each day with excited anticipation of pets we'd be able to place in new homes as well as possible new rescues at the public shelters, today all I could think about was the terrible thing that had occurred here last night—another murder—and how that would affect so many lives, including, perhaps, more little teacup dogs needing to be rescued.

I didn't have time to dwell on the bad stuff for very long.

Ironically, as I'd suspected, the extra news about HotRescues had called attention to the fact that we did in fact have some small dogs that needed new homes.

We were packed that day with visitors who clamored to put in applications for our temporary inhabitants. Some were even interested in larger dogs. And nearly half a dozen of our cats, too, were the subjects of possible rehomings.

All staff members who were around that day, and those volunteers with any experience in counseling, were recruited to give tours of our shelter to visitors. They each knew the drill. There were certain questions we asked of all comers who expressed an interest in adopting. Animals couldn't be taken home who'd be left outside all the time. If there were other animals in the house, we'd need to make sure they got along all right with any potential newcomers. Every other person in the household had to meet the dog or cat under consideration before the adoption could go through. We reserved the right to make home visits to see the environment where our animals would go despite our doing so less frequently now than we used to.

These questions all had to be incorporated into our informal interviews as we introduced people and animals.

We didn't necessarily allow adoption by the first person or family to put in an application for a cat or dog. And since these little teacup dogs were in such demand, we often had a choice about which home was likely to work out best.

We were busy enough that I chose not to personally introduce anyone to HotRescues or our residents. Instead, I wandered and observed and, frequently, interrupted a visit being hosted by one of the people I trusted.

Bev, one of our most senior and longest-term volunteers, knew enough to shepherd a young pair of newlyweds toward Hale, a terrier mix. I joined them by his kennel near the front of our enclosures, where Hale had been put to spotlight him to visitors.

"You know what?" Bev said as I joined them. "Even

though these nice people came here to see some of our little dogs, Hale didn't let them go by without saying hello."

"He's like that," I told the couple. They both looked to be in their early thirties and wore glasses, almost resembling each other with their shirts tucked into their jeans. "He's really a wonderful dog. Do you happen to own your own home?"

"Yes," said the man. "It's got a nice fenced yard, too."

I smiled. "Sounds good. Bev, why don't you take them into our picnic area and let them get to know Hale better?"

Even though Bev was short and thin and a little bit stooped, she knew how to handle even the most energetic dogs. Hale was only moderately excitable, and I watched as Bev grabbed the leash from around her neck to secure him. As soon as he was out of his kennel, the young couple both knelt and fussed over him as if he was the sweetest dog in the world. Maybe he was.

But the great thing was that I thought Hale might be finding a new home at last.

And he wasn't the only one.

Both Pete, our handyman, and Mamie, my former mentor, were inside the cat house with people who'd come to visit dogs but had been waylaid by the sight of our kitties through the window. I also stopped in there and talked to them. I felt optimistic that both of these visits would lead to adoptions.

Finally, I made it to the small-dog building. The downstairs was filled with people who'd wanted to visit our teacup pups. A number of our volunteers were showing them around, including Ricki, a dedicated African-American animal lover who was studying to become a veterinary technician, and Sally, who was even younger but hung around the shelter after school and on weekends.

Sally motioned for me to join her at the side of the room, out of earshot of the people she was hosting. She was pretty,

of Hispanic background, and wanted to work at HotRescues or another no-kill shelter someday.

"So many people here," she said. "The ones I brought in
seem like a good fit for one of the little dogs. They appear
mostly interested in Diamond." That was the name we had
given to the really cute white shih tzu. "But from what I'm
hearing, they're not the only ones who want him. What
should we do?"

I told her to have those who were genuinely interested in
adoption, and who seemed like good dog parents, fill out an
application. Then I'd have to go over all the forms we
received, preferably with Dr. Mona's input, and decide who'd
win the adoption. "I don't like doing things like that, but at
the moment it's our reality. Still too much interest with too
few dogs."

That told me I needed to make a phone call—one I
would have looked forward to a lot more if Teresa Kantrim
hadn't died here, whatever the cause.

For the moment, I edged my way through the crowd,
whispering what I'd said to Sally into Ricki's ear, and that
of Gavin Mamo, our trainer, who'd come here to give les-
sons today but was instead also showing off potential
adoptees, and every other HotRescues person here. And
then Nina issued a page from the welcome area for someone else to show visitors around.

Looked like I'd be a friendly hostess today, promoting
the adoption of our residents, after all.

Much later, when our visiting hours were finally over, I sat
at the table in the welcome area with Nina, who was staying to help me go over the applications. Most were for our
little teacup dogs. And nearly all of them looked good.

I had a feeling that we'd be rehoming at least half of them as a result of today's visitors.

"I've separated the applications by dog," Nina told me. "And I also put them in descending order, with the one I thought the best fit for each on top. Dr. Mona's also put notes on each, and she did get to speak with quite a few of the potential adopters."

"Thanks," I told her. "I'll look them over now. And it's fine for you to go home."

"You're sure there's nothing else you'd like me to do?"

She'd pushed her long hair away from her face, but her bangs still framed it. She appeared a bit frazzled, though not nearly as much as she used to.

"No, I'm fine. I'll check out the applications, then call the top contenders to come in and talk to me in the next day or two. Thanks for all your help."

I'd already thanked everyone else who'd shown visitors around, in a brief group meeting once we'd closed our doors. Some of the volunteers had left. Others were helping Pete clean kennels and feed our residents.

I knew everything was under control, and Nina grabbed her purse and left a few minutes later.

I was alone. And wondering about the investigation into Teresa's death. But I was too busy to worry much about it—although I was reminded each time I passed our quarantine building and still saw police tape over the door.

I'd watch the news tonight. And even check out sites on my computer, once I had time.

But I'd recognized something else. A lot of the applications looked good. Really good. As I'd figured, at least half of our little teacups were likely to find homes fast. It wouldn't take long for the rest, either.

We would have lots more room soon.

Which meant I had to make that anticipated phone call now.

Heading for my office, I checked on Zoey. I'd left the poor girl in there all afternoon, but I didn't want her involved with the chaos within our shelter. First thing, I took her out to the kennel and let her loose in an area that we encouraged our dogs to use as a bathroom.

When Zoey was finished, we returned to the office and I checked the time. It was six thirty here, which meant it was eight thirty in Missouri, in the central time zone. I didn't think it was too late to call Juliet Ansiger.

But I wasn't looking forward to speaking with her. She obviously knew Teresa Kantrim, since Teresa had been involved in caring for the teacup dogs whose initial destinies Juliet controlled. Since the death was in the news, Juliet had to be aware of it. But I'd no idea how close they were.

I would try to keep the conversation businesslike, in the interest of the rescued pups. But for those little dogs' sakes, I had to see about moving another group out here.

Which also caused me some worry. If the Faylers were murder suspects, would they be allowed to fly at all?

Well, one thing at a time. I checked my files for Juliet's number, and then I called it.

She answered quickly.

"Hi, Juliet," I said. "This is Lauren Vancouver, in California. I wanted to—"

"Give your condolences? Well, they don't do much good now, do they? What happened to Teresa? She was really unhappy when she learned we were sending some of our dogs to La-La Land, and it sounds as if she was right."

Chapter 12

I remained silent for a few moments, deciding how to handle this conversation.

If this woman had been friends with Teresa, I wanted to show sympathy. And, in fact, I did feel bad for anyone who lost another person who'd been close to them. I'd had it happen, too.

Like my beloved first husband, Kerry Vancouver, who'd died. Too bad I'd replaced him with an utter jerk, Charles Earles, to try to give my kids a father. That had ended in a much-needed divorce.

But all of that was only a fleeting thought. I had other things to focus on.

Such as the needs of the rest of the small dogs in Juliet's area who, through no fault of their own, could be suffering. Or who might even die, as Teresa had, if everything went wrong.

But if everything went right, they could wind up out here,

where, especially after yesterday, I felt certain that I could find them new, good homes. Quickly.

I therefore swallowed the irritated retort that sprang to my lips, and instead said, "I'm really sorry for your loss, Juliet." I let a second go by, then added, "Were you aware that I found . . . poor Teresa?" Much to my surprise, or perhaps not, I stumbled over the last couple of words as my throat closed in sorrow. I hadn't known Teresa well, and what I'd seen and heard from her had suggested we'd never become close friends. But at least part of who she was included being a dog lover. And if her miserable attitude was the result of her being stymied in her own goal of founding a no-kill shelter in an area with need of one . . . well, I couldn't hate her. The world had suffered a loss by her death, and potentially so had a lot of needy animals.

"You found her?" Juliet must have heard not only what I'd said, but also how I'd said it, since her own words sounded choked.

"Yes." The word came out softly, and I continued, "She'd been here at a party at HotRescues, celebrating the release from quarantine of the dogs she'd accompanied from your area. We had such a celebration . . . and it had definitely been something worth celebrating. But then—"

"The news said she'd apparently been poisoned. Was there something served at your party that could have caused that?"

"Of course not." I didn't allow myself to snap. "If so, don't you think there'd have been other people who'd at least have gotten sick?"

"Possibly." She waited a beat, then asked, "Do you know who might have done it? I heard on the news that the investigation is ongoing, and that the police have zeroed in on a person or persons of interest—but there's nothing that I'd say is useful, at least not yet. Are your cops—I mean, I've of course heard of the Los Angeles Police Department. They're sometimes on TV shows and all. But are they actually competent?"

"Are we back to the La-La Land misnomer?" I leaned forward on my desk, my head in my hand. Zoey saw the movement and came closer, and I swept my midsize dog up one-handedly onto my lap. I wanted to hug her, because I needed a hug. "I've got a friend who's an LAPD detective, and I've also had other contact with them. Yes, they're more than competent." But like everyone else in the world, they weren't perfect or immediate. If they were, I'd never have gotten involved in solving murders before.

Or be considering getting involved with Teresa's— assuming the determination was that she'd been poisoned. At my celebration. That made it my business.

"I didn't mean to insult you. Or, really, them. I'm just so upset . . ."

"Maybe this will help cheer you a little." I related to her what kind of day we'd had at HotRescues, with all those people coming because they were interested in adopting. "I got adoption applications in on at least half of the dozen little teacup pups you were kind enough to send along to this area. There's a lot of buzz over the rest, too, and I've no doubt we'll find them new homes quickly. That's one of the reasons I called you."

"You'd like us to send you more?"

"Yes," I said firmly. "If you haven't found new homes for the rest of those dogs from that puppy-mill rescue, not just a place to stay for now at a sanctuary, just think of how much better off they could be here. It doesn't make sense for us to have to turn away people who're interested in bringing them home when you've got more who need a family."

"You're right, of course," Juliet said slowly.

I held Zoey even tighter. "Then you'll make some more available if I can arrange for their transportation?"

"I think so. We probably won't have anyone else who can accompany them the way Teresa did, though."

I was relieved, but I didn't express that. "That was my first experience with Airborne Adoptions or any other animal-rescue flight, but it seemed to work out well." I didn't want to be too pushy, or at least not so assertive that I would convince her to tell me to get lost. But I did want to close the deal. "Would it be okay with you if I try to get another flight relay set up for, say, next weekend?"

At first she didn't answer, and I hung on to Zoey tightly as if my warm, furry dog could somehow affect her response. Zoey turned her head and licked my face, as if trying to reassure me all was well.

I hoped it was.

Juliet finally said, "I have to tell you that I have reservations about this. But I gather that all the dogs are fine, despite what happened to Teresa."

"Absolutely. More than fine. They're going to get new homes, some as early as tomorrow."

"Then, yes," she said. "Let's go for it."

I wished it would be as easy as I'd led Juliet to believe. And maybe it still would be.

I'd need to call Mike Relfer from Airborne Adoptions first to get the ball rolling—or, rather, the planes taxiing.

But the contacts for the last leg of the journey remained the Faylers. And they were persons of interest in Teresa's death.

Would they be permitted to leave town if they'd be back only hours later with a planeload of little dogs?

It was so late in the day that I hesitated calling them. On the other hand, it was a perfect excuse for checking in and asking what was going on in the investigation, or at least about their connection with it.

It was too late to try reaching Tom at the HotPets office. I tried the cell phone number Dante had given me.

It went immediately into voice mail. Did that mean the phone was turned off because the Faylers were under arrest?

Of course it could be as simple as them not wanting to talk to the paparazzi, who'd undoubtedly be calling them with frantic insistence if they thought the Faylers might be the HotPets employees who were considered possible suspects.

I decided to try another avenue. I called Dante's cell phone.

"Hi, Lauren," he said immediately. "Everything okay?"

"Better than okay," I told him. I related how successful a day we'd had at HotRescues with potential adoptions, including the teacup pups.

"I just called the head of the shelter in Missouri where they'd been taken," I finished, "to see about getting more here for rehoming. I think she's on board, but I want to have a rescue set up as fast as possible. Do you think the Faylers will be available to fly the last leg of a plane relay?"

"We'll discuss it with them over lunch tomorrow, if that's okay with you," Dante said. "I've already scheduled getting together with them, and you can join us if you have the time."

"Definitely."

"The Faylers are still free to do what they want . . . for now, at least." I heard concern in Dante's voice. "I know they're potential murder suspects. And Tom's one of my— Never mind." He changed the subject, apparently not wanting to discuss the possibility of one of his subsidiary's executives becoming unavailable permanently.

We talked for a short while longer about HotRescues and HotPets, including HotPets Bling. "So far, our initial local rollout of those collars here has gone extraordinarily well," he told me. "The dog collars, not those special people necklaces, which we're not selling. In any event, that's what we'll be discussing at lunch tomorrow. Our designer, Chris, will be there, too. It'll soon be time to start pushing more into other venues, like Las Vegas. Tom's been following up with the HotPets stores there whose managers received that area's first Bling samples and they're apparently thrilled, too."

"Great," I said. "I'll look forward to hearing more about it."

"Good work with all those adoptions, Lauren. You're doing a great job. And it'll be wonderful to get some more of those little teacups here to be saved."

"Yes, it will." When I hung up, I looked at Zoey. "He's worried, girl, even if he didn't say so. And I hate to see Dante worried."

Chapter 13

Of course, even lunch presupposed that Dante was right and the Faylers were permitted to get together with business associates and friends.

But Dante, with his knowledge and connections, was surely aware of their legal status. Lunch must be doable. Whether the Faylers could pilot a leg of an Airborne Adoptions Rescue, leaving town even for less than a day, might be another story.

The next day, on my way to lunch, I realized that it promised to be interesting in more ways than one.

Since I'd last spoken to Dante, I'd been home with Zoey for what I'd hoped would be a good night's sleep. Instead, my mind kept me awake with thoughts on rehoming dogs, getting more little dogs out here to save . . . and murder.

I'd then spent my morning at HotRescues, finished reviewing some applications and set up a few adoptions for that afternoon and more for tomorrow. Zoey was still at the shelter, and I would return to work, and her, as soon as I could.

But now I was driving toward Beverly Hills and the HotPets corporate offices. Dante had chosen a restaurant near there for us to meet.

I soon reached the high-rent, boutique-filled area, where the people who strolled along were dressed as if they'd bought all their clothes in the expensive designer shops. Some were probably just tourists filled with wishes, but they'd at least realized how near Hollywood they were and dressed the part.

Assuming their jeans were high-end and not the economy kind like mine. But I'd at least buttoned a professional-looking olive-green blouse over my HotRescues T-shirt.

I knew that parking wouldn't be easy, so I decided to splurge and drove into the restaurant's lot, where a valet all but bowed to me as he took my keys and my car.

Not my usual way of doing things, but I was, after all, about to dine with one really successful man and some of his staff. I might as well get into the mood, even though it would cost me.

But knowing Dante, the charge and tip would be reimbursed. He was that kind of person. He'd even given me a couple of raises when I'd needed extra money to send my two kids to college. This amount was chump change to him.

The restaurant was called BH Sinful. It was in the middle of a block and didn't look especially sinful, or even especially good, from the outside. But I had no doubt that Dante had eaten there before. It was only about three blocks from the tall building where HotPets was headquartered.

I pulled open the glass door and went inside. As I'd anticipated, it was crowded. It was also decorated as poshly as—well, a Beverly Hills restaurant. There were a lot of tables but not too crowded together. Each sported a silky-looking beige tablecloth, and many were occupied by decorative china plates and a crowd of diners eating from them. There was a combined aroma of grilled meats, citrus fruit, and expensive perfumes and aftershaves, but subtle, not overwhelming.

I quickly spied Dante holding court at a table at the far end of the dining room. "Thanks," I told the approaching maître d'. "I'm joining the people over there."

The suited man gave a large grin. "Oh, you're with Mr. DeFrancisco. Welcome."

If I hadn't been sure Dante had been here before, I would have been now.

I edged my way through the busy restaurant, ignoring the loud hum of conversations as I approached the table, aiming for the empty chair across from Dante. Both Faylers were already there, but not Chris. Seated beside Dante was his assistant, Sheila, and she had a regular steno notebook in front of her, not a laptop or iPad. Old-fashioned or not, I assumed this was a working lunch for her.

"Hi, Lauren." Dante stood, and so did Tom Fayler, who pulled my chair out gallantly.

"Hi." I looked around to include everyone. A server handed me a menu and asked for my drink order. I chose water. "What's good?" I asked Dante.

"Nearly everything," Sheila responded. She, too, had been here before, then. Did Dante treat his assistant often? When I saw the prices, even at lunchtime, I figured the staff wasn't likely to frequent the place often except on an expense account or boss's treat.

The group discussed possibilities, and I decided on a Cobb salad. Chris joined us as the server returned with my water and to take our orders.

Unsurprisingly with this group, the conversation turned immediately to HotPets Bling. And animals, of course. At least for the latter, I felt right at home.

Dante intended to publicize how the Bling campaign had led to increased interest from local people in adopting, especially small dogs like those shown in the ads. That would be good for encouraging even more people to adopt—and it wouldn't hurt Bling sales, either.

They were generating a model for other cities, too, as the Bling collars were rolled out.

Sheila continued to take notes as Tom and Chris batted ideas off Dante. Even Naya jumped in with suggestions.

And me? All I did, for the moment, was grin. This was good stuff. I loved anything that helped to save animals' lives.

Our meals were soon served. Unsurprisingly, my salad was delicious. The others had chosen everything from appetizer-sized plates to enormous burgers. It all looked great. No wonder Dante chose the place.

As we ate, the conversation started up again. I still stayed out of most of it, and Naya also didn't get very involved. She sat on the opposite side of Chris from me, so it wasn't particularly easy for us to converse, but I nevertheless started talking with her. I needed to know what was going on with Tom and her, and if they could fly again very soon to help save more of those little dogs.

"You know," I began, "we're well on the way to adopting out those little teacup guys you flew here. We have applications on at least half of them already."

"That's wonderful!" Her face lit up, emphasizing what I'd noticed before: her expression looked strained, her face more lined than before, and she really wasn't a whole lot older than me. "I'm so glad we could help."

"I was wondering if you could help again."

Her blue eyes widened. "I can't tell you how much I'd love to. Maybe . . ." She looked toward Tom, but he was talking with Dante. She turned again toward me. "Things are . . . well, you've probably heard in the news. We're 'persons of interest' in Teresa Kantrim's death."

Chris's attention was apparently caught by that. He'd been staring toward Dante and the others, but he looked at Naya and then toward me. "The cops interrogated me, too," he said.

The conversation between Dante and Tom didn't stop, and now there were two discussions at the table.

"Why do they seem to be focusing on you and Tom, Naya?" I asked.

She gave a little shrug of her narrow shoulders. "That Teresa—I certainly didn't wish her dead, but she acted so . . . well, nasty to us. Not just in the plane, but afterward, too."

"Yeah, and people heard it." That was Tom. He and Dante were now looking toward us. "Someone must have told the police, and they somehow assumed that gave us a motive to kill her. But if I killed everyone I know who's nasty, there'd be a lot fewer people around me." He gave a smile that I figured was intended to convey humor, not irony, but it fell short. "I'm not speaking of anyone here, of course."

"Of course," Dante said.

"I just wish I'd understood what she was talking about," Naya said. "She kept saying things like, 'I know what you're really doing.' And, 'If you don't help me, then I'll make sure things go bad for you.' But when I asked her to explain, she'd just smile really nastily, and say, 'Oh, you know exactly what I mean.'"

"And the cops think that something so obscure would have given you a reason to kill her?" I knew I sounded amazed. I shouldn't have. I'd unfortunately been involved in helping to solve enough murders lately that nothing should surprise me about the process.

"I guess so." Tom no longer sounded humorous. "I kept suggesting that they look into other people, like her boyfriend and cousin, and those other people who came here from her area. They knew her a lot better than we did. Maybe one of them hated her, or had some real reason to kill her. We certainly didn't."

I didn't mention that I'd spoken with her boyfriend, Mark—or that I hadn't completely ruled him out, either.

"That's such a shame." Sheila, no longer taking notes, shook her head. "I just hope the police come to their senses and leave you alone."

"Yeah," Chris said. "We've got Bling to create and sell. We don't need that kind of distraction. Teresa had nothing to do with us."

"Except that she flew with Tom and me," Naya reminded him.

"Have the police given you orders not to leave town?" I asked Tom. "That's what they all say on TV to people they claim are primary suspects."

"Not really. But I think I'd want to tell the detectives in charge of the case if we decide to leave town even briefly."

"I hope you have their phone number or e-mail address," I said, then explained how I hoped to do another plane relay of teacup dogs from the Missouri rescue as soon as the next weekend. "First, though, I guess I'd better ask if you're willing to do it."

"Absolutely," Tom said. Then he looked at his wife. "You agree, honey?"

"Yes," she agreed. "As long as it doesn't get us into any more trouble."

When Tom said he'd check with the detectives and confirm whether they could do the run this weekend, I wondered if I could help. Could I come up with other suspects and motives the professionals hadn't thought about within the next few days?

Dogs' lives could be at stake. And so could the Faylers'. They were nice people. Animal lovers.

They needed to fly next weekend for lots of reasons. And they'd be a lot more likely to be able to go if someone else hit the cops' radar harder than they did.

Maybe I could help.

Chapter 14

For now, though, I accompanied the gang back to the Hot-Pets offices.

Dante had indicated that he wanted to talk to me. Which was a good thing, since I wanted to talk to him, too. And not with this crowd around.

I left my car in the restaurant parking lot. I wouldn't be long.

The building wasn't far away. Unsurprisingly, it's an attractive office structure, even for Beverly Hills—six stories high, with a glass and concrete façade that has lots of character, not just an up-and-down look to it. Dante checked me in with the downstairs security guard. That was when Naya gave Tom a quick kiss and left.

I joined everyone else in the elevator, which only stopped on the top floor, where the HotPets executive offices were located. I hadn't been here for a while and immediately noticed the signage they'd posted for HotPets

Bling in a wing of the main offices—no digital lighting, but a definitely noticeable indicator of pride in this new subsidiary, considering the size of both the sign and the apparent square footage designated for this new venture.

I'd always figured that Dante was well liked by his employees, and this visit confirmed it. Every time we got near anyone, they hailed him with friendly greetings that all seemed genuine, not like just sucking up to the boss.

"Need me for anything?" Sheila asked as we reached the CEO's office suite.

"Not right now," Dante told his assistant, "but stay tuned. There are some things pending this afternoon, and I'll buzz you as soon as I have some free time to tell you about them."

"I'll be waiting," she said, "but not idly." She shot her boss a grin, then turned and walked away.

I followed Dante inside his office. Not surprisingly, it was pretty nice, with a sleek wooden desk with hardly anything on top, surrounded by chairs and a sofa that all had matching carved legs. They looked antique—and pricey. But price never seemed to matter to Dante.

And, nice guy and animal lover that he was, he was always ready to give away some of what he had to save animals—and help people.

He waved me to one of the chairs and took his own seat behind his desk. "Excuse me for a second." He ran his computer mouse along his desk, presumably checking the screen for important e-mails. He then glanced at his phone. The message light was blinking. I'd no doubt that at least some of those callers had something imperative for him to deal with, but he didn't check.

Instead, he looked at me. From the time I'd met him a few years ago, when he'd been seeking someone to run

HotRescues, I'd considered him a handsome guy, with his wavy, dark hair and intense, deep brown eyes. "So, Lauren," he said, "what's on your mind?"

"I'd rather hear what you wanted to talk to me about first, Dante. Mine can wait."

"So can mine—maybe." He leaned forward, increasing that intensity in his gaze. "I really liked how that first rescue of those teacup dogs went. The whole idea of a network of pilots shuttling animals from areas where they're not wanted to places they'll find new homes—I definitely like that. I want to help support it."

"Great!" I said excitedly. "HotPets' reputation for helping needy animals will soar even more than it already does. And HotRescues' ability to get involved and save pets would benefit from it, too."

Internally, though, I pondered for a minute. What did Dante have in mind? Would he put his own pilot Tom Fayler in charge of whatever HotPets would do? But who would run HotPets Bling, then?

And who knew if Tom could fly much longer—assuming he even could now?

"I'm going to look into this more. I'd like you to introduce me to the person in charge of Airborne Adoptions. Maybe I'll invite him out here for a meeting sometime. Meanwhile, since Tom and Naya are too busy to do all the flying I'm hoping will be done in Southern California by this service—assuming they can continue at all—I'll check with Tom for names of friends we may be able to recruit here. We'll probably have to ease into it, though—find the right people to help and all that."

"Sounds good. And if I can do anything besides introductions—like helping to coordinate which animals can be sent where for new homes—I'd love to do it."

"As long as it doesn't take too much time and distract you from HotRescues."

"I was just about to mention that." I smiled at him.

"Anyhow, I'll follow up with Tom on this later. I don't want you to get your Airborne Adoptions contact too excited until I've looked into the possibilities, though. Why don't you stop in Tom's office before you go and sound him out on what he thinks of the idea?"

"I know one restriction he's likely to want."

"So do I," Dante said. "Don't necessarily allow people to accompany the animals, especially those who could become murder victims."

"My thoughts exactly," I said.

"So . . . what did you want to talk to me about?"

I laughed. "Pretty much the same thing you wanted to talk to me about. It's such a shame in so many ways that this long-distance rescue was tainted by someone associated with it getting killed. But I wanted to verify with you that you've no problems with HotRescues getting involved with more of that kind of animal rescue."

"You've got my opinion," Dante said. "Go for it!"

"I just hope Tom and Naya will be able to help with the relay I intend for next weekend." I stood. "I'll do all I can to make sure of it."

"I knew there was a lot I liked about you, Lauren." Dante stood, too. "When it comes to saving the lives of animals, you don't let anything, not even a murder, stand in your way."

Tom Fayler's office was a lot smaller and much less decorative than Dante's—unless you counted the Bling. As the manager of the subsidiary, he had used the theme to a wonderful degree, with magnified photos on the walls of a lot of the designs I'd seen on the collars: faux jewels in the shapes of dog bones and ears, dog faces, and more. Though for all that, his desk was fairly ordinary, and so were his chairs.

He waved me to one distractedly as I came in and asked if he had a few minutes to talk. "Sure, Lauren. Just give me a minute."

He was working on his computer, too, with a smartphone beside him on his desk. His attention seemed to jump from one to the other.

I sat for about five minutes, feeling antsy about this delay. I had to get back to HotRescues. I was about to stand and excuse myself when he finally moved his gaze toward me.

"Sorry, but I was on the phone before and had to follow up with a few things. The good news is that neither Naya nor I are under restrictions from traveling—yet. We do have to give all details to our lawyer and the people who've been questioning us—when and where and how long and why. Will the next trip be the same as last time?"

"As far as I know." I knew I was smiling. "Then you are definitely available?"

"For now," he said. "The trip this weekend should be fine, as long as I continue to keep them informed about every aspect of it. Later on . . . I just don't know."

"Well, your boss hopes you'll be able to help set up an ongoing system of rescue flights." I told him what Dante had said. "He doesn't want you doing them all and taking too much time away from HotPets Bling, of course. You'll need to find out more from him, and I'll be putting him in touch with the person in charge of Airborne Adoptions."

"Sounds great!" I hadn't seen Tom smile much lately, but he did now.

"Can I ask a favor?" I looked at him, then scanned the pictures on the wall again. "I'm really impressed with the Bling. I know you don't manufacture it all here, but is this where Chris and the others design the collars?"

"Yes, and they do put together prototypes for our manufacturing facility—it's not in China but actually nearby, in the City of Industry. It's good for us to be able to observe any time we want."

"Great idea! Maybe I could visit someday."

"Absolutely. Right now, go ahead and make plans for the next rescue by plane. Naya and I will look forward to it."

As long as no one like Teresa got on the plane with them— or died afterward, I thought. But I didn't need to say it.

The sudden pang of sadness that twisted Tom's face for a moment let me know that he'd thought it, too.

Chapter 15

It was now late afternoon. I'd already called Mike Relfer of Airborne Adoptions to let him know what was happening—without mentioning Dante yet. I requested that he get a relay team of pilots prepared to bring a lot of small dogs from Missouri to L.A. again, once more incorporating the Faylers' help for the last leg.

I'd also called Juliet Ansiger to tell her I was nearly positive we were on for a new rescue next weekend. She promised to have another dozen dogs available.

Apparently she, like Teresa, retained some skepticism about how we'd do. There were at least another dozen who'd need to be rehomed. But I didn't argue with her. The important thing was saving as many as we could, as quickly as we could.

Would I be able to do this yet again?

I'd certainly try, since from the way Juliet described the

sanctuary now housing the remaining teacup dogs, they were treated well enough but hadn't much human interaction.

Dogs need people. People need dogs. And I do all I can to help fulfill both of those needs.

I'd keep in touch with Mike and Juliet, and with the Faylers and Dante. But for now, I had some time available to do my real job—run HotRescues.

And at this moment, that meant getting a lot of adoptions completed.

I went through the applications again in the order Nina had stacked them. I felt ready to process about nine of them, including seven involving the teacups we currently had available.

With more coming in, those had to be handled first. I looked through them once more, then began calling the applicants, scheduling them to come in, starting with a couple later that afternoon, and the rest the following day, except for some who could only make it on the weekend.

"Busy time," I told Zoey as I hung up after leaving a message for one of the prospective adopters. "Isn't that great?" Zoey looked up at me with her soft brown eyes and wagged her tail, as if answering me. I glanced at the time. The first adopter would arrive in half an hour. That gave Zoey and me time for a quick shelter walk-through.

I ran into Pete first thing, since he was cleaning one of the kennels nearest the entrance. I waved at both him and Shazam, a Doberman who had resided here for too long. But, miraculously, one of the non-teacup applications was for him, and it looked good.

Shazam, named after a comic book character who was a wizard, was about to have a magical new home!

"We've got some teacup adopters coming in this afternoon," I called to Pete. "Shazam's new family will be here tomorrow."

Pete gave a thumbs-up and smiled. "Things are really hopping around here, Lauren. All good."

"All good," I echoed, and Zoey and I continued on.

We had to hurry toward the end, since there were a lot of volunteers around that day despite it being a weekday, and many had stopped me to chat with them. All wanted information about how the teacup rescue and rehoming was going.

Eventually, Zoey and I were back in the welcome area just in time for our first adopter of the day to join us.

I'd met Marshall Droven briefly during our party. He was in his early twenties, lived alone in an apartment that permitted pets, and had fallen for Onyx, a black Pomeranian.

Marshall was of moderate height and thick build and wore a vest over his T-shirt. If I'd thought about it when I'd first seen him, I'd have figured him for a guy who'd want a Lab or shepherd, not a tiny dog. But I'd learned in my many years of running a shelter that it's not always possible to predict people's tastes in their soon-to-be best friends.

"Hi," I said after he introduced himself. "Let's chat for a little while, and then we'll go get Onyx." We sat down at the table below the window in the welcome room.

I introduced him to Nina, who returned from a walk around the shelter just as Marshall and I were getting started. And then we went through his application again so I could ask a few questions.

"What do you sell on the Internet?" I asked, since he'd filled out the line for his profession with "online commerce." I would actually have figured him for still being in school, but he might have chosen not to go to college. Or maybe he was working his way through school.

He smiled, showing gleaming white teeth. "Whatever will make me some money." He went on to explain how he frequented garage sales, estate sales, and thrift shops to find treasures he could post on eBay and other sites.

We asked about careers on the HotRescues application because we preferred not adopting to people who'd leave their new pets—especially puppies or kittens—alone for large amounts of time each day. Marshall's responses to this and other questions made sense, so we soon headed into the kennel area and the building where our small dogs were housed.

"Great place," he said as we walked past enclosures where some dogs were playing with volunteers, and others barked as we went by.

"It sure is." I grinned.

I introduced him to Pete, who joined us as we went around the corner and entered the building housing the small dogs.

I took Onyx out of the enclosure he shared with two other teacups and handed him to Marshall. He smiled at the little dog, looked into his eyes, and tucked him under his arm. "You're coming with me, guy."

I thought about how cute, black little Onyx had looked with a HotPets Bling collar at the party, although all those collars were on loan and had been returned to Dante and his HotPets crew. I wondered if I should have some at HotRescues to give away or sell with the teacup dogs.

I mentioned the collars to Marshall. "Have you seen those ads with little dogs wearing them?"

"Of course I have," he said with a laugh. "That's why I fell in love with the idea not only of owning a dog, but a small one. Onyx and I will stop at a HotPets on the way home to buy one. Thanks so much, Lauren."

"You're welcome. And please keep in touch. Send us some pictures as you and Onyx get better acquainted, okay?"

"I will."

Marshall left a short while later with Onyx, plus a collar and leash and some food to start with, all, of course, from HotPets.

I felt the same bittersweet pang I always got when one of our wards left to go to a new home. I hadn't had much opportunity to get to know Onyx, but I wished him the absolute best life possible.

Our next adopter came just over an hour later. Janice Crift had put in the winning application for Sapphire, who wasn't blue like the gem she was named after but rather a brown Chihuahua.

Janice looked younger than the age she had put on the application, which was twenty-one. She had smooth skin, a ready smile, and long brown hair that looked similar in shade to Sapphire's.

She'd been greeted by Nina, who came to my office to get me. Zoey accompanied me back to the welcome area.

"Hi," I said to Janice, who was already seated at the table. I'd brought her application with me and sat down across from her.

"Hi, Lauren. I'm really glad to be here. Can't wait to get Sapphire."

I smiled. "Just a few details to go over first." I started discussing her application with her.

Like Marshall, she lived in an apartment that accepted pets. She had brought a copy of her lease to prove it.

She, too, worked at home—doing medical transcriptions. I'd have thought someone her age would want to be

out and about in the workforce, but when I asked her about
how she enjoyed her job, she said she loved it—and she'd
love it even more with the company of Sapphire.

Once again, everything seemed to be in order. "Let's go
get Sapphire," I told her, and she did a celebratory fist pump.

It was later in the day now and quieter in the halls. The
dogs and cats were being fed by Pete and the volunteers
who helped him, but most of the volunteers had already left.

"He's really cute, too," Janice said when we neared the
kennel that held Ruff, a shaggy bearded collie mix, before
turning the corner and heading toward the building for
small dogs. Ruff hadn't been here long, and I doubted he'd
take very long to rehome. He was sweet and had an energetic but loving personality. "Could I visit him?"

"Are you interested in adopting him instead of Sapphire?" That could happen, but if someone appeared to
waffle between dogs, I always made them wait and consider which would be a better fit.

"Oh, no," she said hastily. "I'd love to adopt all of them, and
he's particularly appealing. But Sapphire's the one I want."

I wasn't so sure about that. Yet when we were in the
small-dog building and I'd taken Sapphire out of her enclosure, Janet crooned over her, hugging the small brown Chihuahua against her cheek, tearing up a little when she
received doggy kisses on her chin.

I let her walk Sapphire through the HotRescues grounds
toward the office, and she didn't spare a glance toward
Ruff's kennel as we passed. I, on the other hand, tossed
Ruff a sad but warm smile and thought, *It'll be your
day soon, boy*. He stood and wagged his tail, as if he'd
heard me.

I soon had another of those bittersweet moments as Sapphire headed to her new home with Janice.

As I had with the last adoption, I asked Janice to keep in touch, send pictures, and let us know how things went.

Then they left, and I returned to my office. I had lots of things to do there.

And being emotional wasn't among them.

Chapter 16

A light blinked on my office phone, showing I had a message waiting. Zoey was there, lying under my desk. "Why didn't you answer for me?" I asked, and laughed when she stood and walked up to me with her head down, as though she thought I'd really scolded her. "You're a good girl," I assured her. "I know you'd have done it if you could."

The message was from Naya Fayler. "Tom and I want to chat with you about this weekend's plane flight," she said, and the cheerful tone of her voice sounded false.

Did they have to pull out? I hoped not, for the sake of the next planeful of dogs—and for the Faylers. There could be other reasons if they weren't able to fly, but the most likely one would be that the cops told them not to.

No use speculating. I returned the call.

Naya answered on the first ring. "Hi, Lauren. Before you ask, we're still on for this weekend—at least so far. The detectives who've been questioning us know what we're planning and haven't said not to go, but they also have insisted that we give them every iota of information we have about times, locations, flight paths, whatever." Her laugh was mirthless. "I wouldn't be surprised if they made us carry some kind of transponder that would let them know where we are at every moment."

"But it's a good thing, isn't it, that they haven't told you to stay?" *Or arrested you*, I thought. That appeared to be what they were hoping to do, with all the grief they'd been giving the Faylers.

On the other hand, since they hadn't, they must not have had the kind of evidence they needed to try to convict one or both of them. That's what I'd learned from TV shows and from my past nosiness in murder cases.

"Yes," she said, "it is. But I also wanted to let you know that Tom and I have been checking with some of our friends who are also pilots in case this isn't the last flight of this kind you'd like us to do. Dante knows about it, too. He's been working with Tom a lot on expanding what we're doing for Airborne Adoptions, and they've both talked to the guy in charge, Mike Relfer." So I wouldn't need to introduce Dante to him after all. "We haven't gotten anyone to say for certain that they're in, but we'll keep you both informed." She paused. "I really love doing this. I just hope we can continue. And—" Her next pause was a little longer. Had our connection died?

"Naya?" I asked. "Are you still there?"

"Yes." The word came out as a sob. "Lauren?"

"What, Naya?" I asked softly.

"I honestly didn't like that Teresa." She spoke more forcefully now. "She kept making all those really odd insinuations. I had no idea what she was talking about. But that wouldn't have given me a reason to kill her. Tom, either. And we didn't. But the police—" She stopped talking.

"The police don't believe you," I finished. I did—or at least I wanted to.

What I also wanted was to save all those dogs in Missouri, and find them wonderful new homes. I wanted to protect Dante's operations from further disruption by the ongoing interrogation of the head of his new, potentially highly profitable HotPets Bling subsidiary, Tom—and his wife, Naya.

And that, unfortunately, meant that I also really wanted to help solve Teresa's murder . . . as long as the killers really weren't Tom and Naya. But I wouldn't feel certain of that till I learned who the real murderer was.

I soon hung up with Naya. I wanted to talk with Dante. But first I began a computer file as I'd done before when I tried to solve murders. I started it by listing all the people I thought could be the killer, in the order of who I thought was most likely to have done it to the least probable.

Number one, despite our earlier conversation, was Teresa's boyfriend, Mark. Next came that couple from Missouri who'd been here for the party when the dogs were first released from quarantine, Stu and Rhoda Krieg. I'd heard that the police had talked with them, but despite the animosity I saw between Teresa and them at our party, they apparently weren't suspected any more than the Faylers—or if they were, they, too, apparently remained free.

I felt sure Antonio would notify me of any arrests in Teresa's murder, even if he couldn't discuss details.

I then added Teresa's local cousin, Elsa. I'd no good reason to suspect her, but she knew Teresa better than most of the people on my list.

That included Naya and Tom. Also Juliet Ansiger, although she was way near the bottom. She hadn't sounded upset with Teresa, and as far as I knew, she'd remained in Missouri.

My list wasn't especially long, and I really didn't know much about any of my suspects, except, perhaps, the Faylers.

I had to fix that—or at least determine ways to talk to some of them.

Was Mark Black still in town? I didn't know.

What was Elsa's last name, and how could I get in touch with her? I didn't know that, either.

This situation felt really odd to me. Not that I enjoyed getting immersed in murder investigations, but in all the others I'd helped to crack, I'd known more of the players, or at least had known where to find them.

I tried Googling Mark Black. There were certainly a lot of men with that name. Some in Los Angeles. Maybe, with some time and ingenuity, I'd figure out which was the right one from Missouri and learn his phone number.

And Elsa? Without her last name, I'd really no way of finding her.

What could I do?

"What do you think, Zoey?" I asked. She barked.

I looked at the time. It was past seven o'clock. I knew we should go home soon so I could feed her.

But her bark also reminded me that she probably had to go out. And the best place to take her was one of the areas within our shelter where our residents were allowed to run around.

At this hour, I was also likely to see Brooke or whoever was staying overnight on security detail—assuming she was already here.

And I really hoped it would, in fact, be Brooke who'd be here. And that she would have Antonio with her.

"Just a second, Zoey," I said, and phoned Brooke, leaning down to pat my dog and urge her to patience.

"Hi, Lauren," Brooke said almost immediately. "Is anything wrong?"

"Not here," I said. "Who's staying here tonight?"

"Me," she said, and I felt my breath rush out in relief.

"Are you here yet?" I asked.

"I'm about five minutes away. Are you still there?"

"I sure am. I need to talk to you—and Antonio. Will he be joining you?"

"What's going on, Lauren?" She sounded more amused than irritated. As our security director, she knew the kinds of things I might be asking her, either about our animals' safety or . . . something else.

"Why don't you call Antonio and ask him to bring us all some dinner?" I asked. "On me." I'd feed Zoey here. Unsurprisingly, we had a lot of dog food around, and it was excellent quality, since it came from HotPets.

"I'll call him," she said. "But would you care to elaborate on what this is all about?"

"No," I said. "See you soon."

"I know it's not my responsibility," I told Antonio a while later. The three of us were eating upstairs in the main administration building, on the conference table in the middle of the room. Lots of people who'd adopted pets from HotRescues smiled down at us from photos on the yellow walls. It was because of those pets, and the many more to come in the future—especially those from the teacup rescue—that I felt I had to do this. "But an executive at HotPets is involved, and the murder took place right here." I waved my arm expansively, to take in all of my shelter. "I want to help figure this out."

He laughed. "I know you do, Lauren. And all of us in the department appreciate it, and the murders you've solved in the past. But—"

"Sure you do," Brooke said dryly. "That's not the way you've described it to me." She raised her eyebrows and smiled. Her highlighted brown hair enhanced her features as always, and she wore her uniform, consisting of a traditional black T-shirt that said SECURITY STAFF, over matching black jeans.

Brooke, a former P.I., had been ill the first time I'd met her. She had come here to relinquish Cheyenne for rehoming since she didn't think she would survive much longer. Instead, I'd found her help—with Dante's assistance—and she'd regained her health, kept Cheyenne, and been hired here at HotRescues as our primary security provider.

She had brought Cheyenne today, and Zoey and he were at the side of the room lying on the floor near each other, obviously bored with the conversation. Both had already eaten.

The look on Antonio's jagged features was no longer amused. "Okay, I've taken a little heat over encouraging you now, and before on other cases. I don't mind that. But this case is still under investigation, and nothing has been determined yet—except that Teresa was, in fact, killed by cyanide poisoning."

"All the more reason to just give me a little information to use as I'm looking into things. I'll let you know if I find anything useful so you can take credit for it. That's not what I'm after."

"I'm not, either. But I don't want you to put yourself in danger or to interfere in a police investigation."

He sounded like Matt did when he was trying to discourage me from checking things out my own way. They were both officers, though of different organizations. They had their own official agendas.

I had my own unofficial one. But even so, to get what I wanted, I had to figure out a compromise.

But Brooke was the one who got Antonio back in the spirit of things. "Look," she told him, "you can just save Lauren a few steps here, and if she learns anything useful, everyone will benefit. Do you think that your not answering her questions will stop her from pursuing this?" She looked toward me, and I shrugged as I grinned at her. "Now, don't you get all smug, Lauren." My grin faded. "Antonio is right. And so is Matt. And—well, me, too. The good thing is that we're all concerned about you. The bad thing is that you seem to forget that you're not an officer of the law or otherwise trained to protect yourself or others. If Antonio does get the information you've asked for, you'd just better do as you promised and keep everyone informed about what you're up to and what you learn. Agreed?"

I was taken aback by what she said and by her take-no-prisoners attitude, as if she were the boss and I were her employee, instead of vice versa.

On the other hand, I supposed that what she said was right. And an indication that she, like Matt and Antonio, gave a damn.

"I agree," I said sheepishly, leaning against the table and taking a sip of my cola, to give myself a breather. Then I turned back toward Antonio, who sat at Brooke's other side. "So . . . how soon can you get me the information?"

Chapter 17

Antonio was quick. I had to grant him that.

While Brooke and I cleaned up after our dinner, he went downstairs. I assumed he was making a phone call, and that assumption proved true, I learned when he met us as we walked down the steps behind the dogs.

"Okay, here's what I found out." He glanced at a small pad on which he'd apparently written notes, as Brooke took the trash both she and I had been carrying and headed out toward the covered garbage can in the parking lot. "Mark Black has been told not to leave town, and he is staying with Teresa's cousin Elsa Martin in Hollywood. They've both been cooperating with the investigation. They remain persons of interest but appear to be less so than some other people connected with the case."

"Like the Faylers," I surmised.

"That's right. And also that brother and sister who were here at the party, the Kriegs."

"They're brother and sister? I assumed they were a married couple." Whoever they were, they'd clearly had a gripe with Teresa, so Antonio's reference to them wasn't surprising.

"No, they're siblings. They both attend USC and share an apartment near the campus."

That was most likely why they'd left Missouri. But they hadn't left their biases there.

"I don't suppose you have phone numbers or addresses that you can give me," I told Antonio as Brooke returned inside, giving both Zoey and Cheyenne, who'd stayed with us, a pat.

"Nope. I've already given you more information than I should." He paused and glared at me with his edgy brown eyes. "And you remember your promise, don't you, to keep me informed about everything you're up to?"

"Yes, I remember. And—Antonio, I really appreciate your help."

As he, Brooke, and Cheyenne left the building to check out the shelter before retiring for the night in the security quarters, I gathered Zoey's leash and my own thoughts.

Was I really doing the right thing by pursuing this? In the other murder cases I'd gotten involved with, I'd had a closer relationship to the suspects—or at least in most of them.

But I wasn't only doing this for the Faylers, I reminded myself as I opened the door to my Venza and let Zoey jump in. All of HotPets was somewhat involved, and I definitely owed its CEO a lot.

And besides . . . the faces of the teacup dogs who'd already arrived here inserted themselves into my mind yet again. Others like them also needed help, and my assisting the Faylers could lead to their obtaining wonderful futures.

I vowed to dig out the contact information for all the

people Antonio and I had discussed and to make some calls tomorrow morning.

The next day, Mark Black walked into our welcome area at HotRescues late in the morning. I hadn't expected him, but I was glad he was there.

I would get his phone number this time.

Nina, at our entry desk, had sent an e-mail to my computer as soon as Mark walked in the door: "Do you know why Teresa's boyfriend is here? Is he going to become as intrusive as she was about our little dogs?"

I responded quickly, "We won't let him," then hurried to greet him, Zoey at my heels.

He'd seemed rather ordinary to me before, with his thin build and large and expressive brow. Now, I almost expected devil's horns to emerge from somewhere beneath his milk chocolate–colored hair.

Which told me I'd already drawn a conclusion regarding his guilt. Even so, the police had questioned him but hadn't taken him into custody. They were the experts. I was only an interested bystander who wanted to protect the Faylers for reasons of my own. Assuming they were, in fact, innocent.

"Thanks for coming," I told him, attempting to smile. "How have you been? I imagine that things have been difficult for you. I'm sorry for your loss." Even though I hadn't known Teresa well and hadn't especially liked her, she'd been this man's girlfriend. I had seen him after Teresa's death but hadn't expressed my condolences.

Besides, I wanted to see his reaction.

"Thank you." He bowed his head as if in pain. Genuine, or an act? When he raised it again, he looked me straight in the eye, his gaze sad. "Lauren, can we talk?"

"Sure. Would you like to come into my office?"

"Could we walk through HotRescues instead? I like your shelter, and maybe seeing all the animals will help cheer me a little."

"All right."

I left Zoey in Nina's care, wanting to fully concentrate on my pending interrogation.

As we walked out the door into the first shelter area, I said, "You've been here before, so I won't turn this into a tour, but feel free to ask any questions. Do you have a pet at home?"

"I do—an Irish setter mix named Bopper. My family's taking care of him while I'm here. I didn't think this trip would be good for him, since it was such a long drive. And it's a good thing I didn't bring him. I'd no idea I'd still be here—and for such a hard reason."

His dog wasn't teacup size. I wasn't surprised. And the segue from his response into my further questions wasn't difficult.

"Once again, I'm sorry—even more so because Teresa died here. I just wish I really knew what happened, who hurt her."

We were on the walkway between the kennel area and the first building on the right, which contained the HotRescues security facilities. The cameras might be on and recording, but no one would be watching them. Nor would they capture our voices. Not that I expected Mark to blurt out a confession right here, but just in case . . .

"Me, too," he said, "although I think we both know." He'd stopped walking and turned to face me. "From the time I got here, she kept talking about Las Vegas, and transferring the dogs into the Faylers' plane, and the fact that they were so obviously hiding something, although she didn't tell me what it was. Do you know?"

"I heard her insinuations, too," I told him, "but, no, I've no idea what she meant."

"I told the police that, hoping they'd let something drop, but I got the impression they didn't know, either. But I'm going to find out."

Interesting. I still didn't feel sure about his innocence, but I now had the impression that he, too, might be conducting an investigation into Teresa's murder—or at least that he wanted people to think so, possibly to shift their suspicions away from him.

I decided to play along, at least for now. Act like we were both on the same side—as he appeared to be doing with me.

"To be honest with you," I said, "my hope is to clear the Faylers of suspicion, since they're now helping to bring rescue dogs here for Airborne Adoptions. Plus, as I'm sure you're aware, Tom works for HotPets, and most of HotRescues' funding comes from the CEO." That was a matter of public record, so I wasn't in any way harming Dante by mentioning it.

"I know. I've checked. Cute dog." Mark's gaze had moved beyond me to the nearest kennel. Inside was Shazam, the Doberman.

"Yes, he is. Sweet, too. He's about to be adopted—going home today."

"That's a good thing in more ways than one. I won't be tempted to bring him home with me."

An attitude like that made me feel like my impression of him was thawing. I had to remain cautious. It could all be an act.

But acting friendly with Mark Black remained on my agenda, too. If he was guilty, he'd probably drop a clue. I'd need to be able to recognize and interpret it.

And if he wasn't—well, maybe we could form some kind of alliance to dig up the truth.

"As you said, it's a long ride," I reminded him. "Besides, how would Bopper feel if you brought someone else home with you?"

"He's pretty good about getting along with other dogs we meet, but you're right."

We started walking again.

"About the Faylers," he said, "I honestly don't know— not yet, at least—what Teresa was talking about. But I gathered it had something to do with that flight, or something they discussed . . . but she didn't go into detail other than to say she was going to do something about it. She hinted it would be something she'd be happy about. Maybe saving more animals? I just don't know." He looked at me. "Any ideas?"

I wouldn't have told him even if I'd known anything— but I didn't. I shook my head. "Sorry. I wish I did."

We started walking again, and I pointed out how great our volunteers were about getting inside the kennels and socializing their inhabitants.

"I'm becoming even more impressed with HotRescues, Lauren," he told me. "But I'd still like some answers."

"Me, too. In fact—well, you know better than me, but what is Elsa like? I mean, Teresa was staying here with her cousin. Did they get along all right?"

He laughed. "Elsa is probably the least likely to have killed Teresa of anyone. Not that Teresa didn't give her a hard time. She gave me and everyone else a hard time. But Teresa did have a good heart, especially when it came to protecting animals. And Elsa? Well . . . you know what? Are you available for dinner tonight?"

"Maybe, but—"

"I'll get Elsa to come here and we'll all go out and talk." My expression must have seemed dubious, since he added, "Believe me, I'm not hitting on you. Teresa and I—Anyway, bring a date if you want. We'll all talk about what happened and who we think did it. Not that we'll reach any good conclusions, but I'm sure I'll prove to you that whoever killed Teresa, it wasn't Elsa."

"All right," I said. "Let's do it."

We continued our stroll around HotRescues, and I pointed out more of our attributes, introducing him to dogs, volunteers, and staff—and even cats, after we turned the corner to the other part of the shelter and our building that housed felines.

I felt certain that Mark intended to put me off guard with our pending dinner so that I might start to doubt that he could have killed Teresa.

But I would keep an open mind.

Chapter 18

From later that morning through the afternoon, my time at HotRescues was delightful. Six adoptions! I barely had time to breathe, and loved it that way. Of course I skipped lunch.

The first two adoptions involved more of the little teacup rescues. One, Rhinestone, a pale brown Pekingese, went home with a senior couple who'd bonded with her right away. The other, Garnet, a tiny reddish male poodle, was adopted by an attractive twentysomething woman who was a computer programmer and worked near her home.

The next adoption was particularly special to me. Shazam, the well-trained Doberman, finally went home with a couple who were engaged and about to be married. They seemed so thrilled to be increasing their new family this way, since they'd immediately fallen in love with Shazam, and they promised to leave him with the bride's loving parents during their honeymoon.

Next, one of our cats, Abyss, a part Abyssinian with a dense, attractive coat, was adopted by a college student who said she needed company at home while she did her homework. Abyss had a caring personality but was also independent, so it seemed like a good fit.

And then two more teacup dogs, both Yorkies: Aquamarine, who had a long brindle coat, and Topaz, whose fur was primarily yellow. Aquamarine couldn't stop licking the face of the stocky young man who picked him up. I had initial reservations when the guy immediately rubbed his mouth with a sanitary wipe, but he laughed and said that, though he was a germophobe, he hoped that owning a dog would help cure him. The guy lived in a Valley apartment that allowed pets.

Topaz's new owner was a young woman who also had a nearby apartment. She giggled a lot and looked adoringly at the small Yorkie, hugging her tightly as if she worried about losing her.

As I watched them leave our welcome area, I heard Nina behind me. "What a day. Are you okay, Lauren? You look exhausted—rightfully so."

"What a nice compliment," I said, sinking down onto a chair at our table beneath the window. "But, yes, I'm really tired. In a good way. So many new homes just today. I'm so happy for the animals."

"Me, too." She came out from behind our leopard-print counter and stood there with her hands on her hips, grinning. "Too bad all days aren't like this."

I rose, too. "I need to go get Zoey and take her for a walk. Maybe if we did so many adoptions every day, I'd be used to it enough not to feel pooped. Wouldn't that be great? I'd love it. But I still have half of our teacups to send home—and I'm hoping for another rescue this weekend."

"Those Bling ads keep going," Nina said. "I see them on TV and on a lot of streets in commercial areas. That's so good for finding little dogs new homes, and it's likely to stay that way."

"I agree." I picked up the paperwork I'd been collecting for all the adoptions and started walking toward my office and Zoey. It seemed that the ads were attracting more young adult adopters than any other age range, but I supposed that made sense. Younger people were more attracted to contemporary technology like the digital HotPets Bling outdoor ads.

Even so, I decided I'd start asking the teacup adopters how they'd heard of HotRescues and why they'd chosen the small rescued dogs over others, just because I was curious.

I perked up considerably that evening when Zoey and I met Matt and his dog, Rex, at our house. Together, all four of us headed to the family restaurant with the dog-friendly outdoor patio where I'd arranged to join Mark and Elsa for dinner—and some serious discussion about Teresa.

They were both there already, and they had saved an outdoor table despite how crowded the place was—both with human patrons and their companion dogs. The patio was large and surrounded by tall hedges, and there were no other tables available.

I had previously warned Mark that we'd have our dogs with us, but not any that Teresa had flown with. Matt and I had changed out of our respective uniforms and were both dressed casually.

So was Mark, in jeans and a St. Louis Cardinals T-shirt. Elsa, though, wore a skirt and blouse.

When I had met her before, I hadn't paid a lot of attention

to her appearance—mostly because I'd only seen her around her cousin Teresa, whose personality, as abrasive as it was, far overshadowed the quiet Elsa. Or so I'd thought.

Now, though, Elsa seemed more outgoing. As Matt and I sat down at the round table and the dogs lay down at our feet, Elsa said, "It's good to see you again, Lauren. I really liked visiting HotRescues. How is the shelter doing? Have you gotten rid of many of the dogs that Teresa brought here?"

I didn't contradict her and say that her cousin hadn't brought any of the teacup pups here, but had accompanied them while griping over the fact that they were being flown to La-La Land. "About half of them have been adopted so far," I said, looking up from the menu to watch for her reaction. "We also have adoption applications on a few more. So although we don't consider that anything like 'getting rid' of them, we're happy to say that we've been able to find quite a few of them new homes already."

She didn't comment on that but seemed to have all her attention suddenly grabbed by the menu. I took the opportunity to study mine as well. When the server came by, I ordered a diet soda to start with.

After the server left, I exchanged glances with Matt. He never liked it when I got involved with attempting to solve a murder, no matter how involved my friends or I happened to be. We'd exchanged more words over the current situation, since I barely knew the Faylers. But I'd done as he'd previously asked and let him know what I was up to, and why.

He did understand my concerns about HotPets, Dante, and the dogs marooned halfway across the country after their rescue. But he had insisted on joining me here tonight.

Which was fine with me. Although I seldom admitted it to him, I appreciated his concern. I appreciated *him*. I still wasn't sure where our relationship was going, but it was definitely a relationship.

"So," Matt said, looking toward Mark, who sat beside him. "I understand that you've been questioned by the police about what happened to Teresa." I'd already told Matt about my discussions with Mark, but it didn't hurt to go over the subject again. And again. Maybe the answers would change. "Is that why you're still in town? I know she was your girlfriend, and I'm sorry for your loss."

"I'm still here partly because I've been told to hang around, but I'm also hoping to learn the truth. Or get it confirmed."

"That's right," Elsa cut in. For the first time, I actually studied her. It didn't surprise me that I hadn't taken in her appearance before. Her looks were plain, and she hardly wore any makeup. Her nose stuck out a bit, her lips were narrow, and her cheeks were a little sunken. Even her hair wasn't particularly memorable, a pale brown, unstyled mop. "Getting what happened confirmed is the key." She picked up the glass of water the server had put in front of her and took a drink. "We all know what really happened."

"Actually, I don't," I informed her mildly, although I found her attitude almost as irritating as her cousin's had been. Was she now sliding into Teresa's shoes? "What do you think happened?"

"It was those pilots who killed poor Teresa." She took another swig of water as if she wished it were alcoholic. "When she got here, Teresa didn't stop talking about how awful her plane rides here had been, especially the last leg. She kept saying things were really off in Las Vegas when those Faylers met up with her and the dogs. They didn't even talk to her at first, mostly just meeting up with a bunch of people who were evidently there from some pet stores, even though she'd been waiting awhile for them to arrive.

After that, she said things were really miserable. She hinted that she'd seen some pretty nasty stuff but wouldn't tell even me what it was."

"Me, neither," Mark cut in. "I had the same impression, and she usually told me everything, but not this time. But I had no idea what she was hiding."

I determined to speak with the Faylers again as soon as I could, to see if they had any idea what Teresa had been talking about. Or not talking about, as the case may be.

"She was just so . . . well, so preoccupied this trip," Elsa went on, then shut up as the server brought our meals.

We ate in silence for a few minutes—at least at our table. A couple of other tables near us had children and their parents at them, and several of the kids seemed very wound up and vocal. That didn't seem to faze either Rex or Zoey, though. That was partly because they both were good dogs . . . and partly because Matt and I rewarded them with treats we had brought along to encourage them to stay down and quiet.

Then I asked Elsa, "Did Teresa visit here often? You seemed to be pretty close."

"No, she didn't." Elsa looked down at her plate, which held a double hamburger. "We saw each other now and then. I just wish—well, she didn't give me much notice that she was coming this time, which I, of course, understood under the circumstances. I'd been glad, since we used to be closer. But this time . . ."

Her voice trailed off, which only made me more curious. "Did you feel less close to her?"

"Of course not," Elsa snapped, then seemed to regain her temper. She sighed. "Look, I have a life, too. I'm a schoolteacher, and although it's August and classes don't start for another couple of weeks, I've still needed to work, show up at school for meetings, work on lesson plans and all. I really didn't have time to be Teresa's chauffeur while she was here, but she didn't have a car and she was so nervous about driving around big L.A., since she comes from a small town . . . well, I decided to help her out."

"I'm sure she was very grateful," I said mildly, suspecting that what I said wasn't true but wanting to gauge Elsa's reaction.

"She should have been but she wasn't," Elsa snapped, and then bent her head. "Teresa . . . she was used to getting her way. About everything. And she didn't get her way about starting her own pet shelter back in Missouri, at least not yet. She was rather difficult while she was here. I sympathized, of course."

"Of course," I echoed.

"You think I didn't," Elsa snapped once more. "I did. But I really hated having to just act like, well, her servant."

"So why did you?" That was Mark asking. He'd been living at Elsa's, too. Hadn't he seen this? Why was he asking?

"It was a good thing you arrived when you did," Elsa said. "I'd been all ready to kick her out of my place, tell her to go rent a room and a car and all. But then you started chauffeuring her around in your car, so things were a little less crazy."

"But you still argued with her a lot," Mark persisted. "Why?"

"You heard," Elsa all but shouted. "She kept telling me what to do, how to live. Why did I have such a small apartment? Why did I give her a hard time when, during the school year, I undoubtedly was a doormat to kids, so I was used to listening to other people? Why didn't I have a dog? And all that."

She picked up a French fry and dipped it into the ketchup on her plate, staring at it instead of at anyone at our table.

"What did you tell her?" I asked.

"I told her to go and . . . well, I'm not going to repeat it here, but it was pretty nasty. And she, she . . . she just laughed."

"I see," I said. Elsa had clearly been pretty angry, because I gathered she'd used swear words—perhaps some that everyone heard these days, but as a teacher she clearly found them upsetting.

"But I didn't kill her, if that's what you're thinking." Her tone was belligerent, and she stared from me to Mark to Matt, and back to me again.

"I wasn't thinking that," I lied. "But . . . well, you were at the party at HotRescues that night. Were you arguing with Teresa then?"

"None of your business," Elsa said. And that was pretty much the last thing she said for the rest of the meal, except for asking people to pass things and anteing up for her part of the bill.

I had a strong feeling that Elsa Martin was moving up several notches on my suspect list as soon as I got home.

But as it turned out, I didn't get anywhere near the computer that night.

Matt and I discussed the dinner conversation on the way back to my place, both dogs in the back of his car.

"So . . . I think either of those people could have killed Teresa," he said, "not necessarily the Faylers."

"My thoughts exactly," I said. We talked over Elsa and her attitude, and how Mark had pressed her some when I wasn't doing it—but was that just to move our suspicions away from him and onto Teresa's cousin?

"But we've heard more than once," I said, "about how Teresa and the Faylers argued on the flight from Vegas. Elsa mentioning how Teresa kept grumbling about the Faylers without saying anything specific could have been her way to shift blame elsewhere, just as Mark may have been doing."

"Agreed," Matt said as I used the electronic gadget I'd brought along to open the gate into my secure community.

I knew what I wanted to do next. And that involved Matt's staying the night, which he did.

But as soon as possible, I had other plans in mind for pushing my investigation forward.

Chapter 19

I'd checked with Dante first, of course, but he had no problem with my talking to Tom Fayler alone in the HotPets Bling area of the corporate offices the next day. I'd been honest with Dante. I wanted to talk not only about the upcoming weekend's rescue flight, but also more about Teresa Kantrim and what had happened to her—as well as the Faylers' conversations with her.

I headed for Tom's nice corner office at the far end of the area dedicated to the Bling label. On my way there, I peeked into a number of open doors and also looked at the name cards on the walls outside the rest. Since this was a subsidiary of the major organization, they didn't seem to have a separate accounting staff, but the people officed here apparently included planners and retail liaisons and an advertising staff, as well as designers besides Chris Mandrea.

When I reached Tom's office, the door was open. I knocked on it as I peeked in.

Tom stood up from behind his very messy desk and walked over to me. "Lauren, how good to see you. Sheila told me you were on your way."

I figured that Dante must have told his assistant to let Tom know what I was up to once I'd called him. "I hope you have a minute," I responded. Or five or ten.

"Of course. Please have a seat."

I'd already rehashed in my mind the results of the conversation we'd had during lunch a couple of days ago. Naya had done most of the talking for the Faylers. As I recalled, she'd said that Teresa kept making odd references and accusations that they hadn't understood, but she wouldn't explain them.

"I'm here for a couple of reasons, Tom," I began, sitting in the un-blingy green upholstered chair across from his desk. "Mostly, I want to help Naya and you. At least that's what I want if you aren't, in fact, Teresa's killers. But if you are, I don't really expect you to admit it to me."

"Understood. But whether you believe it or not, it wasn't us." I was used to seeing Tom smiling, but he wasn't grinning now. His cheeks didn't look as wide now, and his face looked gaunt beneath his short graying hair.

I leaned forward, wanting to look as sincere as I felt. "I want to believe you. You save animals and you work for HotPets, and those add up in your favor. But I don't really understand what went on between Teresa and you, and—"

"Neither do we," he interrupted. "Look, Lauren. We're a pretty tight group here at HotPets. Dante has talked a lot about you and all the great things you've done for HotRescues. He's also mentioned that you've gotten involved as an amateur in solving murders, of all things. I was really glad to hear you were coming today, because I was hoping to . . . well, ask you to solve this one. It wasn't me, and it wasn't

Naya, so if you could figure out who really killed Teresa, that would be fantastic." He half stood, raising his moderate-sized body, clad in a similar dressy shirt and slacks as I'd seen him in the few times we'd been together lately. Although he still wasn't smiling, I read hope in his gaze.

"I don't do it by choice, exactly, and you're right. I'm an amateur." I wanted to warn him. I couldn't exactly say I'd be able to figure things out and save Naya and him—and I now believed, since he'd asked me to get involved, that nei-ther of them was likely to be the killer.

Although I knew what Matt would say to me right now. Tom might be attempting to put me off guard, so I should watch my back and assume nothing.

But that was Matt. "Why don't you tell me all you remem-ber from the time you met Teresa," I said. "Maybe some-thing will give a hint as to why she acted so belligerently and strangely with you. And that might give a hint about what she did or said with other people—and led to her murder."

I sat there with Tom for maybe three quarters of an hour, listening and asking questions.

And drawing no conclusions.

He had someone bring refreshments, so I sipped on black coffee and nibbled on cookies as I listened.

Naya and he had arrived at the Las Vegas airport a little late the day they were transporting the dogs. "There was a backup taking off in Van Nuys because of mechanical trou-bles one plane developed while taxiing." I hadn't known that, because I'd left when they'd entered their plane. "Every-thing worked out all right, but the rest of us had to wait."

All the other Airborne Adoptions flight segments had been on time—Missouri to Oklahoma City to Albuquerque.

By the time the Faylers had arrived in Vegas, the last plane before theirs, the one from Albuquerque, had been there for probably an hour. The pilots had walked the dogs, had made sure they had water, and had generally taken good care of them.

But they hadn't been the only ones on that plane. Teresa had been along for all of the flight segments.

According to the pilots on the flight from Albuquerque, she, too, had helped to take care of the dog passengers. But she had apparently gotten bored. She went inside the terminal and the nearest hangars, claiming she'd needed to find restroom facilities, and maybe she had. But she had spent more time away from the plane than she had helping the dogs she'd professed to care about.

When the Faylers landed, they met the Albuquerque pilots right away, who'd described how they had cared for the dogs while waiting. They had acted suitably impressed about the HotPets connection and had oohed and aahed over the HotPets Bling collars.

It had soon been time to transfer the little dogs to the Faylers' plane. "And talk about oohing and aahing," Tom said with a wistful smile. "Naya and I . . . well, we were so pleased to see all those little dogs and knew we were helping to save them."

They'd left them alone in their Cessna, but only for a short while.

"Those pilots warned us that there was someone from the Missouri shelter traveling with the dogs, and that we should wait for her before taking off again."

Which had been fine with them, despite it being unexpected. They hadn't intended to leave immediately anyway.

They had called ahead, so the four managers of the local HotPets stores knew they'd be late and had arrived at the airport around the same time. The Faylers hadn't checked for where their unexpected passenger was; instead Naya and Tom had done as they'd originally planned: they brought out some boxes of the HotPets Bling dog collars to show the store managers and give them a few samples. They'd discussed marketing and promotion strategies inside a nearby hangar where there were seats.

The private-flight section of the airport had been busy, with lots of landings and takeoffs, as well as local personnel helping to load and unload the planes, including the Faylers'.

Eventually, a strange woman had come up to them at their meeting. She had introduced herself as Teresa Kantrim from Missouri, and said she had flown in on the plane from Albuquerque and intended to ride to L.A. with them to ensure that the dogs were being well treated.

"And how was Teresa during that initial meeting?" I asked.

"At first, she was friendly. Smiled a lot. Shook hands with the HotPets store managers and acted charmed about the HotPets Bling necklaces which we showed her. We'd brought a lot to show these guys but were taking some back with us. When we got ready to go, we did as asked and made room for her in the back of our plane, and she helped as we walked the dogs once more. The other Airborne Adoptions pilots had already left, but we said good-bye to the HotPets people and got on our way."

It was on the plane toward L.A. that Teresa had first gotten snippy. "She started poking us by saying she knew what we were up to, she wanted more, she wouldn't tell anyone if she was treated right—but she wouldn't explain. And then she totally shut up, after saying it wasn't over."

"Hi, Lauren." Chris Mandrea had just entered the office.

He sat down in one of the chairs beside me. "You're all talking about Teresa Kantrim again, aren't you?"

This was a good opportunity for me. "Yes, we are. I don't suppose you know what she was hinting about."

"Not really, but she kept pushing about it after I first met her, too, and when I asked her what she was talking about she got really nasty."

"Same here." That was Sheila Sheltron, who had just walked in the door. "I'd never say anyone deserved what happened to Teresa, but if she acted that way to everyone she met here in California, I can't say I'm surprised. She was also complaining all the time about you, Lauren, and how you'd been pushy about getting the dogs here and that, even though HotRescues had a good reputation, you'd never be able to take care of all of those rescues and find them suitable homes. What a nasty piece of work she was."

This conversation was interesting, but it wasn't netting me any helpful data for figuring out who had killed Teresa.

I wanted to press the Faylers some more, without promising to help them. I still didn't think they'd killed Teresa, but I couldn't prove who else had done it because I really didn't know.

Could I add Sheila and Chris to my suspect list? Not likely. Although—

"I agree," Chris responded to Sheila. "You know, she found out that I was the head designer for the Bling collars and used the opportunity to tell me what a waste they were. Collars already existed that had shiny designs in them. And how dare I be involved with an organization that was so wild to publicize their product that they endangered little dogs?"

"Endangered?" Sheila all but shouted. "All HotPets did was to make little dogs more popular around here. They were *endangered* in her part of the country. We—you, Lauren—were saving them."

I couldn't disagree with that. In fact, I very much agreed with it.

But Chris's response had made me wonder. Especially when he continued to express his anger, especially about how the woman just wouldn't shut up, even when there were a lot of other people present, like at the HotRescues party.

Surely that wouldn't have given him a motive to kill her.

Or would it?

His anger made him more of a suspect than the Faylers, based on what they had described.

I wasn't sure yet exactly where, but I would be adding Chris Mandrea to my suspect list.

Chapter 20

My mind was reeling as I headed back to HotRescues that afternoon, but I was quickly distracted from the murder as I saw the wonderful chaos there. Even though it was a Thursday and not a weekend, a lot of people were visiting. I could tell by the number of cars in our parking lot.

"Our volunteers are really busy today," Nina warned me as I entered the welcome area. "We've gotten half a dozen applications already, too—mostly for the remaining little dogs."

"I'll take a look at them. Are any of the applicants still here?"

"As far as I know, they all are. Most of them wanted to hang out with the dogs they hoped to adopt—maybe to ward off others who were interested, too."

Interesting. No one had mentioned, at the HotPets office, that there was a new round of Bling ads going out, but maybe the existing campaign hadn't stopped attracting people to taking home teacup-sized dogs.

"I think I'll go take a look. Is Zoey in my office?"

"Yes. I shut her in there. There was a lot going on, and I was afraid she'd get an application put on her!" Nina smiled so I knew she was joking, but I also realized that, with all the tumult going on at HotRescues, Zoey was better off staying out of the way.

I did go in to see her and give her a hug, then said, "Stay, girl. I'll be back soon." Of course, she obeyed.

I went down the hall and out the door into the kennel area. It wasn't as jammed as when we'd held the party here, but there were still a lot of people around—which was a good thing, especially in that location, since it was where medium to large dogs were housed. Maybe this group was working its way toward the building with the small dogs, but perhaps some would fall in love along the way. Or even in the cat house around the back corner.

Almost as soon as I got outside, Mamie Spelling approached from the crowd. She looked harried, which wasn't good for this senior volunteer who'd had some mental issues that had led to her being an animal hoarder. I didn't think she'd start hoarding again—no, I knew she wouldn't, because I'd helped to arrange her current living situation in a senior center that allowed few pets—but I didn't want her former confusion to return.

"Hi, Mamie," I said. "Everything okay?"

"Sort of. But—do we have any of those HotPets Bling collars for sale here?"

We did have an area where adopters could buy a few things, like leashes, collars, and food, but only regular collars—so far. "No, we don't," I told her.

"Well, we should. Almost everyone is asking to buy

them, especially people interested in those little teacup dogs." The frown on her wrinkled face as she looked up at me caused her chin to lift almost belligerently, and I kept myself from smiling. No, she wasn't confused at all. In fact, she seemed to have a mission.

"I like the idea," I said without mentioning that I'd thought about it, too. "I'll look into it."

She took me over to a family of potential adopters whom she had introduced to Mabel, the setter mix in one of the nearby kennels. "We'd come here to see the little dogs," the mother said, "but Mabel is so cute . . ."

I could only smile back at her. Her kids appeared to be in their early teens, which could be a good fit with a moderate-sized dog. "Yes, she is. And well behaved. I'm sure Mamie can tell you the process if you're interested in putting in an application to adopt Mabel."

I continued walking through our kennel area, and my smile only broadened. So many people looking longingly at so many dogs . . . I wondered how many adoptions would result.

When I finally reached our building housing smaller dogs, I grew even happier, even as I felt just the slightest amount of concern as Pete Engersol came up to me, his hands filled with papers. "We've got applications on nearly all the rest of the teacup dogs now," he told me. "Some more than one. I was just bringing them to Nina."

"Do the potential adopters seem like good fits?"

"I think so. A bunch of them are still here. Want to meet them?"

"Sure." I held out my hand for the applications. I'd make notes on the ones with which I'd talked to the people who'd filled them out.

Good thing I didn't need to make a decision on the spot,

but of the six remaining dogs from the teacup rescue, five had applications. Of those, four of the people wanting to adopt were still there.

They were all single, living in condos or apartments. Two were men and two were women. Their ages ranged from twenty-one to twenty-six.

Their applications seemed quite good.

And yet . . . were they too good?

I wasn't sure what struck me as being a little off here, but I was glad that I wasn't approving adoptions on the spot. Instead, I talked to the young people individually about where they worked and why they wanted to adopt a dog.

They all sounded good enough that, had I wanted to, I'd have felt fine about letting the adoptions go through fast . . . except that I needed some time to absorb what was going on. I didn't know why yet. Maybe it was just all too many, too fast.

But each time I pulled one of the little dogs out of his or her kennel area and put him or her into the would-be adopter's arms, there were so many hugs and licks that I almost tossed out my misgivings as just a reaction to a bit of stress.

Almost.

As Mamie had warned me, several asked about the Hot-Pets Bling collars, whose ads had gotten their attention and sent them here to adopt. "Do you have any here to sell?" asked Sissy, who had put in an application on Opal, a sweet little white Maltese.

"Not at the moment," I told her, "but I hope to get some soon." In fact, I'd call Dante or Tom a little later, once all this chaos died down a little and I could return to my office.

All the potential adopters seemed to support one another. None was too pushy with me, but the group encouragement somehow made me feel like putting the brakes on even more.

Which I did.

"Sorry, guys," I told them all. "I know you'd like things to go as fast as possible, but that's not how we work here at HotRescues. Why don't you go home now, and I'll be in touch with each of you so you can come back and we'll go over your applications. It shouldn't take long, but I need some time."

None appeared too upset, fortunately, but they traded glances that I read as being not so thrilled by the shelter manager's overprotectiveness.

Well, tough.

Eventually, it was late enough that I could justifiably invite them to leave because it was the end of the day's visiting hours. The animals had to be fed and their enclosures cleaned.

And I needed some time to think.

As I walked back through the shelter grounds, I saw my staff and volunteers also gently herding our visitors out. When all of them had gone, I thanked the HotRescues gang. "This kind of day is a good thing, but not easy," I told them. "I really appreciate your help."

"Not doing it for you," said Bev, her words softened by a large grin. "We're all for getting the animals into new homes."

"Amen," said Gavin Mamo, our dog trainer, who happened to be around this afternoon. He was a large Hawaiian who knew just how to get animals to do what he wanted by rewards, not by any kind of punishment.

"I get it," I told them with a grin of my own. "It's all about our pets." I waved to everyone as I finally headed back to my office.

Zoey was loose now. Nina had released her after the outflow of visitors had passed through our welcome building. She greeted me at the door and accompanied me down the hall where I thanked Nina, who was about to leave.

I'd gathered the applications filled out that day and combined them with the ones other potential adopters had left earlier. Then Zoey and I returned to my office, where I sank down onto my desk chair. I didn't feel as if I'd done very much, but I was exhausted anyway.

My plan was to go through the applications and make notes about what other questions I needed to ask each person or family.

First, though, I had a phone call to make.

Using my cell, I rang Dante. He didn't answer, so I left a message, requesting that he get back to me as soon as it was convenient.

I then called Matt. I didn't reach him either, but I left another message.

Then I got to work studying the applications.

As I'd anticipated, five were for teacup dogs. On impulse, I next called Tom Fayler. He, at least, answered. "We're adopting these little guys out fast," I told him, even though I'd yet to approve any of the current applications. "Are you and Naya still available for Sunday?"

They were, so I did as I had last time and also confirmed once more with Juliet Ansiger that the second batch of dogs would be available to transport, and with Mike Relfer to ensure that Airborne Adoptions had pilots to handle the flights from Missouri to Las Vegas.

All was well.

And on impulse I called Tom back. "Feel free to say no if you'd like," I said, "but I'd love to be a passenger while you pick up the latest load of pups."

"Not to speak ill of the dead," he quipped, "or maybe so, but as long as you promise not to act as nasty as Teresa, you're more than welcome."

"Well, as long as you tell me if I start acting nasty, that's fine with me."

I smiled as I hung up and returned to the applications.

A short while later, my ring tone sounded, and I looked at the caller ID. Matt. We arranged to get together for dinner that night, although he wouldn't be available till late. He'd come to my place with Rex, and I'd bring in a pizza.

While we were ending our conversation, my phone indicated another caller. I quickly said good-bye to Matt and answered. This time it was Dante.

I told him how busy things had been at HotRescues today. "If all goes well, I'll have a bunch of adoptions to finalize."

Which pleased him—and why not? This was his shelter, too.

I then described how eager visitors here seemed to be about buying HotPets Bling collars. "How would you feel about my stocking some to sell?"

"It's a great idea," he said. "In fact, how would you like to join me tomorrow at our City of Industry manufacturing facility to pick up a bunch there for you to sell?"

"Really?" That sounded like fun.

We arranged for a time to meet the next day.

I'd never seen any of the HotPets merchandise being produced before. A lot of it was food, and the facilities were located all over the country.

Then there were the other things pets needed: toys, collars, leashes, and more. Once again, I figured that the manufacturing plants could be anywhere. I hadn't thought about whether any might be nearby. That wasn't necessarily of interest to me anyway.

But the Bling collars? I wouldn't admit to being any

more interested in them than I was with the other HotPets products . . . but I was. They were special.

And the advertising for them had certainly resulted in keeping me busy.

I really looked forward to seeing how they were made.

Chapter 21

I'd passed the City of Industry before but had never stopped anywhere to visit. When I looked it up on the Internet before heading there, I noted that its human population was quite low, but that didn't apply to its population of industrial facilities. Nearly all of its streets were lined with commercial buildings, mostly for manufacturing—not surprising, considering its name.

I programmed the address of the HotPets Bling plant into my GPS before heading there, then drove on freeways that took me east of downtown. As usual, L.A. traffic going in that direction wasn't exactly fast, but I nevertheless arrived there on time.

The building where HotPets Bling was manufactured appeared very unassuming on the outside, as did most of its neighboring buildings. They looked like . . . well, factories.

I parked my Venza in a fairly empty lot at the building's

side, noting that Dante's silver Mercedes was already there. I got out and went around to the front sidewalk.

The structure was long and low and gray, with symmetrical blocks of green windows. There was no grand entryway, just a sidewalk lined with low hedges that led up to a double glass door.

I walked up to the door and found it was locked. I saw a call box on the wall beside it and pressed the button.

"Yes?" said a hollow voice.

"This is Lauren Vancouver. I'm—"

"Come on in, Lauren." A buzz sounded, and I heard a snap like a door unlocking.

Chris Mandrea met me in the small, shadowy entry with decoration-free beige plaster walls. "Hi, Lauren. Dante told us you were coming." The grin on his narrow face was rather pert as he looked me up and down. I felt a little self-conscious in my usual HotRescues blue knit shirt and jeans, but that was ridiculous. I'd been to my shelter earlier and would head there again, and there was no reason for me to dress up here. Besides, he didn't look especially professional, either. He wore a green shirt with the tails out over dark blue jeans.

"Did he mention that I'd like to have some of the Bling collars to sell at HotRescues? People keep asking about them, so I feel I'd be helping both them and HotPets."

"Sounds good to me. Let me show you where we assemble them." He gestured for me to follow him, then opened a door on one side of the room.

We entered a long hall that was lit much better than the entry. It had doors opposite one another in a long row.

"We're just getting started," Chris said, "so only a small part of the facility is up and running right now, but we've got plenty of room to expand if the collars sell well."

"How can they not sell well?" I asked. "People are already climbing over one another to buy them, thanks to your ads."

"That's in L.A.," he reminded me, stopping at one of the doors. "Everyone here wants to impress his friends and neighbors, so the buzz we've started with our ads works great in Southern California." I opened my mouth to respond, and he put one of his long-fingered hands in the air as if to stop me. "I know, word of mouth will help, and there should be a lot of other areas of the country where we'll do well, too. We'll just have to see." He pushed the door open and stood back, politely waiting for me to precede him.

The room was vast. The first part was laid out mostly with noisy machinery. There were quite a few people inside, too, observing what was going on. I saw one guy approach the nearest machine and push a button, so I figured the human supervision wasn't completely extraneous.

The part of the room where we entered had to be the beginning of the assembly line. But things seemed to change near the middle of the large space, since people started outnumbering the machines there.

It appeared that the colorful leather collars were put together with their buckles first, and the designs were added later.

The designs were undoubtedly the most interesting part. I saw Dante off to the side near the room's middle. He apparently noticed me at the same time and waved.

"Let's go talk to Dante," Chris said in my ear so he could be heard over the mechanical din. I nodded, then followed him, watching the gadgets, the people, and a conveyor line of collars off to our left as we proceeded.

"Hi, Lauren," Dante yelled as we got near him. "Is this what you expected?" He was dressed for his main, more formal office in slacks that were probably part of a suit, although he wasn't wearing a tie and his shirtsleeves were rolled up beyond his wrists.

"I didn't know what to expect," I yelled back, "but this is fascinating."

"Come on. Let's not stop here." He started walking away in the direction I'd been heading.

As we passed by, I could see intricate patterns on the computer screens in front of the people decorating the necklaces, in the unique designer shapes of dog bones and ears, rag toys and more. Squinting intensely, those people attached small, gleaming gems within the thickness of the leather with some kind of tool I'd never seen before. I watched as one skinny blond man finished putting a bone together, then placed the collar on a conveyer belt, where a woman removed it and started working on the pointed-ear design that showed on her monitor.

"Amazing stuff!" I said to Dante, knowing that my awe was showing.

"Yeah, it is." He smiled.

"Thanks." That was Chris, and I grinned at the designer, understanding the pride he took in having helped in the creation of these fun collars.

We observed for another twenty minutes, and then I followed Dante out the door opposite the one through which I'd entered the assembly room.

I stopped, looking around this next chamber—not much like the one where the collars were put together, but surrounded with small computer screens that were configured like the digital ads promoting HotPets Bling.

"Wow," I said. "Are all your manufacturing facilities like this, Dante?"

"No, this one's special in a lot of ways. Plus, it's the newest, so we've had fun putting it together with all the best and latest technology."

I didn't mention the fact that people, and not just machines, helped to create the individual collars. But I liked the hands-on approach and figured that, since the Bling collars contained artistry, having human hands finish them was only part of the magic behind them.

"I'm assuming you've shown me this so I'll be an even better advocate about selling the ones you're going to let me peddle at HotRescues, right?"

"You could say that." Dante laughed. "Anyway, I've got to hurry back to the office, but Chris will help you load a few boxes into your car for you, okay?"

"Sounds great!" We discussed for a minute what the sales price should be—the same as in the HotPets stores, since the Bling collars weren't going to help convince people to adopt. Instead, they, and their ads, were a lure that brought people into HotRescues to see the teacup dogs those folks already hoped to adopt.

Dante led me to a storage room filled with boxes of already finished collars. Chris started to follow us in, but Dante said, "Hey, there's something I wanted to go over with you. Let's go outside."

I watched them head down the hall together, and then I started peeking into the cardboard boxes that hadn't been taped shut. In each, one side seemed to have collars of one design, with collars of another design opposite them, all wrapped in sealed plastic bags.

I liked the ones with dog bones and pointed ears the best. But I'd take whichever boxes Chris thought best.

For now, though, I didn't know how long the men would be talking, and I had a somewhat long ride back to HotRescues. I decided to find a restroom.

The facility was a bit of a maze, with all its hallways and locked doors in areas that would probably be utilized as the collars' territory expanded, but were now unused. I admit to being curious about nearly everything, so I decided to explore the building, just for the fun of it.

Although I would have to find a restroom soon.

Okay, I admit to something else: I got lost in the vastness of the place. I decided to backtrack the way I thought I'd come and go back into the room filled with machinery and people, then ask someone where the ladies' was. That wasn't as easy as it sounded.

I gave it a try, though. I also tugged on some door handles, thinking I might have a better shot at figuring out where I was if I could look out a window or two.

Most doors were locked. I did find one that was open, though, and went inside the room. It contained no windows, but on the floor sat some boxes similar to the ones I'd been checking out before. I peeked in the tops of a couple.

Unsurprisingly, they contained Bling collars. The designs were a little different from the ones I'd already picked out. Maybe I could take a couple of boxes of each. These had faux jewels set in the shapes of tiaras and dog noses set into them. Cute!

The boxes were too heavy for me to carry long distances, and Dante had said that Chris would help me anyhow. I left these boxes here and again went in search of a restroom and what civilization there was in this building.

Fortunately, I found a room marked LADIES and went inside. After I'd used its facilities, I felt a lot more relaxed and started out once more in the direction from which I thought I'd come.

"Oh, there you are, Lauren," said a voice from behind me. I turned, and Chris was hurrying down the hall. "I looked for you around where the boxes of collars are stored. Dante told me you're to get three boxes' worth to sell at HotRescues. Are you ready for me to help you out to your car with them?"

"Definitely." I checked my watch. The morning was almost over, and I needed to get back to HotRescues to see if today was as crazy as yesterday.

And maybe sell a few Bling collars along with finalizing some adoptions.

I followed Chris down the hallway and around a corner, and the area did start to seem a little more familiar. He opened a door, and there were all the first boxes of collars that I had looked at.

"This side contains my designs of dog bones and representations of pointed ears," he said, "and the others over there have gems set to look like sticks to throw and dog treat boxes. You're to get three boxes to take along. Which design would you like two boxes of?"

"Well, to have a variety, I'd like the third box to contain the other design I saw as I was . . . er, checking out the facility." I didn't want to admit to him that I'd been lost. "The ones with designs of dog noses and tiaras."

He blinked, and his usually pleasantly smug expression seemed to turn lost, but only for an instant. "Oh. Those. They're off by themselves because they're something new and not ready to sell yet. Sorry. Maybe next time."

"Okay. Let's go ahead and pack these in my car. I need to leave soon. Oh, and Chris?"

"Yes?" That impishness was back on his face. "Are you going to tell me how much you love my designs?"

"Yes," I said, "I am."

Chapter 22

It was Sunday. I was back at Van Nuys Airport with Naya and Tom, standing near their plane. And this time I wasn't just seeing them off.

I was swallowing my fears about traveling in small planes and going with them.

Which made sense to me. I always liked to face my fears and overcome them. This particular one, in these circumstances, begged to be cast aside.

I was going to help save a bunch more little dogs.

"We're almost ready to go, Lauren." Naya positively beamed, with her chestnut hair whipping a bit around her face in the wind from noisy aircraft taking off and landing nearby. This time, her pilot's uniform consisted of black slacks and a lacy shirt adorned with one of the HotPets Bling human necklaces in blue. I had the impression that she was ready to soar, and that the flight would lift away all her cares around here—including the fact that she was a person of interest in a murder investigation.

"Great," I finally replied.

She looked at me. "That sounded lukewarm. Are you sure you want to come?"

"Absolutely." I shifted my glance between Tom and her. "This will be a different experience for me, and I love to take on new challenges."

Tom laughed. "So you consider flying with us a challenge?"

"Only if you don't know how to fly this thing." I gestured toward the small aircraft behind them.

"Oh, we've been doing this for quite a while," he said. "One thing that even Teresa didn't complain about was how we were piloting our craft."

That was true, at least as far as I knew. "I'm ready whenever you are," I assured them both.

I felt pretty good when, a few minutes later, I sat behind them in the plane. They were going through some apparently habitual moves to review equipment, rehashing a memorized list that they then discussed aloud. It sounded as if everything checked out fine. Then both put on earphones. I just watched, telling myself that all of that would make sure everything remained safe.

I hoped.

Several boxes were piled beside me on the second passenger seat. At least one more was in the back along with an assortment of small-dog crates—ones that could hold the dozen we expected to pick up in Las Vegas.

I pulled my phone out of my purse to check the time—10:34 AM. I considered calling Matt again, but decided not to. I'd already talked with him that morning. We had gone out for dinner and a movie the night before and I'd told him then about my planned one-day trip today.

"Sounds like it could be fun, Lauren," he had told me as we both drank large glasses of beer. "But—"

"I know." I'd tried not to roll my eyes. "Be careful."

"Yeah, that," he said, regarding me sternly with his toast-colored eyes. "Especially since I've no doubt you'll try to turn this into part of your amateur investigation into Teresa Kantrim's death."

"Only if it makes sense to ask questions or whatever." I'd tried to glare at him in case he wanted to argue about it, but I wasn't very successful. For one thing, he was one good-looking guy and I felt pretty sure that our evening wouldn't end with the finale of the movie . . . and it hadn't.

For another, even though he'd annoyed me yet again with his fussing over what I did regarding this latest murder I'd stumbled over, I reminded myself that he groused at me because he cared.

He'd left Rex at my place with Zoey when we went out, and both Matt and his dog had stayed the night.

When he was ready to leave Sunday morning, Matt had given me an unforgettable kiss good-bye. "Be careful," he said again.

"I will," I promised.

And, as an encore, he had called me once more around nine o'clock, as I'd left Zoey at HotRescues and gotten ready to drive to the Van Nuys Airport.

"Hi, Lauren," he'd said. "Just calling to check in and—"

"—Tell me to be careful," I'd finished for him. I had tried to sound irritated, but I failed. "I will. Honest. And to prove it, I know we don't usually see each other two nights in a row, but I should be home tonight before dinnertime. I'll still have to drop the dogs off at Carlie's for a checkup, but I'll be available after that. Maybe we can have dinner with Dante tonight so I can fill him in on my day."

"Sure. Call me when you're leaving Vegas."

I'd smiled and set off for the airport. And all that fussing was why, as much as it would have felt good to talk to him now as I fought my worry about flying in this tiny plane, I only thought about him and didn't phone him then. I did, however, call Dante and invite him to join us for dinner. He agreed, and said he would bring Kendra, too.

I admit it. I gripped my armrests as the plane lifted into the air. Maybe I even closed my eyes as I felt gravity letting go of us.

But I opened them again to watch the ground receding as my host pilots talked to each other in a tone that sounded businesslike but not at all disturbed. If they were happy, then so was I.

I stared down at the San Fernando Valley below as we circled, then headed east. The plane was noisier inside than the commercial aircraft I'd flown in before, but not intolerably so.

I thought about where else I could be going in this plane. To Phoenix, where my parents, and my brother Alex and his family, lived? The Browns. That was my maiden name, but I had taken back my beloved first husband Kerry Vancouver's name after I'd divorced the jerk, Charles Earles.

Maybe I should go see my daughter, Tracy. Kevin didn't require a plane ride, since he attended Claremont McKenna College in Claremont, California, which wasn't far from L.A. But Tracy went to Stanford University in the Bay Area.

Letting my thoughts wander like that helped to calm my nerves, at least a little.

Since the Faylers continued to be occupied with their

piloting duties, I watched the ground a little longer, then decided to be nosy and peer into a box of Bling or two.

The first one had very similar contents to the couple I'd been able to take back to HotRescues. We'd already sold collars along with the adoptions of three more of the remaining teacup pups. We still had three little dogs left, but I'd no doubt that they, and the ones we were picking up in Las Vegas today, would find new homes very quickly.

The Bling collars wouldn't hurt that process.

That box had been on top of one on the other passenger seat. I carefully moved it and looked at the box below it, which had been sealed with red tape.

I've already admitted to being nosy. Plus, if some of the boxes were open, there was no reason the others shouldn't be.

Even so, I glanced up front to make sure my hosts weren't paying attention to what I was doing. Then I took a key from my purse and split the tape.

When I opened that box, I was surprised to see that it contained some of the same designs I'd been permitted to bring to HotRescues for sale, all nicely packaged and labeled like the ones I had, but also some of those that Chris Mandrea had said were just experimental so far and weren't available yet, with tiaras and dog noses. They were packaged similarly but were also contained in larger plastic bags.

Of course, Tom Fayler was the head of the HotPets Bling subsidiary. It wasn't surprising that he'd want to show off all the designs, even if they weren't for sale yet, to the managers he wanted to impress and inspire to sell lots of Bling in their stores.

I dug through the boxes a little more. Then I settled back in my seat to enjoy the ride.

Trying not to think about how small this plane was, and how high, and . . .

I felt a lot better when Naya turned in her seat, and asked, "How are you doing, Lauren?"

"Fine. How long have you actually been flying?"

She and I got into a discussion about her lifelong interest in soaring through the air. She had even skydived a few times.

"Have you?" she asked.

My first instinct was to shout, "No way." Instead, I responded, "Not yet. But maybe I'll put that on my bucket list. Flying in a small plane like this has already allowed me to cross something off that list." As I've said ad infinitum, I'm willing to lie if it makes sense to do so. Usually, I do it to protect animals.

This time, I wanted to protect my reputation for coolness.

Tom joined into the conversation, too. I wound up asking how the little dogs had behaved while they were in the air. I had to continually raise my voice to be heard as we flew, and I also leaned forward as far as I could without loosening the seat belt.

"Noisy at times." Tom also spoke loudly, as did Naya. "We held a couple on our laps, but I'm sure the rest were even more scared. Also, we didn't have anything to relieve the air pressure in their ears if they were uncomfortable. That was one thing Teresa helped with. She pulled a few out of their crates when they seemed to need attention and held them, one at a time. Talked to them. I really think she liked dogs—although she didn't let up much on her gibes at us without giving us any real reason for them."

I remembered Matt's cautioning me to be careful if I got into amateur sleuthing about Teresa's murder. But I was being careful, not accusatory, and I couldn't ignore an opportunity to learn more, especially from the people I was hoping to prove were innocent—assuming they were.

"You said before that she kept alluding to something she claimed you were involved in that she knew about, right?"

"Yes," Naya agreed, "but I don't understand why she didn't explain."

I didn't, either. "Did she say why she kept pressing you about it?"

"Not in specifics," Naya responded, "but I kept getting the impression she thought we'd be so concerned about whatever it was that we'd offer to pay her to keep it quiet."

So the woman might have been attempting to blackmail them for . . . what? And depending on what it was, that could have provided a motive for them to murder her.

"Have you tried to figure out what she meant?" I asked. "Something about the little dogs, maybe?" Although I couldn't come up with even an idea of what about them might have enough value for the Faylers to pay her to shut up about it.

"We've talked about it so much . . ." Naya sighed. "With the police asking us questions over and over, you'd think we'd come up with something, but we haven't."

This wasn't getting us anywhere . . . except toward Las Vegas. The next time I looked down, we were flying over a desert.

And much sooner than I expected, we started our descent into McCarran International Airport.

Chapter 23

The landing was quick and gentle, just the way I'd hoped. We were here! I couldn't wait to jump out of the plane and see the next batch of little dogs for whom I would find great new homes.

Had they arrived yet? I assumed so, but I asked Tom if he knew.

"They're here," he said. "I asked the traffic controllers if the other plane acting on behalf of Airborne Adoptions had landed, and they said yes. Naya and I will meet with the HotPets store managers here first, though, before we bring the dogs on board. You can go meet the other pilots right away, if you'd like, and help them with the pups." He gestured toward another small plane on the tarmac.

"Will do," I assured him.

Because of the way the plane was configured, it was easier for me to get out first, followed by the two pilots. I offered to carry a box of collars down the steps, but Tom said they'd had help last time and probably would today. The local managers had gotten some baggage handlers to remove the boxes.

He was right, since as soon as the three of us were on the ground, a couple of guys in airport uniforms came over and talked briefly with Tom, then went up the steps.

Before they came back down again, Tom and Naya were met by three people to whom they introduced me—all associated with local HotPets stores.

"So glad to see you both again, Tom and Naya," said the only woman among them, Wanda, who wore a long sweater despite the day being Las Vegas–desert hot. "Are we getting closer to being able to sell the HotPets Bling collars here yet? I've given a few away as promotions and everyone wants more—especially when I show them the ads you've done in L.A." She smiled hopefully, her brown eyes wide behind thin, black-rimmed glasses.

"Me, too," said Bud, who looked awfully young to be a store manager. But I'd no doubt that Dante had checked him out scrupulously.

"That's what they're here for, guys," said Jose, with a broad grin extending the hint of beard on his round face. "Right?" He looked at Tom and Naya.

"Discussing that is one of the reasons," Tom said. "Let's go talk about it." He turned to me. "I've told those guys to put the boxes in the back of their vehicle for now and leave it parked here. They can cover the boxes with a tarp so they won't be obvious." He gestured toward a small motorized contraption nearby, then turned to the store managers. "We'll grab a smaller cart so you can take the ones I'm leaving to your cars when we're done talking." The group then headed along the tarmac to the terminal.

Another plane landed nearby, its sound almost deafening,

and the wind it created bouncing even my very short dark hair around. I held my ears, careful to include my hair, as I walked toward the other small plane nearby that Tom had designated.

Two men stood outside it, talking. "Hi," I called as I approached. "Are you with Airborne Adoptions?"

One of them, who looked quite senior and had no hair to blow in the still potent wind, smiled. "Yes. You, too?"

"Indirectly." I held my hand out. "Lauren Vancouver. I'm the chief administrator of—"

I didn't have to finish. The other gentleman, also bald but a lot younger, said, "HotRescues, right? We've heard about how you got this rescue together. My kudos to you, Lauren."

He introduced them both. They were Nelson and Dwayne Hannover, father and son, and both loved animals and flying—a good fit. They lived in Albuquerque, and this was their seventh Airborne Adoptions flight.

Both men looked like carbon copies of each other, except for their ages. They wore similar dark blue jeans and silver flight jackets. Their smiles were identical and showed off teeth that were large and bright white. They were the same height—maybe four inches taller than my five foot six.

The major difference was that Nelson's face had the look of age: divots around his long nose and mouth, and wrinkles beside his eyes. Dwayne clearly knew what awaited him in another twenty or thirty years.

We spent the next half hour removing a dozen animal crates from their plane and walking the little dogs who occupied them, handing each some treats and hugs, and making sure, before we put them back inside, that their crates held bowls containing water.

"You're sure you'll be able to find homes for all of them?" Nelson asked, bending to hug a Chihuahua who resisted going back inside her crate. Who could blame her? "It won't be a lot longer, precious," Nelson told her, then pushed her gently inside. He quickly locked the gate, then turned back to me. "I mean, your reputation precedes you, and we know you initiated this rescue, but . . ."

"But you haven't seen the ads that have made this all possible," I said, walking a little silky terrier around in circles near him. I described the HotPets Bling TV and digital-sign promos with their adorable tiny dogs. "Nearly everyone in L.A. is apparently ready to adopt teacups," I said. "I've had no trouble finding homes for the first little dogs. We named them after jewels, and that might have helped, too."

"Are the ads really that spectacular?"

"The ads are. And the collars are really nice, too. Would you like to see some?"

"Sure. Let's take these guys over to the other plane first."

I helped them carry crates while talking soothingly to the little dogs inside. They each carried one crate in each hand. I only handled one at a time so I could keep it near my face and watch each of my small charges.

Their plane wasn't parked far from the Faylers,' but there was a runway in between. It took some time to move the dogs, since we had to avoid a couple of taxiing small craft. I wanted so badly to hold the pups' ears so they wouldn't have to suffer the noise that we did—worse for them, considering the sharpness of dogs' hearing—but there were too many of them and too few hands, and we'd put them back in their crates after walking them.

"This'll get better, too," I told those I took care of.

Since I hadn't seen the Faylers exit the terminal with the HotPets personnel, I figured I could show off some of the collars on my own. "Are you ready to see those HotPets

Bling collars?" I asked the Hannovers after we'd moved all the crates onto the tarmac near the wheels of the Faylers' plane.

"Of course," Nelson said.

"Any possibility of our buying a few to take home with us?" Dwayne asked. "We could show them off. Will they be available online or in New Mexico HotPets stores?"

"You're asking the wrong person," I said. "But I'd imagine so eventually, though not today."

I looked around to see if the Faylers were returning yet, but I didn't spot them. I felt sure that they, and Dante, wouldn't mind if I showed off some of the HotPets Bling to people who might talk about the collars in an area where they might not be available for a while. The buzz might make them all the more popular later, when they could be bought anywhere.

Only then did it dawn on me that I didn't see the baggage vehicle where the boxes had been temporarily stored. I started to panic on Tom's behalf as I looked frantically around. One just like it was parked against a nearby hangar. Could that be it? I hurried toward it without telling Dwayne or Nelson what I was up to.

Fortunately, it was the same one. A tarp over the contents in the back pulled up easily to reveal the familiar three boxes.

"Here they are," I called triumphantly as the Hannovers followed me. I pulled the flaps off the nearest carton and brought out a couple of the collars of the most familiar type, in shades of blue and yellow, decorated with the shining false gems in the designs I'd seen most often.

The two men each took one from my hands and looked them over. "I'm not usually excited about dog collars," Dwayne said. "Who is? But if I was going to make a big deal about any, these could be it. They're really nice, as long as they're for little cutesy dogs, not the working dogs we tend to own."

"Maybe," I said. "That's probably why the ads I described focus on the little guys."

About a minute later I noticed the Faylers leading the men and woman who'd met them before toward this area. So they didn't get upset the way I had, I waved to them, pointing toward the baggage vehicle. They headed this way.

One of the men was pushing a cart, the kind that's easily available in the baggage claim areas for a price. When they reached us, Tom and Naya showed off the collars, including the ones the Hannovers passed to them.

"Like these?" Tom asked Nelson.

"We just told Lauren how nice we think they are—for little dogs, like the ones we flew here."

Naya looked at me. "I see a lot of crates under our plane. Are all the dogs there?"

I nodded. "They've all been taken care of, too." I mentioned the walks, treats, and water.

"Then let's get them inside and head home," Tom said.

We all shook hands with the Hannovers and the HotPets folks. Tom picked up the box of collars I'd unsealed previously. He pulled out a couple of the types of collars that were in the other boxes, too, to show to the HotPets managers, but he didn't display any of the ones I'd been told weren't available yet. When he then returned them to their container, he carried the box into the plane. The store managers received the other two boxes and split their contents, all in the same designs Tom had just shown to them.

"Now, you be sure to get our Bling campaign started here right away," Jose told Tom.

"That's right," Wanda seconded him. "We're really eager

to do more than just show those collars off. We'll sell a lot of them, I'm sure."

"I'll let management know," Tom assured them. "They're aware of my contact with you here, and I'm pretty sure we'll get the green light soon."

"Be sure to keep us posted," Bud said, looking from Naya to Tom and back again. "And our three stores are just a drop in the bucket around here. There are more than a dozen HotPets, and we'll do well selling those collars."

They said their good-byes—farewells, really—and left the tarmac.

Tom, Naya, and I then took the dog crates one at a time into the plane.

I couldn't help it. As we loaded the dogs, I asked Tom, "Obviously the collars were a major subject of your conversations, but did anyone mention another aspect of your last trip here—Teresa?"

We were both inside the plane then, and he looked at me ruefully. "Oh, yeah. Those managers all asked about what happened."

"They'd met her even before you did, hadn't they?"

He nodded. "I think she gave them a hard time, too, since they'd all had to wait for our late arrival on the last flight."

"Did they have any ideas about who might have disliked her enough to kill her?"

"Not that they told me about—although I had the sense that they were glad she was murdered in L.A. and not here, since that way none of them could be accused."

"Unlike you and Naya," I said.

"Yeah, unlike us." His tone, and expression, were grim.

We finished loading the dogs after that with no further discussion of the last voyage.

The flight back to L.A. seemed a lot quicker than the one to Vegas. Maybe that was because I had such delightful company in the back of the plane.

Not that I had anything against the Faylers, but holding a tiny poodle on my lap, followed by a Chihuahua and a bichon frise, then passing them around so the Faylers, too, had company sitting on their laps as they flew, then trading them for three more little guys . . . well, that was even more spectacular than the view below.

When we landed in Van Nuys, the Faylers helped me load the dog crates into the back of the HotRescues van.

"Thanks so much for letting me come along," I told them as we stood in the airport parking lot.

"Thank you for all you're doing for those little guys." Naya nodded toward the closed back door of the van. "They're all so wonderful. I'd love to adopt another one."

"But our little Marvin is quite a handful," Tom interjected. "Our daughter's been great as our sitter when we've taken these trips, and we're ready for another whenever. Assuming we can, of course." He paused, his glance at me rueful. "Thanks also for being a whole lot nicer a passenger than our last one on this kind of trip."

"You're welcome." His words slapped me with another reminder of how much I wanted to help them clear themselves of any suspicion in the death of Teresa Kantrim. Having spent this additional time with them, I was even more convinced of their innocence. "Look, now that you've done the same thing again, did it bring to mind anything at all that Teresa said or did that could help lead to who really killed her?" Though Tom and I had talked about it before, Naya hadn't been involved in that conversation, so I looked mostly at her.

But she shook her head. "I wish. How about you—did you get any ideas?"

I shook my head. "Sorry. But I'll keep looking into it— as long as I have your assurance that it really wasn't you."

Naya looked hurt. Tom looked peeved. "I thought we'd convinced you of that before," he said.

"Just checking," I said lightly, then smiled. "It's time for me to take these little guys to the vet for a standard checkup. They should be back at HotRescues in our quarantine area within a few days, then available for adoption about a week later."

"Are you planning another party?" Naya asked. Her tone was soft, her expression too bright to reflect what she was really thinking.

The strain was back, and I'd helped to remind them, too.

"Could be," I said. "I'll let you know."

"Oh—and Lauren," Tom said. "Once Dante gives the go-ahead and we roll out our HotPets Bling campaign in Las Vegas, I wouldn't be at all surprised if there's a surge in adoptions of teacup-sized dogs there, too. If you know any shelter owners there, you might warn them."

"That's exactly what I have in mind," I assured him.

Chapter 24

"They're all adorable. Just like the last bunch." Carlie had just finished doing a preliminary health check of each of the latest dozen dogs I'd brought in for her assessment.

We sat in her office at The Fittest Pet Veterinary Hospital. It wasn't a very large room and in my opinion didn't mirror the charm of the rest of the one-story pink stucco facility, but it was utilitarian, with a nondescript desk and somewhat comfortable chairs facing it.

Still, it seemed rather a let-down for a TV star like Carlie to spend her time in such an ordinary environment when not curing animals or advocating their proper care on her show, *Pet Fitness*.

"I'm not going to argue with you," I told her. "In fact— want to place a bet about how long it'll take me to find them all new homes?"

"Only if I can put my money on the lowest number of days. Do you have any left from the first group?"

"Three, but a couple already had applications, and when I checked in with my HotRescues gang while you were examining the dogs, I was told that an application was being filled out for the last one, too."

"So . . ." She checked written notes she'd made in a folder. "Twelve little dogs again—a poodle, two Yorkies, one Pekingese, one Pomeranian, two Chihuahuas, one bichon frise, one shih tzu, one Maltese, and two silky terriers, if I've got them right." She looked at me for confirmation.

"Sounds right, but my list was done in a hurry when I parked here and got help bringing them inside. I'll confirm it with your bill and also double-check when I get them to HotRescues."

"Should be okay to take them in a few days, assuming nothing changes. They all seem healthy, but we'll need the results of their blood tests to feel more sure. Are you going to name these guys after bling, too?"

I laughed. "I talked to Nina about that, and she's been sounding out our volunteers and staff. We'd have to dig pretty deep, so to speak, to come up with another dozen types of jewels we like, so the consensus appears to be naming these teacups after—guess what?"

Carlie laughed. "Tea?"

"You got it," I told her. "They're working on a list for me now."

"Good thing your adopters don't have to keep the names you pick if they don't want to," Carlie said. "I mean, I'm assuming there'll be an Oolong and an Earl Gray."

"And a Jasmine. That one could be a keeper."

Carlie placed her file on her desk and leaned back. "So when are the HotPets Bling collars going national?"

"I'm not sure, but Matt and I are having dinner with Dante and Kendra tonight. That's one of the questions on my agenda. The HotPets managers in Las Vegas are raring to go. I've seen the manufacturing facilities in the City of Industry, and I gather it won't take long to ramp them up to increase production exponentially. Obviously the sales have been great in the test market here—but what do I know?"

"That's what I'm asking." Carlie smiled. "And here's another thing I'd like for you to question Dante about: I'd like to do a segment of *Pet Fitness* on your amazing phenomenon—the creation and promotion of the Bling collars here leading to the adoption craze for little dogs, the Missouri rescue, the Airborne Adoptions flights—the whole thing. I've got my producers on standby to air it nearly as fast as it's filmed, both to help publicize the dog rescue and because it'll undoubtedly boost my ratings—not that they're hurting, mind you."

"I didn't think they were. But, sure, I'll ask Dante. It sounds like a win-win-win-and-more-wins situation for everyone, especially the dogs."

"And you? Have you figured out yet who killed Teresa Kantrim?"

Had I discussed my latest investigation with Carlie? If so, I hadn't told her much. But she knew me well. "Still working on that," I told her.

Having dinner with Dante and his girlfriend Kendra doesn't happen often, but when it does, I know he'll be in a good mood. Plus, he'd acted pleased that Matt would be with us, too, as I'd hoped.

The four of us have a lot in common, after all. We all make our livings via the pet industry, although we run the gamut of aspects of it.

Dante, of course, founded and is the chief executive

officer of the entire HotPets chain. He also champions shelters, since he founded and now pays for HotRescues. That's my great love, too—private shelters. Matt works for the public sector, and he's particularly proud of the improving, although far from perfect, no-kill attitude that L.A. Animal Services has undertaken.

And Kendra both pet-sits and acts as a legal advocate for animals.

Tonight, we met at a premier Greek restaurant in the San Fernando Valley, and all of us were primed to discuss HotPets Bling and the many, possibly unexpected, results of its success—like what had happened in the animal-rescue community in L.A. as a result.

I'd dressed up for the occasion in a navy skirt and silky blue blouse, and although I wore pumps, they had low heels, as much for comfort as appearance.

Kendra, though, wore stilettos with her tailored dress, even though she wasn't as formally clad as she'd been last time I'd seen her. Both men had donned suits, and although I kept it to myself for now, I thought that Matt looked particularly delightful.

The last time I'd seen Kendra, she had brought her Cavalier King Charles spaniel, Lexie, to the party at HotRescues. "We're thinking about another party next weekend when the latest group of teacups is ready for adoption. You can bring Lexie then if you'd like."

I'd taken Zoey home before coming here. Matt had left Rex at his place, and since we were eating in the Valley, I doubted they'd be my overnight guests tonight, although watching Matt and appreciating how wonderful he looked all dressed up . . . well, I hoped we'd get together alone again soon.

Dante had ordered us a bottle of Greek wine, and we all

toasted one another and HotPets Bling as we sipped the delightful varietal out of crystal glasses while sitting around a round table covered in a white damask cloth.

The restaurant was moderately busy, although the tables were spaced comfortably apart, also attesting to the place's upscale nature. The servers were all dressed in white shirts, black trousers, and white pocketed aprons.

We started out with hummus and pita as well as a calamari appetizer, then ordered an assortment of entrées that we would share.

Dante was treating, as he always did. It was a festive night, complete with delicious food.

And wonderful conversation, as I filled them all in on the latest Airborne Adoptions flights. "I'm especially thrilled to have been on the last leg of this relay," I told them all.

Not that any of them had any reason to know of my now-conquered—well, mostly conquered—fear of flying in small planes.

I described how things had gone in Las Vegas, too, and how enthused the three HotPets managers were to get started actually promoting and selling the HotPets Bling collars.

"Any idea how soon that will happen?" I asked Dante.

"Within the next couple of weeks," he said. "I'm stepping up the schedule since those same managers and even more from that area have started their own campaign to light a fire under me."

"Sounds painful," Matt said, but of course he was smiling.

Kendra looked a bit skeptical, a frown of concern on her pretty, youthful face. "Are you sure you're ready?" she asked. "And just as important, is Las Vegas ready for you?"

Rather than looking at Dante, she cast her blue-eyed gaze on me. I knew what she was asking without words. "If you're wondering if the pet-shelter community there knows

what's about to hit them, I doubt it. But I'll be communicat-
ing with some of them and they can spread the word."

"And it's a good thing," Matt reminded her. "I don't
know what the statistics are for adoptions in the Las Vegas
area, but they surely have a fair number of small dogs."

"Probably," Kendra agreed. "I do think they should be
warned about what this community experienced, though. I
love the positive result, but it's only fair to share it so they
can be prepared." This time she looked at Dante, who
regarded her with an approving smile.

"I agree," he said.

"Now let me ask you one more thing: Are you ready to
share the possibilities of HotPets Bling with the rest of the
country, too?"

I told them all about Carlie's request to do a feature
about the HotPets Bling phenomenon on her show.

"I think it's too soon," Kendra said. "Wait till the national
rollout is ready."

"I disagree," Dante told her. "Let everywhere else hear
about it and anticipate. Carlie can always do a follow-up
when we're ready to go national." He looked at me just as
our appetizers were served. "What do you think, Lauren?
Would she be willing to do that?"

"I'll check with her, but I know she's always looking for
fun topics for her shows. HotPets Bling can surely give her
two segments, and maybe even more."

"Great. Let me know what she says."

We all proceeded to eat then, and HotPets Bling and
Carlie's show were no longer topics of our conversation.

At least not until it was time for dessert—baklava and
Greek lemon cake that we all shared.

"So Lauren," Dante said, "any idea when Carlie will want
to film her show?"

"Soon, I'm sure. Should she contact you?"

"That's fine. Better yet, have her call my assistant, Sheila. I'll warn Sheila about it. I assume Carlie will want to film at a HotPets store or two, and possibly at our manufacturing facilities. We'll need to have some restrictions on that, since our designs and process are proprietary, but we can talk about that. Will you accompany her?"

"If I can, depending on her timing. It should be fun to watch." At Matt's amused smile and Kendra's questioning gaze, I added, "From a distance. I have no intention of getting on camera."

They all laughed. So, after a moment, did I.

"One question for you," Dante added after we'd all settled back down and were eating and sipping our strong coffee once more.

I suspected, with that lead-up from him, that I wasn't going to like the question. Which I didn't. Especially with Matt there.

"Since you accompanied Tom and Naya on their plane both ways and saw the venue and some of the people in Las Vegas, did you learn anything that might help you figure out who killed Teresa Kantrim?"

Another question like Carlie's. They both knew me too well.

Dante's gaze looked innocent, but I caught a hint of steel behind it. The manager of his most potentially successful subsidiary at the moment was under suspicion of murder, and Dante knew that I'd solved some before—and that I'd stuck my nose into this one, too.

I felt Matt's glare as he aimed it first at Dante, then at me, as they both awaited my response. Kendra appeared completely interested. She'd solved a bunch of murders, too, but none recently, the lucky thing.

She was aware I'd somehow taken over for her. And, considering her romantic relationship with Dante, I felt sure she'd want all the stops pulled out by anyone trying to protect him and his pet-supply empire.

"Not really," I told Dante. "But I gather that, for now at least, the cops aren't breathing too heavily down Tom's and Naya's necks about it."

"It had better stay that way," Dante said. His brief stare at me suggested that I needed to ensure it would. Which I absolutely couldn't do.

But neither had I given up on trying to find out what had happened. I owed Dante a lot, and I liked the Faylers.

At the moment, though, I had no further leads. And with the authorities not being too pushy, I hoped maybe we could all just ignore the situation for a while.

I should have known better.

Chapter 25

The next day, I was at HotRescues. Where else? And, as always, I was delighted to be there. It was my second home. Maybe my first, since my kids weren't around.

I'd taken my walk through the entire facility with Zoey and all was well, as the kennels were being cleaned and the animals fed.

Nina had just arrived, and it soon would be time to open for visitors.

Back at my desk, I had already gone over the applications for the proposed adoptions of the three remaining small dogs, as well as a couple more for cats.

There was something nagging me about those teacup-pup applications, but I hadn't yet put my finger on it. All of the applications sounded good enough, though.

And it certainly would be a fine thing to have this lot all accounted for when we were able to bring the rest from Carlie's here for their quarantine.

I heard Nina greet some people in our welcome area, but I was far enough down the hall that I couldn't make out what she said.

Until she started yelling. "No, just wait here. I'll see if—"

I stood, and so did Zoey, who'd been lying on the rug near my feet. She let out a bark, so I knew she'd been startled, too.

Before I got into the hallway, I was confronted by Mark Black. He'd packed his skinny form into a loose L.A. Dodgers T-shirt and cutoff jeans, and he glared down at me as if he was really peeved.

His just being there, defying Nina and showing up at my office, made me really peeved, too.

Zoey sensed it as well. She remained close beside me, her hackles raised and a seldom-used growl emanating from her throat.

"What are you—?" I began, but he cut me off.

"I've been in this town long enough. The cops aren't letting me go home, and I'm tired of hanging out with that miserable Elsa. But one thing she and I have in common? We want justice for Teresa."

"I can understand that," I shot back. "So why don't you just turn yourself in and admit that you killed her?"

He did remain fairly high on my suspect list, after all. I figured the authorities had kept him in their radar for the same reason.

But if he truly was innocent, why was he here at HotRescues today, yelling?

Heck, even if he was guilty—why was he here?

"I didn't kill her!" His shout was loud, and he clasped his hands into fists at his sides.

Zoey's growl grew louder, and I knelt to hold her back—and also, I hoped, to make a change that would ease things up a bit.

At the same time, I saw Nina hurrying down the hall. "Our security people are on the way," she called. I knew she'd gotten in touch with the company that backed up our own security staff, EverySecurity, since Brooke and her people weren't around during the day unless we knew in advance they were needed.

"Great." I faced Mark again. "You don't have much time left here, so why don't you tell me what you want from me?"

"Fairness." He did, at least, back down a little. "I know you're local and that you're friends with a cop, or at least someone who works here is. That has to be why they don't arrest the people who killed Teresa and keep coming after Elsa and me."

I snorted. "It may work that way where you come from, but not around here. It doesn't matter who you know here. If they have enough evidence to arrest someone, they do it. Since you're still free—and I gather that Elsa is, too—then they don't necessarily think you're innocent, but they don't have enough on you to bring you in. The same apparently goes for everyone else in the case, assuming that no one has been arrested."

"Then I need to go talk to those pilot jerks. I know you know them. They were at your party. I got their names from the news reports, but I haven't been able to find them."

"Not that I'd tell you where they are, but what would you do if you did locate them?"

"You will tell me." His arms raised and I had the sense that he was going to grab my throat.

"Nope," I said, and brought out my not-so-secret weapon, my cell phone, and began snapping pictures of him. "You want to wind up in jail anyway? Go ahead and attack me. I'll have proof of it."

That made him hesitate—and apparently EverySecurity

was a lot more efficient now than it had been when I'd first needed their help some time ago. A man came barreling down the hall with Nina, who'd disappeared for a moment, right behind him. She must have let him in and showed him where to go.

"Back off!" the guy hollered. He was in a suit that had an insignia on the jacket pocket. I recognized it, though not the burly man wearing it. Not surprising, it was the Every-Security logo. He grabbed Mark and whirled him around to face him—probably not too difficult, judging by the difference in their sizes. Mark was way thinner, and I figured his real estate job didn't require him to work out or train in self-defense. "Now why don't you just leave, mister? Otherwise I'll need to call the cops."

"You mean you're not a cop?" Mark sneered. He looked the guy up and down. "Not good enough." He nodded.

I could see the anger churning on the security rep's thick features, but despite what Mark said, he was clearly good at what he did.

"What counts is that I'm better than you, bud. Now, are you leaving or am I taking care of that for you?"

I saw Mark's hesitation. In a moment, he turned back toward me. He sucked in his lips and closed his eyes. "I'm sorry, Lauren. What's happening to me—well, it's not your fault. And you didn't have anything to do with my losing Teresa, either. But it's all so hard . . ." To my surprise, he began to cry.

"All right, Mark," I said softly. "I think you'd better head back to Elsa's now, or wherever you're staying."

"That's part of the problem," he sobbed. "She's throwing me out. I'm tired of her, too, but I have to stay in town and I have nowhere else to go. No money, either. I don't know what to do."

If he'd been a dog or cat, I'd probably have felt sorry for him. Well—in fact, even despite his nasty actions here, I did feel a little sorry for him.

But I had no answers or even suggestions about what he could do.

"Maybe you could try again with Elsa. Even if you can't pay her, maybe there's something you can do around her place—cleanup work or . . . whatever." I knew I was stumbling, and I hated to be less than firm. But despite how angry I was with this man, how furious I was that he'd threatened me, I couldn't completely discount my sympathy.

"I miss Teresa," he cried. "That's the worst of it."

"Okay, guy," the EverySecurity man cut in. "That's all a shame, but it's time for you to leave."

I did in fact hear voices from the welcome room. I didn't see Nina and assumed she had gone there to greet visitors.

"Good-bye, Mark," I told him.

As he was led down the hall by the security guy, he turned back for an instant. He opened his mouth as if he was going to say something else, but then he shook his head and let himself be shown out.

After assuring Nina and everyone else that I was okay, I returned with Zoey to my office. And just sat there.

I was angry. I was afraid. I was also still a bit sympathetic.

And I was also determined once more. Not that it was my responsibility, but I really wanted to learn who had killed Teresa. That way, I might help to calm Mark—and get him out of here so I never had to see him again. Assuming he really was innocent, and I wasn't sure of that.

I would also help the Faylers and thus, indirectly, a lot more small dogs and, even more important, Dante.

So what should I do now?

That became obvious to me the more I sat there. It wouldn't involve doing anything, for now, that I hadn't already considered.

But I had already gotten everyone I'd come to believe were potential suspects in Teresa's murder together once before. I would do it again, in about a week.

That was when the latest batch of small dogs would be through with their quarantine.

I seldom threw parties, either at home or here at my shelter.

But I was about to throw one again.

Chapter 26

I immediately called Carlie to discuss when I'd be able to pick up the little guys and put them into our quarantine area here.

Sitting forward in my chair, elbows on my desk, I held my breath when she answered. What if any of them turned out to be ill?

But they all were fine. "Even so, why don't you leave them here for a few more days?" Carlie said. "Till Friday, maybe? Just so we can keep an eye on them."

"That's only to be extra cautious, right?" I asked. "I mean, you don't see any indications of problems, do you?"

"No," she said. "And to be honest, it's also so some of my staff can have more time to play with them. They're all adorable. In fact . . ."

She let a second pass, and I knew that was due to Carlie's tendency to be dramatic. She was, in fact, the star of a well-regarded TV show.

"Yes?" I prompted.

"I suspect that you'll get an application or two from some of my staff. And beyond that, I have a request."

"For what?" I asked suspiciously.

"I want to film that show about your HotPets Bling and teacup adoptions phenomenon right away. It's big here in L.A., and it'll get even bigger all over the country, I'm sure of it, if Dante rolls out those collars with ads like the ones he's done locally."

"He is, and soon, I gather. I've asked him. At least, it'll start soon in Vegas and go from there."

"Great. So when can I start filming?"

I laughed. "Tell me where you want to film and what you'll need from HotPets Bling and from me. I've checked with Dante and he's okay with the idea. I'll give you his assistant's contact information so you can set it up."

Unfortunately, though, it took a while to get Carlie's filming scheduled. In fact, more than a week had passed. I'd already picked up the little dogs from her clinic and kept them in our quarantine area, and the next day, which was Friday, they would finally be available for adoption. I'd planned my party for Saturday to celebrate.

But now, I had just pulled my Venza into the parking lot of the City of Industry Bling facility.

Carlie and her filming crew had apparently arrived just a minute before I had, since they were exiting a couple of vans and removing equipment.

"Are we all set?" Carlie asked, approaching as I stepped out of my car.

"Yes." I'd already told her I had discussed the visit and filming again with Dante after Carlie had talked to Sheila about scheduling it. Dante had been pleased, even though the show would be aired nationally and the rollout wasn't yet ready to begin.

But it would be sometime in the not-too-distant future.

There had been ongoing discussion about when to film where, and Carlie had suggested a couple of different schedules. Dante had chosen one where the filming here, which would be brief, would be done today, then the crew would go to the HotPets headquarters.

So as not to divulge any manufacturing secrets, this would just be an outdoor scan of the plant plus a short introduction to what was inside, not including rooms where the Bling collars were actually put together.

That might be of interest to Carlie's viewers, particularly when combined with more fascinating things like interviews with Chris Mandrea and some of the Bling executives. The factory building wasn't much different from others, especially around here, but people might enjoy learning that some place that looked this blah could result in large quantities of gorgeous dog collars.

The local staff had apparently been warned of our coming, since two people met us just outside the entry door. I recognized them from my prior visit but didn't know their names. Both wore blue coverall uniforms. The older fellow, with mussy gray hair, introduced them. "I'm Al, and this is Jimmy. Dante told us to expect you and to show you all you want to see, but he also let us know what you could take pictures of for your show and what you couldn't." His dark eyes stared a challenge toward Carlie. "I've seen your show. Love it. But you do ask a lot of questions."

Carlie laughed. "Yes, I do. It's part of the gig. But I also respect privacy, at least to some extent. I won't do anything here that conflicts with what Dante is okay with."

They all got to work then, everyone but me. But I did as I'd promised and called Dante to let him know what was happening. "Just filming the exterior now," I assured him, watching that very act happen while I remained in the parking lot. "And your guy Al made it clear he's keeping his eyes on the filming and won't let Carlie or her crew overstep the bounds you established."

He laughed. "Well, we're ready for your buddy Carlie here, too. Almost. I need you to bring a box of the collars along when you come. I'll want to provide samples to Carlie and her gang, and we're a little low here."

"Fine," I said. "But you'd better tell Al or Jimmy. I don't want them to think we're stealing anything."

"No, we definitely don't want that," he said.

The filming at the factory, though limited, took about an hour. The camera crew shot a lot of footage of just the outside, even though it didn't move or change, although I suppose the lighting morphed a little as the morning sun moved higher into the sky at noon.

Inside, there was a little more of interest, or so I thought, despite the restriction of staying in the hallways. But there were signs on the various doors that were fair game to be filmed. Some people, too, were curious and left their posts, where they had been attaching decorations onto the collars.

Finally, as we prepared to go, Al told everyone to wait there but me. He'd talked on his cell phone a few times during the shoot, and at least one call had to have been from Dante, since he said, "Dante told me to give a box to you to take to the HotPets headquarters. Take your pick."

I couldn't tell from the outside how gorgeous the contents were, so I did look at the labels and chose one randomly from the bottom, in a corner. Or maybe not so randomly. The packing tape on it was red, not clear like the rest, and that small difference attracted me, since I'd also seen one like it on the plane. Al carried it out and put it into my Venza for me.

"I take it that you know where the HotPets offices are, right?" I asked Carlie.

She nodded toward the person who was getting into the drivers' seat of the van she was riding in. "I do, plus we've got GPS. See you there soon."

It took nearly an hour, thanks to traffic. But once we got to the offices, Dante's assistant, Sheila, took us to a conference room where a nice buffet lunch had been laid out for us.

"Dante figured you'd all be hungry," she said, gesturing toward the spread as if she were a model on TV showing off some noted chef's cuisine. And she did look like she could be a model, in one of those corporate catalogs perhaps, considering how nicely she was dressed, in a professional black suit. "Enjoy yourselves. He'll join you in a few minutes, then introduce you to some of the Bling people you wanted to interview." She was looking inquisitively at Carlie. "How did you get into a TV show like this? I heard you're also a veterinarian."

Sheila wound up sitting down at the conference table in the room alongside Carlie, who seemed quite happy to explain how she'd been fortunate enough to have an executive at the Longevity Vision Channel bring his beloved dog into her clinic with some pretty scary medical issues caused by allowing the dog to roam free in his neighborhood. She'd cured the dog but had also reamed the exec out for endangering his cherished pet that way.

He'd thought she should trumpet her ideas to the world—and set that up. The rest was history.

I wasn't sure that was the true story, but it was the one she used these days, and it sounded really good.

A short while later, Dante came in, along with Chris Mandrea and Tom Fayler. Although Carlie had met all of them, Dante introduced her film crew to his staff members. They discussed the interviews that Carlie intended to conduct, including asking who'd come up with the idea for the Bling collars. That had been Chris, who had only just started working for HotPets in the marketing department at the time. He gave his usual impish grin as he described his vision, as well as his delight at being able to use his artistic talent in such an unusual way.

And why had Tom been chosen to run the subsidiary that manufactured the collars? He described the successful pet-grooming chain that Naya and he had run for years and then sold at a healthy profit. Not wanting to rest on those laurels, he had approached his friend Dante to discuss the possibility of a job—at the right time, as it turned out, since the idea for the Bling collars had just been suggested.

When lunch was over, Dante took us to his office, and the production guys set things up for the interviews. I watched from off camera and, even though I knew pretty much who was going to say what, I found the interviews quite fascinating.

They lasted for most of the afternoon. I'd anticipated that and had told my crew at HotRescues not to expect me back until fairly late. In addition to being curious about how things would go, I'd been the liaison between Dante and Carlie and wanted to see for myself that the process was handled well, especially by Carlie and her people.

And everyone rose to the occasion, and I thought things went absolutely wonderfully. Even Dante allowed himself to be interviewed, but he modestly deferred a lot to the Bling subsidiary people, acknowledging their prowess in design, hard work, and, so far, marketing.

On camera, Chris didn't act at all modest, but I figured that was his artistic pride coming through. He said he expected a lot and so far was achieving it. But there was a lot more to come.

Tom was much more reserved, but he, too, expressed how much he expected the HotPets Bling label to achieve.

When the interviews were finally over, I figured that Carlie had a lot to work with on her show, especially since she intended to visit some local HotPets stores and interview the managers about the Bling sales. Plus, she'd use shots of dogs of all shapes and sizes wearing Bling collars, not just teacup dogs.

But she would also feature the TV ads and digital billboards on her show, the ones that had made teacup dogs so popular around here.

Eventually, she and her crew packed up and got ready to take their equipment back to their vans. "Thanks so much for your cooperation," she said to Dante. "And may I buy a few of the collars from you to use in my filming?"

"For publicity like this, you can have them for free. Wait just a minute."

He got the box that we had brought from the factory, or at least it appeared to be the same one since it had red packing tape on it.

I accompanied them out to their vans, in a nearby parking lot for which we'd all paid exorbitantly.

"Thanks to you, too, Lauren. And I can't wait till your party on Saturday to celebrate and showcase your newest set of teacups for adoption."

"Me, too," I told her. "See you then."

Chapter 27

But as it turned out, the next time I heard from Carlie was early the following morning while I sat in my office at HotRescues, having just done my first shelter walk-through of the day.

"Hi, Carlie," I said. "Everything okay?" Since I'd just seen her yesterday and we didn't have any animals under the care of her hospital at the moment, I hadn't anticipated talking to her again until our party tomorrow.

"Well . . . I think so."

That wasn't like Carlie. She almost never waffled about anything.

"Look . . . Lauren, could you come over here to the hospital? I want to show you something, and I think it would be better to do it in person."

I couldn't imagine what she was talking about, but she wouldn't elaborate. "Sure. Want to grab lunch together?"

"That's a great idea." She sounded relieved.

When I hung up, I looked down at Zoey, sitting on the floor beside me looking as quizzical as I felt. "I can't explain it," I told her. "But I'll let you know later what she's hinting about."

About half an hour later, I heard voices in our welcome area and walked in that direction. Two women stood there, perhaps mother and daughter, and they looked worried.

I smiled encouragingly, but before I said anything Nina told me, "These nice ladies have been looking everywhere for a small dog to adopt. And, yes, they've seen the HotPets Bling ads."

The younger woman gave a shrug and a half smile. "We'd considered adopting a dog even before that, but we wanted to finish some remodeling in our house. And now it's done, but I guess there aren't any cute little dogs we can bring home."

I looked quizzically toward Nina. She said, "I told them we didn't have any available right now but would as of tomorrow."

"You're sure?" asked the older lady. "We had a couple of shelters tell us that kind of thing and it turned out they apparently started scrambling and making calls after we left for the day but never found any dogs to bring in and show us."

"We're sure," I said. "We have a dozen little guys who are really eager for new homes, but they've been in our quarantine area to make sure they're healthy before we send them on their way. You can check them out tomorrow, but I'd suggest that you attend our big coming-out party that evening. We're going to celebrate their lives and let people start filling out adoption applications then."

"Really?" said the young woman. She looked at the older one. "We can come back then, Mom. And even though it won't be a surprise for Denny, we can bring him along, too, to meet the dogs."

"If Denny is a member of your household, we'll want him to meet the dog you choose anyway before you take him or her home."

"He's my son," the younger woman said. "He's ten years old. Very sweet. Very responsible."

"That sounds great." She'd obviously gotten the gist of what I wasn't saying, too. Not only did everyone in the household usually have to meet a prospective pet, but I maintained the right to refuse an adoption if I didn't like someone or think they'd take good care of the animal. "I could get someone to take you around HotRescues now so you could take a look at some other animals needing homes. We've seen a lot of cases where someone comes in thinking they know just the kind or size of pet they want, then falls in love with one who's entirely different."

"Well, sure," the older woman said. "Wouldn't hurt."

"Wouldn't hurt," her daughter agreed.

"Then wait a minute and we'll get a volunteer up here to be your tour guide."

A familiar refrain, yes, but it worked a nice percentage of the time. I hoped these two ladies, who seemed to have potential as adopters, found the newest member of their household that afternoon . . . or on Saturday.

By the time I'd finished interacting with them, it was time to go see Carlie. "You stay here, Zoey," I told my sweet dog. I wasn't sure where Carlie and I would have lunch.

Even more important, I had no idea what she wanted to talk about, and figured any kind of distraction wouldn't be a good idea.

I drove to Northridge and parked in The Fittest Pet Veterinary Hospital parking lot, then went into the reception area.

"Carlie's waiting for you, Lauren," the vet tech currently acting as receptionist told me. "I'll go find her." She excused
herself, and I took a seat in the waiting room between a man
holding a crate from which a lot of meows were emanating,
and a young woman with a pit bull mix on a leash. Interesting, I thought. Sexual stereotypes would dictate that these
two pets have their ownership reversed. But that was old
stuff. Today, anything goes.

In a couple of minutes, Carlie, in her white medical
jacket, appeared in the doorway. "Hi, Lauren," she called
to me. "Come on in."

She had decided we would picnic in the central outdoor
area of her animal hospital. Fortunately, part of it was seg-
regated from where dogs were most often taken to do their
business. On the other hand, that kind of thing didn't
bother me. I'd been in the animal-care field much too long
to have a delicate stomach.

There was a small picnic table with a bench where we
sat, and Carlie brought out a couple of plastic bags with the
logo of a nearby sandwich shop on the outside. I got my
choice of pastrami and tuna salad and chose the first.
Although she'd brought iced tea, too, I decided that bottled
water was fine with me.

Knowing I didn't have to change clothes to impress
Carlie, I'd remained in my blue HotRescues staff shirt and
jeans, which worked out fine for sitting on a bench. We
organized ourselves and extracted our sandwiches from
the bags before I said what had been batting at my mind for
several hours now. "So, what's up, Carlie?"

"I'll show you after lunch," she said. "But—"

"But what?"

She looked across the table toward me with troubled

violet eyes. "Something seems a bit weird, and I'm not sure what you should do about it."

"What *I* should do about it? What is *it*? And why is it my problem?"

"It's not your problem. Not exactly. But it affects Dante. Or maybe I'm wrong. Maybe he knows . . . but it doesn't make any sense."

I almost stood up then. "Carlie, you're never this cryptic. Why don't you come right out and tell me what the heck you're talking about?"

She closed her eyes for a moment, and when she opened them her expression looked both troubled and sympathetic. "You're right. And I can't be sure my cameraman was correct. But he's not always been a cameraman. He was in the jewelry business for quite a few years. His family's business." The last couple of sentences were low enough in volume that I actually did stand and lean in so I could hear her.

My mind churned, and my body tensed. I suddenly thought I knew where she was going with this. If so, she was right in many things. It made no sense. And Dante . . . ?

But I went around the table and let her whisper in my ear. "I'll show you in my office. But Lauren? Darius, my cameraman—he says that some of the jewels on those collars aren't just paste. They're real."

When we were done eating, we went into her office.

Not that I'd recognize a real gem, but what if she was correct?

I hadn't heard that HotPets was considering selling another level of Bling collars. Not that Dante would necessarily tell me, of course. But if so, he surely wouldn't have given Carlie a box containing collars decorated with actual jewels.

I took a look at the collars she proffered to me, holding them over her desk. "This one seems to have just the artificial stuff," she said, indicating the blue leather one that had been in her left hand, "but this one, my cameraman said, has real diamonds and rubies among the paste." This time, she moved her right hand, which held a black collar with embedded stones.

The designs on the blue collar were ones I was quite familiar with: the dog bones and upright doggy ears. I'd taken some of them to HotRescues to sell.

I recognized the designs on the black collar, too, though— tiaras and dog noses. I'd seen some of those in the remote storage room in the City of Industry facility, as well as in the boxes of collars that rode with me in the backseat of the flight to Las Vegas.

"I know you said your cameraman had the background for checking out real versus fake jewels, but . . ."

"But nothing." Carlie scowled at me. "Have it confirmed professionally if you want. Or don't. I'm just passing along the information I was given."

I'd rested the collars on my side of her desk, and now I raised my hands in a conciliatory gesture. "I'm just puzzled, that's all. No one would necessarily tell me that they'd decided to ramp up the value of the collars, or some of them at least. But I'm still surprised that I didn't have any inkling of it. And why would Dante have given these to you without telling you the value?"

"I'm surprised, too," Carlie said. "You're not only in the inner circle of HotPets, with your connection with Dante, but also with their Bling subsidiary since you've become buddies with the guy who runs it. Somewhere along the line, I'd have thought someone would have told you, or you'd at least have overheard a conversation or a rumor or something."

"Right," I said. My mind was racing. Should I just call Dante and casually mention that I'd just learned of the possibility, thanks to Carlie? Should I go there with one or more of the collars that appeared to be decorated with the real things?

What should I do?

I expressed my quandary aloud. Whether she was irritated by my questioning or not, Carlie was my dearest friend—plus she was a really smart lady.

"I'm not quite sure how to handle this. Should I act like it's a major issue when I talk to Dante about it, or laugh about the possibility, or—?"

"Why not make an appointment to see him at his office, as soon as he's available?" Carlie suggested. Her expression had grown sympathetic. Our friendship was prevailing. "Just take one of the collars with real jewels. Hide it in your purse. And then broach the subject, see what his reaction is, and you'll know what to do next."

Chapter 28

Things got a lot more baffling after that. I excused myself from Carlie's office, since I wanted a little privacy. Then I went out into the hallway and stood in a corner.

I called the HotPets headquarters and asked Sheila if I could speak with Dante. He answered immediately.

"We've got some confusion going on here, Lauren," he told me before I could say anything. "The Bling folks say that the wrong box of collars was given to Carlie for her show. There are some designs that are just in the preliminary stages that they're not yet willing to disclose even in L.A., let alone nationally. Could you have her exchange that box for another one?"

That didn't tell me anything about what Dante knew or didn't know. Or what I should do next.

Except that Carlie's idea about visiting there might help me figure out if this was anything I should pursue any further.

"Sure," I said cheerfully. "I just happen to be at her

veterinary hospital now." What a coincidence—not. But I didn't tell him that. "I'll let you know if she has any problem with that, but otherwise I'll just take the box she has back to you, then bring whichever one you say is appropriate to her on my way back to HotRescues."

I hung up and returned to Carlie's office, telling her what Dante had said.

"Is it okay for me to exchange those boxes, as he requested?"

"Sure, with one condition."

"What's that?"

"You tell me what the heck is going on."

I got in to see Dante right away. The price of my entry was toting back the box of collars in question. Sheila looked at me quizzically as she showed me inside.

Dante greeted me, took the box and laid it on the corner of his desk, then began to pace his office, alternating his glares between the offending Bling and me. He wore a black shirt and matching trousers today—all dark, which added to the darkness of the room's atmosphere.

"Something's really strange, Lauren," he told me unnecessarily. "I decided to wait until you got here, but I'm heading to the factory this afternoon. Problem is, I'm not really sure who to talk to."

"Who let you know about the . . . er, problem with these collars?"

"One of the shift managers. But I had a sense that he was just repeating what he'd been told, and I couldn't trace it to the source of the matter. Yet."

I drew in my breath. He needed to know the worst of it, too. "There does appear to be a real problem with these collars, Dante."

He stopped pacing. Now the glare in his intense brown eyes centered on me, as if I was the cause of whatever was going on. "What?" he demanded.

I related to him what Carlie had told me. "I can't be sure, of course, but she felt her cameraman had the right kind of background to recognize and test real jewels. You might want to have those collars checked out before you head to the factory."

"What? That makes no sense, but, yeah, I'll look into it, just in case. I've got some contacts in the jewelry business." He had contacts everywhere, so that didn't surprise me. "Which are the collars that you think have the real things attached?"

I repeated what Carlie had told me about that, too, pointing out the ones with tiaras and dog noses. "I saw some with these designs in the boxes taken to Las Vegas the last time, too. I've no idea if they had actual jewels in them, of course. One of the boxes had been sealed with red tape, like the one I just brought back from Carlie's. I saw one like it in a room at the City of Industry plant, too."

"Looks like I'd better find out if there are any more boxes like that around."

Another thought struck me. "Do you suppose some of the collars with real jewels could also have been on the first flight?"

He was apparently on the same wavelength. "I just thought about that. I've no way of knowing for sure. But—"

"But if so, what if Teresa Kantrim somehow knew or suspected it? That might have been what she was goading the Faylers about."

"Yeah." His tone was grim, and the rage in his expression would have worried me if I hadn't gotten to know him a bit, as my employer and the HotRescues benefactor, over the years. He wasn't directing his anger at me.

But if he had been, more than my position could have been in jeopardy.

"Are you going to question them about this?" I asked. I probably should have backed off, but even though I was only peripherally related to this situation, I wanted answers, too.

"Of course. But . . . well, I'd be surprised if Tom was behind this. Trouble is . . . well, hell. I don't want any of them to be behind it." He had stopped pacing and slammed a fist down on his desk. It must have been a hard blow, because the sound reverberated and made me jump.

I took a couple of deep breaths. Something had occurred to me.

"Were you planning to come to my party at HotRescues tomorrow to honor the latest batch of little dogs, who're finally out of quarantine?"

His glare ended in a blink, as if he was incredulous about the non sequitur. But it wasn't a non sequitur. In fact, it was very much related to what we'd been talking about.

"Yes," he said slowly. And then he stopped.

The rage on his handsome face was slowly replaced by a smile. "Interesting idea, Lauren," he said, his mind obviously retuned to the same wavelength as mine. "I'll check on how genuine those stones are. And I won't push anyone for answers, not yet. But what I will do is make sure that everyone at HotPets who has anything to do with the Bling line comes to your party, too. Do you know how to approach this?"

"No. I just got the idea. But why don't we brainstorm ahead of time, see what we can come up with."

"Gladly." He came around his desk and put out his hand

for me to shake. "I like the way you think, Lauren. And not just about animals."

I smiled back even as my mind raced. Could I live up to his expectations and figure out a way to get the results we wanted?

When my kids were little, I used to love to cook for them. I'd try all kinds of recipes, and, often to my surprise, they liked most of them. Maybe it was because the things I tried contained ingredients that I already knew were their favorites.

But I hadn't seen either Tracy or Kevin for over a month now. Their being away at college did that. Kevin used to come home around one weekend a month, but now his visits were less frequent.

And I hardly ever cooked for myself.

I'd invited Matt over for dinner that night, though. After dropping off the box of neutral Bling collars that Dante had given me for Carlie, I spent a little time at HotRescues, then Zoey and I headed home.

I had decided to make my own version of chicken escabeche, a conglomeration of several recipes I'd found online, one with the meat ultimately resting on seasoned black beans. There'd be a salad first, and store-bought cupcakes for dessert.

I'd also told Matt to bring Rex along. That was an automatic invitation for them both to stay overnight.

I was just finishing the chicken dish when my phone rang. Matt was at my complex's gate. I buzzed him in, and a few minutes later my doorbell sounded. Zoey, as always, started barking, and we both headed toward the front door.

"It's okay, girl," I told her. "You're having company tonight."

To my delight, not only did Matt look handsome and sexy in his work shirt and jeans, but he also surprised me by handing me a small bouquet of daisies. "Thanks for inviting me, Lauren," he said. And when I closed the door behind him he gave me such a hot, sexy kiss that I figured I could have cooked the rest of the chicken by holding it in my over-heated hands.

Not that I tried.

I sent Matt into the backyard with the dogs until I had set the table and was ready to serve dinner. I'd considered eating in the dining room, but Matt was practically family. Instead, I set things up to dine in my kitchen at the small table.

I called the gang inside, checked the water bowl for Zoey and Rex, and gave them each a biscuit. Then I directed Matt to sit down.

He dug into the salad with gusto, then complimented me profusely on the chicken dish.

Then he said, "Okay, Lauren, what's going on?"

I'd been eating without looking at him . . . yet. But now I met his gaze with an expression I hoped looked com-pletely innocent. "I miss my kids, but I enjoyed cooking for you tonight. Do you really like the chicken?"

"I love it, but that's not what I meant. I know you have an ulterior motive for softening me up with food. That's not something you usually do."

"No, it isn't, but it doesn't mean—"

"Sure it does. We've known each other long enough now that I can read at least some of your signals, inten-tional or not. Is this something about your looking into that latest murder?"

I thought about denying it, but I'd have a hard time backing off the lie later. I'd promised before to at least let him know what I was up to so he could back me up—or at least worry about me. In fact, that had been a major reason for this dinner.

I pasted a rueful smile on my face—not rueful about my intention of looking into those collars and who was responsible for them . . . and if their existence could somehow have been related to Teresa Kantrim's murder. No, I was rueful that I'd been so obvious.

But on reflection, just serving a dinner at home shouldn't necessarily have been a clue about anything. It was actually more of a statement about my relationship with Matt that he had correctly interpreted it that way. Wasn't it?

"Okay," I said. "You're right. Will you promise not to say anything to anyone but me about this? There's something going on at HotPets that I'm helping Dante with." It might expand into the murder investigation, but it might not, too.

"What's that?"

"Do you promise?"

He laughed. "Of course." He reached across the table and put his large, firm hand on my wrist as I used my fork to cut my chicken. He squeezed gently. "Am I going to be mad about this?"

"That's up to you," I said, "but I hope not."

"Okay. Tell me."

"Well, you're coming to the HotRescues party tomorrow, aren't you?" I was only equivocating a little as I decided on the best way to approach this with him.

"Of course. I may not be there for the whole thing, though, since there's a SMART training session tomorrow." And the Specialized Mobile Animal Rescue Team was one of the L.A. Animal Services teams that he supervised.

"That's fine. I'm not sure what the timing will be for my inquiries, anyway, or how I'll handle them."

"What inquiries?"

I took a deep breath, and said, "Dante's still having them checked out, but there's . . . an issue about some of the HotPets Bling collars, and I'm going to see if I can find out anything about their origin tomorrow by asking some questions."

"What issue?" His tone and expression were so suspicious that I'd have laughed if I hadn't known that would only make him madder.

"Well . . ." I told him then about Carlie's cameraman's discovery of the not-so-fake jewels in some of the collars. "Dante has some friends who know about jewels and all, so he'll confirm whether that's true or not by tomorrow. But if so, it'll be kind of fun to check out what some of his folks know at my party tomorrow. I've invited a bunch of people from HotPets who are involved with the Bling collars, like I did last time."

"I get it. Maybe I can help, too, at least while I'm there."

"Maybe," I agreed, relieved at his tone. He wasn't angry. In fact, his expression had turned thoughtful. And he looked so good while thoughtful that I considered going over to his side of the table and giving him a kiss.

"I'm figuring you're somehow going to turn this into part of your investigation into who killed Teresa, right?"

Damn. He was at least as observant and intuitive as Dante. Probably more so. I knew that. And I should have known better than to think he wouldn't realize how I was potentially equating the two maybe-not-so-separate issues.

"And if I am?" I intoned belligerently.

"If you are, I'm definitely going to get involved," he said.

This time, his expression was so intense—and caring, at the same time—that I did stand and approach him.

Fortunately, we were both done with our meals. I whisked our plates into the sink so the dogs couldn't get to them, and then I took Matt's hand and led him from the table.

Chapter 29

Here we were again. It was another Saturday, a few weeks after the last party, and HotRescues was about to host another similar event.

I'd be releasing the next batch of little dogs from quarantine so they'd be available for adoption.

And I still didn't know quite how to question the people connected with HotPets for information I sought, for Dante's sake and maybe the Faylers' if they truly weren't involved.

I sat in my office now with Zoey at my feet. I'd spent a delightful night with Matt, fed all of us breakfast, including the dogs, and sent him on his way to his job. Of course I anticipated he'd be here at HotRescues a little later, for moral support at least.

At the moment, I faced my computer and looked at which of the latest teacups had been given which names of tea varieties. We had Breakfast and Earl Grey, Yorkies; Chai, a Pekingese; Chamomile, a Pomeranian; Citrus, a bichon frise; Greenie and Lemon, Chihuahuas; English and Irish, silky terriers; Icy, a poodle; Jasmine, a shih tzu; and Oolong, a Maltese. All were healthy. All were adorable. And all were highly adoptable.

That process would start today at our debut party for them. In the meantime, we'd adopted out all of the little dogs from our past rescue. This was all working, as it should have.

The ads for HotPets Bling collars continued on billboards and on TV.

But what was the real story behind the Bling collars that contained not fake, but real, bling?

And did that have something to do with Teresa Kantrim's murder here at HotRescues after our last party?

I admitted to myself, but not anyone else, that I was a little nervous about this gathering. Surely no one else would wind up dead . . . would they?

Enough of that. To make sure the Bling was a topic of conversation at the upcoming party, I was wearing my Bling necklace over my HotRescues blue staff T-shirt. I was about to change out of my usual jeans into nicer slacks, and I'd wear a dressier shirt with my tee underneath.

As I stood to begin removing my pants, a knock sounded on my closed door. Good thing it hadn't happened three seconds later.

Zoey stood from where she'd been lying on the rug and approached the door, but she didn't bark. She did look from the door to me expectantly, though.

"Yes?" I called out, not inviting whoever it was in, although it was most likely Nina.

It was. She poked her head in as she opened the door. "Guests are starting to arrive, Lauren. I'll stay here to greet them, but I'd like to get a stream of volunteers started to come up here and show them into the back."

"Fine," I said. "Give me a minute to change, and I'll go get the stream started."

That was easy enough. I even helped show people into HotRescues myself, along with Mamie, Ricki, Bev, and more volunteers, plus Pete and even Angie, Gavin, and Dr. Mona. Most of my regular gang was here for the party, which made me feel good. Nina and Mona were wearing their HotPets Bling necklaces, like I was.

I was surprised to see Pam here. She was the volunteer who'd apparently given Mark Black an alibi for the night of Teresa's murder. She hadn't been back here since then.

When I spared a moment to try to take her aside, the young, pretty volunteer's pale brown eyes teared up as she said, "I know what you want to talk about. I only spent a little while with Mark, and I didn't like the way he acted, so I got away from him. I don't know what he did after that. I didn't want to talk about it, so I didn't come back here—but I missed this place."

"You're always welcome," I told her, and didn't ask any more questions. She'd told me enough, and I assumed she'd done the same with the authorities.

Quite a few of the people who arrived were strangers who'd come because they had heard on the news and online that we had more of those cute teacup dogs like the ones in those ads for sparkling HotPets collars.

Yeah, those sparkling collars.

The next time I walked people into our busy kennel area, where the volume of conversation was increasing exponentially, there happened to be two college-age boys who just couldn't wait to see our little pups. Really? As I took them past our medium-to-large-sized dogs who greeted them from behind their own glass-fronted enclosures, both appeared delighted to see the animals I'd have considered more the type for these guys, who undoubtedly wanted to appear macho to attract lovely young women. Even so, they only smiled and looked at the front-end dogs, then both looked at me expectantly, and I led them through the increasingly dense and chattering crowd.

Soon, I had them just outside the building where the tiny dogs were kept, now that they were out of quarantine. "We're going to have a little ceremony in"—I looked at my watch—"twenty minutes. For now, I'd suggest that you hang around here, grab some refreshments." I pointed toward some tables in our outdoor dog-meeting picnic area. It was even more crowded over there. I supposed everyone was wasting time there until the unveiling.

Why weren't they visiting our animals?

Actually, a lot of them were. It probably wasn't easy to get up close to the kennel doors, even in this area around the corner from our entry. And I did see people waiting in line to get inside the cat house.

Some of those people milling around where the refreshments sat were EverySecurity personnel, undercover to watch and make sure no one poisoned what we were serving—just in case some random poisoning was what had happened to Teresa. Which was very unlikely.

I left the college guys and started maneuvering through the crowd, stopping to say hi each time I got near a volunteer or staff member who was also trying to be a host.

Senior volunteer Mamie was gabbing with three young people, a guy and two girls. One looked familiar, even though there was something different . . .

Oh, yeah. The guy looked like the young man who had adopted Onyx, the black Pomeranian who'd been one of the first of our initial group of teacups to find a home. I didn't recall his name, and I could be wrong—although I seldom was. He looked around the same height and somewhat heavy weight, and his facial features appeared at least similar. As I recalled, he'd dressed somewhat upscale for wearing a T-shirt, with vests each time he had come here. This guy had on a tank top. And didn't the first guy have light brown hair? This one's hair was longer and darker.

Maybe he didn't look much like Onyx's new dad at all.

I approached him and his friends, though. Just in case, I asked, "How's Onyx? Or did you keep that name?"

For just an instant, I thought I saw an expression of shock pass over his face, although it didn't last long. "Sorry," he said. "Onyx? What do you mean?"

But I did see some looks I couldn't interpret exchanged between his friends.

"Did you adopt Onyx?" Mamie asked, excited. Her eyes glowed in her lined face, and she clapped her wizened hands together. She loved animals, especially her own dog, Herman, and every one of our pets was important to her. She got so attached to some that she even cried while she smiled when they went home with new families.

She hadn't had time to get so close to any of the teacup pups, but that didn't mean she didn't care about them.

"I don't know anything about some onyx," the guy protested, but I still thought I saw a hint of fear in his eyes.

Something was going on here. I wanted to pump them for more information about who they were and why they were here, but I didn't get an opportunity to.

Dante had arrived.

He had turned the corner from the older part of our shelter. With him was Kendra, but neither had their dogs with them this time.

Also walking near them were others from HotPets, pretty much the same crew who'd been here for the last party, I believed, but some additions, too. The Faylers, both of them. Also Chris Mandrea, and Dante's assistant, Sheila. Others I'd seen at the HotPets Bling factory, including designers who worked with Chris, and even some who might be part of the assembly-line crew.

Interesting.

And who among them knew about the genuine jewels in some of the collars? All of them? One or two? What was the reason?

Leaving Kendra with the rest of the group that crowded together in the swarm of other people, Dante approached me. He had clearly come from his office, since all he needed was a jacket and a tie to be completely dressed up for business.

I wove my own way through the masses, smiling at anyone who met my eyes. These people could be future parents of HotRescues residents. Or they could be contributors. Or both.

No matter what concerns were gnawing at my insides, I wasn't about to act unfriendly to our invited, and uninvited, guests.

"Good morning, Lauren." Dante raised his voice to be heard above the noise around us. But then he drew closer and lowered it as he spoke into my ear. "How are you going to play this?"

"Honestly? I haven't come up with any great ideas. Have you?"

"Just talk generally about the collars and how they

apparently raised people's awareness about shelters in general and saving small dogs in particular."

"Right. And . . . ?"

"That's all for now. I'll keep an eye on my crew, and you can, too. If nothing else, I want whoever's doing this to know we're watching the collars and how they sell, as well as the little dogs we've helped to promote."

"You really think anyone will give himself or herself away by some kind of horrified reaction?"

"No. But I know these people fairly well. And I also have another idea if we don't make progress with figuring this out today."

"Glad someone does," I retorted.

He backed away and gave me a smile that looked full of irony. "I never thought you'd admit you had no ideas about anything, let alone a solution, Lauren."

"I admit nothing." I crossed my arms and ignored his laugh as he strode back toward his crowd, the rest of the people apparently recognizing him or sensing his power, since they got out of his way.

I noticed that the rest of *my* crowd had just arrived. Carlie and Liam had just entered our side plaza, and Matt was with them. Somehow seeing all of them boosted my morale, especially since Carlie, too, wore her Bling necklace that resembled the collars. I didn't know yet what I was going to say, but I'd figure something out—and watch Dante's people as I did so.

I waved as I edged my way through the crowd toward the building that housed our small dogs. Carlie and Liam headed in the same direction. Good. I'd have some help.

I saw that Pete must have anticipated what I was up to, as our senior handyman also drew near the building I was aiming for. Ricki and Nina, too.

In a short while, I met up with my group inside the small-dog house. Some of the little pups were yapping, apparently with glee that there were finally people around them.

I grabbed some leashes off the hook near the door and passed them around. "It's about that time," I said to the people, then repeated it, in more of a baby-talk tone, to the dogs. "You're about to be introduced to the world as their potential babies," I explained to them.

Even if they didn't understand my words, my tone must have resonated for them, since even the ones who'd remained still and quiet started to jump behind the glass doors to their enclosures.

It didn't take long to get them out and leashed. We all held more than one leash as we returned to the door.

"Will you make a speech again this time, Lauren?" Carlie appeared to beam, and I knew that this animal champion was as glad as me that this latest group of little dogs was healthy and ready to find homes.

"I sure am." But I didn't mention that it might sound a bit odd when I got on to the subject of the collars. She'd figure that out for herself.

"Everything okay?" Matt bent over to ask quietly. He was at my side, dressed in his L.A. Animal Services uniform. At the same time, the little Pekingese whose leash he held, Chai, started pulling to catch up with the other dogs.

I held the leashes of two small pups: Lemon, one of the Chihuahuas, and Oolong, the Maltese. They, too, were tugging, although not in the same direction.

"I think so," I replied. "Ask me again in about twenty minutes."

I immediately regretted that I'd said that. He probably would. I might not have an answer for him, any more than I'd have answers to all the questions doing backflips in my mind.

But I did pull gently on the leashes I held and led my charges out the door. I was followed by everyone else who was in control of, or was controlled by, some of the little dogs.

I stood just outside the building for a few moments before starting to yell, "Hey, everyone. Listen up! I really want to get this party started—the right way."

Other people started repeating my request until the idea finally went viral enough to get the crowd quieted somewhat. Then I began a spiel like the one I'd done at our last party.

"Okay, everyone. Thanks for coming. This time, I want you all to welcome to HotRescues our latest teacup rescues." I pulled notes out of my pocket and looked at them, then read off the names of the types of tea we had named the dogs in this group after. "They're really 'teacup' this time. This latest gang is out of quarantine now and ready to find new forever homes. Time once more to celebrate. I have a few things to say first, though."

I watched as the people who'd looked like they were ready to walk off mostly stood still. At the same time, I noticed that the crowd now contained two new arrivals— Mark Black and Elsa Martin, Teresa Kantrim's people. What were they doing here?

Was it because Teresa had been killed after my last party?

Were one or both planning on killing someone else—or was I just hoping they were the guilty parties?

"I want to especially thank Dante DeFrancisco, CEO of HotPets, who is an invaluable asset to HotRescues," I continued with no hesitation, despite my gaze pulsing back and forth along the crowd. "Although it's his fault that the little teacup dogs are so much in demand. Everyone in L.A. loves the ads with those little dogs wearing HotPets Bling collars."

I waited for a few seconds as people nodded and smiled and otherwise acknowledged what I'd said.

I tried not to be obvious as I centered my gaze on the gang from HotPets, but they all appeared as interested as everyone else. No one seemed concerned at all.

That was when I went into an ad-lib description of the collars. "For any of you who haven't seen them in person, they're absolutely amazing. We have some of the designers here today." I pointed in the general direction of the HotPets crowd. Now, at last, some of them appeared to squirm. But that didn't necessarily mean they were admitting to doing something strange to the collars. "I mean, they've come up with symbols that really lend themselves to being captured on dog collars in brilliant stones that look like real jewels."

I noticed how Dante, though grinning at his staff, also seemed to be scrutinizing them. But was this doing any good whatsoever in figuring out who was involved?

I didn't think so.

I went on like that a bit longer, praising the collars and how they looked and how cute the designs were . . . and how real the jewels looked. That should have evinced a reaction from the culprit, but I didn't see it.

Whoever it was, was good. And maybe I was just getting frustrated enough to want answers to everything immediately, but, right or wrong, I was sure that Teresa Kantrim's death was somehow linked to this additional mystery.

Not that I understood how . . . yet. But I'd figure it out.

I had to, for Tom and Naya's sake. And, more important, Dante's.

I realized, though, that I'd gone on long enough. Time to wind down—and let this enthusiastic gang meet some teacup dogs. Especially since the ones I'd been holding, now under Matt's control, looked as antsy as the rest of them. Some probably needed a good walk to relieve themselves. Others were sniffing the crowd and wanted to go visit.

And since they all needed good homes, it was time to let our nice, big crowd get to meet them, too.

"Thank you all for coming," I finished. "Now, come meet our latest rescued dogs."

I told Matt to let my volunteers and staff work on those introductions, but, nice guy that he is, he started talking to some folks about the little dogs whose leashes he still held.

Slowly, I made my way toward Dante and the rest of his group.

They were all talking, and I thanked them for coming. I couldn't resist saying that I was eager to sell more HotPets Bling collars as we placed these dogs in new homes.

I didn't catch any more reaction then than I had while gushing over the collars in front of the throng watching me.

But I wasn't through. "Okay, which of you is going to admit that the HotPets Bling collars, or at least some of them, contain real bling?"

"You mean actual jewels?" Dante's assistant Sheila, who stood near Kendra and him, appeared stunned. She, too, was wearing a HotPets Bling necklace over a nice black dress. She looked at her boss. "Shouldn't HotPets be charging a lot more for them?"

Dante laughed. "Maybe so." He kept his tone light, as if he thought what I said was a joke. But I noticed his eyes shift among his staff.

I just smiled at the group, too, as I regarded them. But I kept irony in my smile, so whoever was involved would hopefully suspect that I did, in fact, know the truth.

Which also meant I'd better watch my back. I didn't want to wind up like Teresa if the two issues were, in fact, related.

But no one leaped forward and admitted to the truth of the bling, let alone to being a murderer. Dante eventually dismissed them with a suggestion that they, too, take a look at the latest group of little dogs.

I eventually got Dante and Kendra off alone. I knew she wasn't guilty. She didn't work for HotPets, she loved Dante, and she was a lawyer as well as a pet-sitter. Not that I believed all lawyers were good people, but I'd always found Kendra to be fairly down-to-earth.

"Anything seem helpful to you?" I asked quietly.

A look of anger passed over Dante's face. "No," he said. "If whoever's involved is here, he's damned good at hiding any reaction."

"Then we'll just have to figure out something else," I said. I wasn't about to tell him what I had in mind, but I did have a thought.

Maybe now that these guys were out of quarantine, it would be a good thing to do another airplane rescue.

I noticed then that Mark Black and Elsa Martin were making their way toward me.

"Nice party," Elsa said. I listened for sarcasm in her voice but heard none. "Even though Teresa wouldn't have been glad to have more of her dogs brought here, she'd have been happy that they were likely to find good homes quickly."

"That's right," Mark agreed. "But . . . well, I believe she was killed here right after your last group of little dogs came out of quarantine." He looked at me for acknowledgment, and I gave it. "I assume you have a lot of security here tonight, right?"

"Is that a threat?" I asked.

"No, just a suggestion." But his grin made me shudder.

Chapter 30

Just in case, we did have extra security at HotRescues that night. Not only Brooke and Antonio, but EverySecurity sent additional patrols to our facility after the one at the party.

No one came by who shouldn't have. There was no danger.

But I still felt relieved when all was fine at my shelter that night and the next day.

I also felt angry. And frustrated. I really needed to solve that murder before we could go on with things as they used to be.

And I wanted to help Dante and his mystery about the HotPets Bling real, live jewels.

I still figured the two issues were related. If I solved one, would I have a solution to the other, too?

I was determined to find out.

My best idea about how to deal with them required another rescue from Missouri of at least some of the remaining teacup dogs. Since the latest batch here at Hot-Rescues was out of quarantine, I called Juliet Ansiger first.

Fortunately for me, but unfortunately for the poor little dogs, there were still another eight teacup rescues at the animal sanctuary. Some other groups, mostly in the east, had taken in the rest.

"You're prepared to bring in that many more?" Juliet asked. On the phone, I couldn't tell whether she was incredulous or thrilled or both.

"Yes," I said. "I've a feeling that the dozen just let out of quarantine will find homes quickly." That feeling was hope. And I also had some applications already that I would follow up on later today.

Even so, we had room and could make more if necessary.

She agreed to have them ready for Airborne Adoptions on the following Sunday.

My next call was to Mike Relfer of Airborne Adoptions. "Sure," he said. "We'll do it. This is amazing—so many all at once like this. At least I think we'll do it. I need to make sure we have enough pilots available and that they have enough fuel."

I crossed my fingers hopefully as I said, "You know, Dante DeFrancisco will probably help with the cost."

"Oh, yeah, Dante," Mike said. "Nice guy. He's been in contact with me about what we do, and what we need to continue to do it."

"I'm not surprised. He's funded the last leg of our two previous rescues, and I know he's happy with the results. I'll check with him."

Which I did just after I hung up with Mike.

I also told Dante my intentions of using this rescue to help figure out who was behind the Bling situation.

He of course agreed and offered to pay for it. "What do you have in mind?"

"Still working on that, although I have some ideas. Just make sure that the Faylers can do the flight segment again and that they intend to meet up with HotPets store managers to show off Bling collars."

"Which ones?" he snorted. "The ones with real gems, or our actual items for sale?"

"Exactly," I said noncommittally. "If it's like last time, I suspect there could be some of both—or at least we'll not tell anyone otherwise."

"Ah . . ." he said. "And that's how you're going to figure out what's what?"

"That's how I hope to," I acknowledged.

After we hung up, I called Mike once again and told him the good news. "Your pilots on each of the legs can rest assured that at least their fuel will be taken care of. Do you think you can put together a group?"

"I'm fairly sure of it," he said. "I'll let you know if I have any problems."

When I hung up with him the second time, I felt pretty good. That was because I at least had plans in the works that might lead to some of the answers I sought.

But I had other issues to contend with that day. And so, rather than just going out to visit our residents once more, as I probably would have on a normal day, I checked some computer files.

What was the name of the guy who'd adopted little Onyx? My records showed he was Marshall Droven. I kept the file open on the computer and printed out his contact information.

I didn't intend to call first, but I'd go visit Marshall and

Onyx. I recognized that, in the middle of the day, no one might be home, but he had said that he was in Internet sales, so, since he worked from his apartment, he could be there.

I'd at least be able to check out his living situation to some extent. He'd said he lived in an apartment that allowed dogs, and he had shown me his lease to prove it.

But an hour later, I wished I'd done as permitted by our adoption application and gone to see his home before letting him take Onyx.

I'd driven to the address he had written down. It wasn't an apartment but rather a mailbox drop-off location within a big-name printing and mailing store.

"Onyx!" I whispered frantically, hitting the steering wheel of my Venza with the flat of one hand. Where was he?

And what the hell was going on here?

I decided to wait till I was back at HotRescues and in front of the computer—and Droven's application—before calling Brooke, but my anger must have shown on my face and in my attitude.

"What's wrong, Lauren?" Nina asked as I stomped through the welcome area.

Zoey came out from behind the desk where she'd been with Nina, but even she didn't get close to me.

"I'm mad at myself," I told Nina. I was even angrier with Marshall Droven. I almost never second-guess myself, but I was doing so now. That made the situation even worse. "I've been too lax in following up on applications lately. I used to go visit people's homes a lot more before approving adoptions. Well, I'm going to do that again now. But I just hope it's not too late for Onyx."

I'd make sure it wasn't . . . somehow. But where was the

little dog? He obviously wasn't living where his adopter had claimed they'd be.

What also worried me was that Onyx might not be the only one. I needed to put together a list of all the addresses of people who'd been adopting the teacup dogs.

Now that I'd started worrying, the feeling mushroomed. I hadn't been overly concerned at the time, but I'd noticed that several of the adopters had similar backgrounds: young, around the same age, some with work-at-home jobs. Theoretically ideal pet owners. And maybe they actually were.

I'd figured that the adorable little dogs in the HotPets Bling ads had particularly appealed to folks like that.

But now I wondered whether there was something else involved.

I was going to find out.

I entered my office rather than doing my usual tour of the shelter. That could wait, especially with the caliber of staff and volunteers who'd be in the kennel area socializing the animals and doing everything else necessary to take care of them.

Including showing them off to potential adopters?

I froze before sitting down. Maybe I'd better go see who was there.

On the other hand, no adoptions would go through without my okay. And I would be a whole lot more careful from now on.

Definitely more careful than I'd thought I'd always been . . .

Damn. I got into the files on the computer once more, then called Brooke.

"Hi," I said when she answered. "I need you to put on your P.I. hat right now." That had been her background before I'd hired her as the HotRescues Security Director.

She must have heard the tension in my voice, since she didn't question what I'd said. "What do you need?"

"I need you to find out who Onyx's adopter Marshall Droven is—his real background, why he gave a private P.O. box as his address, and where he has put Onyx."

I heard her sharp intake of breath. "What happened, Lauren?"

I told her. Then I said, "Just to be safe, I want a background check on the other teacup adopters, as well as their confirmed addresses.

"Really? What's going on?"

"Nothing, I hope, except that there has been a mix-up with Onyx. But I need to make sure."

And before I hung up, I made it very clear to her that I needed all the information yesterday.

I waited for Brooke to appear later at HotRescues. I'd already checked, and she was the security person scheduled to be here overnight.

I'd taken a couple of walks around the shelter by then. Checked on all our dogs and cats. Particularly hung out for a while, without Zoey, in the small-dog house, where I played with our current teacup residents.

We had gotten four applications on them after our party. With all that had been going on, I hadn't reviewed them yet.

Now, I would scrutinize them even more carefully. And for the moment, until I had more information about Onyx, I wouldn't approve any adoptions.

I'm not usually impulsive. But despite the fact that it was eight o'clock on a Sunday night and not an ideal time to go calling on a stranger, it did have its plus side.

From what Brooke had found out—and assuming Marshall

Droven had in fact used his real name—he was a student at Santa Clarita College.

Santa Clarita is just north of the San Fernando Valley. It's reported to be the third largest city in Los Angeles County, one of the fastest growing cities in California. Both statistics surprised me, but I looked it up online before heading there.

I looked up the college, too. It was small, and its majors included liberal arts and technology.

Nothing about dog-adoption fraud, or at least nothing I could see from its Web site.

I doubted that Marshall had any classes that evening. He might be home studying.

He might be out drinking. Or doing something I wouldn't like with Onyx. That was why I'd decided to go right away.

Maybe he really was a dog lover and had felt, somehow, that he had to lie or I'd never have approved him.

Given a choice, I wouldn't approve him now. But I had to see what the situation actually was. If he and Onyx had bonded, his apartment allowed dogs, and he explained his lies in a way that didn't make me want to strangle him—any more than I wanted to now—then maybe I'd just leave it alone.

Maybe.

Otherwise . . . well, if there was a problem beyond his lying, then I'd have to fix it.

Was this somehow related to the real bling collars? I didn't see how, and I doubted it. I'd seen no indication that Marshall had any connection with HotPets, just with Onyx. And he'd come back to look at more teacup dogs, not collars.

Why the heck hadn't he been honest?

Brooke hadn't found his school schedule. I hadn't expected her to, and it was most likely irrelevant on a Sunday night.

But helpful former P.I. that she is, she'd found his address and phone number.

I chose not to call to see if he'd be around. That would allow him to elude me.

Not that I could be certain of seeing him now. But I had to try.

His apartment was on the third floor of a building on a street lined on both sides with similar structures. I wasn't sure if Santa Clarita College provided dormitories, but I'd first driven by the school, saw, in the fading August daylight, the attractive façade of a tall, marble-looking building that shouted academia and was surrounded by other, shorter buildings that helped to bolster the atmosphere.

For now, I parked my car on the street about a block away from the apartment building.

I looked around. I saw a student-aged guy walking a golden mix just ahead of me. Not a teacup dog. It wasn't Marshall anyway. This fellow was skinny and short.

I heard some shrill chattering to my right and glanced that way. Three girls had exited the closest building and were gabbing excitedly. I kept walking.

It didn't take long to get to Marshall's building. It was one where I'd need to push a button to get buzzed in, darn it. Most places were like that these days, for security. I wasn't surprised, and had considered the possibility already. I decided that I was delivering a pizza. No matter which unit he was in, it was unlikely he'd be able to see this entrance from his place. There weren't any windows positioned suitably.

But to my relief, those three girls had been headed to this building. One of them had a key and let the others in. They were so busy still chattering that they didn't notice, or care, that I slipped in with them.

I took the elevator with them. They got off at the second floor, and I continued to the third.

I got out and checked how the apartment numbers went. Marshall's was to the left. I stalked down the hall, getting myself into the mind-set of being prepared to chew him out if he happened to be home.

I rang the bell.

No one answered. But I heard the barking of more than one yappy small dog.

Onyx wasn't alone.

Chapter 31

If someone had another pet in his home, we tried to make sure our adoptee and that animal got along well together.

Marshall hadn't admitted to any other pets.

My irritation grew, and I knocked on the door again. Of course, the yapping inside increased, but no one came to see who was disturbing the peace.

At least not from inside Marshall's apartment. I did hear a door open across the hall and turned, figuring it would be a peeved resident who'd want to tell me to get lost and stop riling the dogs.

She might have, indeed, been a peeved resident, but she was one I recognized. As I recalled, I'd thought she looked younger than the twenty-one years she'd put on her application. She was in a shirt with cropped-off sleeves and jeans and looked pretty young now. Her long brown hair draped around her face and shoulders. What was her name? She'd come to HotRescues at the same time as Marshall and had adopted another of the teacups, Sapphire. Unsurprisingly, I remembered my animals' names better than I recalled people's.

At the instant I turned and recognized her, she apparently recognized me, too. Her face went white as her mouth opened.

"Hi," I said calmly. "Do you happen to know where Marshall is? I have some questions for him. And I think I have some for you, too . . . er, sorry, but what's your name?"

"Janice," she whispered.

"Right. Janice. How is Sapphire?" I had an odd feeling that little Sapphire could be one of the dogs I heard with the one I assumed was Onyx. I believed something was going on here, and Janice's attitude confirmed it, but I didn't yet know what it was—besides their lies about their addresses.

"She's . . . fine," Janice said haltingly. I watched her gaze dart in what appeared to be fright up and down the hall, as if she sought someone to rescue her from me.

Fortunately for me, no one else emerged. Not yet, at least. But I figured they would soon if the dogs didn't quiet down.

"I don't suppose you have a key to Marshall's apartment, do you?" I asked.

"Well . . . yes. How did you know?"

"I just figured," I lied. Since I had no comprehension of whatever I'd apparently uncovered here, I was merely guessing. "Why don't you get the key and we'll check on the dogs, okay? I'll bet your neighbors would like that."

"Okay," she said huskily. As she ducked back into the other apartment, I stepped up to it and stuck one foot inside, in case I had to prevent her from slamming the door shut. But that didn't happen.

In a minute, she returned, a key in her hand. The dogs

had quieted down a little, but I didn't mention that. I wanted to go visit with them.

I'd also noticed that Sapphire hadn't run out the open door, underscoring my belief that she was in the other apartment with Onyx. It sounded like there was another dog in there, too.

Janice preceded me across the hall again, and she opened the door, squeezing her way in so as not to allow tiny dogs to skyrocket into the hallway. I acted as her backup, just in case. And then I followed her in.

Onyx, the black Pomeranian, and Sapphire, the light brown Chihuahua Janice had adopted, were there. So was another little pup, one who looked like Garnet, the little poodle we'd also adopted out from the rescued teacups—to a young woman who was a computer programmer, if I remembered correctly.

"What's going on here, Janice?" I demanded. "Something doesn't smell right, and I don't mean the dogs. Did you all lie on your adoption applications? Should I call one of my cop friends?"

I wanted to scare her so she'd open up. I might take the dogs back, but I probably wouldn't report her—not unless it appeared that the dogs had been abused. They all looked okay, but I still needed to know why they were here and together.

"No, please," Janice squeaked. "It's nothing bad. Not really. We just . . ." She started to cry.

I sighed. Getting information out of a crying child—for she was hardly a stalwart grown-up—might not be easy. "Let's go into the living room and sit down," I said. Through an open doorway I'd spotted a couch in a room with a TV, a sofa, and a couple of upholstered wooden chairs sitting on a hardwood floor, a pretty sparse excuse for a living room.

She obediently led me inside and sat on one end of the stiff black leather sofa. The dogs followed and leaped up beside her. She grabbed Sapphire and began crying even harder into the dog's fur.

I took the other end of the sofa and waited.

When her crying eased a little, I said, "Okay, Janice. Tell me what's going on."

She looked up at me with bloodshot and wet hazel eyes. "We just . . . well, we're all in school, and it's expensive." Her tone had taken on a defensive quality, and her lower lip jutted out.

"So you did . . . something . . . for money." I tried to keep my own voice level, but if she was about to tell me something horrible they'd done with the dogs, I might need to call the police after all—to restrain me from doing something awful to her.

She closed her eyes for a minute and hugged Sapphire against her face again. Onyx and Garnet—for I was pretty well convinced that the little poodle was also one of the dogs I'd rehomed—came over and lay down on my lap. I stroked them as I waited for Janice's response.

When she opened her eyes again, I glared at her and thought I saw her shudder. But she did start talking.

"It was those ads for those nice decorated collars. You know, the HotPets ones with the jeweled designs. The ads had all those cute little teacup dogs, and we kept hearing on the news that people loved the ads as much as we did, and that none of the shelters could keep as many small dogs available for adoption as there were people wanting to adopt them. We just figured . . ." Her voice trailed off.

"Yes?" I demanded, then made myself say in a calmer voice, "What did you figure, Janice?"

"Marshall had the idea. We also heard on the news

about that rescue that brought a lot of small dogs from . . . where was it? Missouri?"

"That's right."

"They said all of them were going to HotRescues, and Marshall told us that if we got some of those dogs, we wouldn't have to pay too much to adopt them from a shelter, but other people might pay a lot of money for those cute little things while it was so hard to find them."

My turn to shudder, and I hugged the pups that were still on my lap. I wanted to yell at her. The money didn't matter; the well-being of those cute little dogs did.

But I mentally patted myself on the back as I stayed outwardly calm. "And is that what you did—adopt them, then sell them?"

"Some of them, yes. But it wasn't as easy as Marshall originally thought. We—"

The front door opened then. We both turned to look up as the little dogs bolted from our laps and ran toward the new arrival. It was Marshall. He didn't look the way he did when he'd taken me in by taking in Onyx—somewhat nicely dressed, with light brown hair—but as he had the last time he'd been to HotRescues and I'd thought I had recognized him, with darker, possibly dyed hair and somewhat grungy casual clothes.

He noticed us immediately, which wasn't surprising. "What the hell?" Ignoring the dogs who pranced around his feet and yapped, he approached us. "What's going on, Janice?" But he was looking at me, not her.

"She came here and heard the dogs and wanted to know what was happening with them." Janice started to blather. "And I thought she needed to know the dogs were okay, and she said she'd call the cops, and—"

"Shut up," he growled, finally looking at the young woman. Not unexpectedly, Janice started to cry again.

He took no time to reach us. I'd stood up, not wanting to be in a position of weakness as he stared down at me, but he was tall and broad enough that I still felt a little intimidated. Only for a second, though.

I placed my hands on my hips and let all the belligerence I felt show. "I don't know what you thought you were doing, Marshall, but I want to know what you intend to do with these dogs—and you'd also better tell me what other ones you and your friends adopted, and what you've done with them."

"That's none of your business," he retorted. "They're ours now."

"Not completely true," I contradicted. "You and all of your friends who are involved signed contracts. There are minimum standards of care in them, and I have the right to take the dogs back if any of those standards aren't met. There's more than that in them, too. I can at least get a lawyer involved and sue you for breach of contract if anything's not met, and I've got all the resources of Dante DeFrancisco behind me if necessary." Not entirely true, although I knew that Dante would back me up. "And there's always the possibility that you broke the law, in which case I'll get some of my cop friends involved. Janice and I already discussed that a bit."

With each word, it seemed, Marshall wilted a little. As I finished, he took a few steps backward, almost stepping on Onyx. I swooped down and picked up the little Pom.

"I didn't mean to do anything wrong," he said to the floor. "I like dogs. I figured I could find them good homes, too, and make some money while doing it. No one would get hurt, especially not the dogs, and I was even sharing with my friends who helped out. We'd all have some help with our school expenses for the coming year."

"Do you all attend Santa Clarita College?" I asked.

"That's right, and the tuition just went up. Again."

That, unfortunately, was the norm for all higher education these days. Probably all education altogether.

But feeling sorry for them did not trump how I felt about what they'd been doing with my little rescued teacups.

"So, tell me what you've been doing with them. How many of my adopted-out rescues are involved, and where are they now?"

"We haven't had as much luck adopting them out as I'd hoped," Marshall admitted. He moved around me and sank onto the couch. Janice, too, sat back down and watched us.

I remained standing, my arms crossed, regarding Marshall sternly.

"Go on," I said.

He explained that he and his friends had adopted seven of my teacups from HotRescues. These three hadn't been rehomed by them, but the other four had: Aquamarine, Opal, Topaz, and Amethyst. "But some of the potential adopters wanted copies of their pedigrees. I know they were rescued from puppy mills, so there was probably some kind of documentation like that, but we didn't get it from you so I couldn't really provide it—at least nothing that would be at all legitimate."

"I didn't get their pedigrees either, if they had any," I told him. Occasionally I received that kind of paperwork in puppy-mill rescues, but it was irrelevant to adopting from a shelter so I never insisted on it, even when I suspected or knew that a dog was a purebred.

He described the way he had checked out the homes he
allowed the dogs to go to. We always charged a minimal
amount for adoptions at HotRescues, and he had been able
to get around a thousand dollars each for the four he had
found homes for. "I gave my friends each about five hundred," he said.

I looked at Janice. "That's a pretty small amount for you
to get to take on so much potential liability."

Her eyes teared up again, and I looked away. Pity had no
place in this room.

We talked a little more about what they'd done and how
they had done it.

Meanwhile, I pondered what I would do to rectify the
situation.

Eventually, I pulled one of the wooden chairs over from
where it sat near the base of the TV mounted on the wall
and sat on it. I turned it to face them and picked up Sapphire, hugging the Chihuahua as I talked.

"Here's what we're going to do," I told them. "First, you're
going to return these three dogs to HotRescues."

"But—" Marshall began.

"I realize you might have bonded with them, and I'll
hold them for a short while. If you meet all my other crite-
ria, then we'll see about whether you can legitimately adopt
them. To keep." I looked at the doleful Janice, who also
nodded. I'd gathered that she left Sapphire here some of the
time so she and the other little dogs would continue to have
their own pack.

"Next, you're going to give me all the information about
who now has the other four dogs you adopted out. I'll check
them out this week. Hopefully, I'll find them all acceptable
and won't have to go through efforts to get the dogs back. If

I do, part of that will be your reimbursing the people who need to return the dogs. Got it?"

Marshall nodded dolefully. "They're all good. I checked them out. But I understand."

"And finally, I want to set up a meeting with you and all the other people who conspired in this. I intend for you to learn more about the process of caring for orphaned pets, and that means you will all need to take our orientation, then volunteer for a minimum number of hours I'll establish at HotRescues. Got that, too?"

"Yes," Marshall said, not objecting.

I looked at Janice. "Yes," she parroted.

We talked for a short while longer. It was getting late, and I wanted to go home to Zoey. But this needed to be as finalized as possible for now.

Eventually, I said good night to the people and dogs. "E-mail me tonight before you go to bed with the information about the people you adopted dogs out to," I told Marshall. His classes tomorrow didn't start till the afternoon, he informed me when I asked. "Good. Bring these guys to HotRescues no later than nine o'clock AM." I figured that would give them time to say good-bye to them, at least temporarily. "Make sure you contact all your friends who are involved, too, so we can arrange for them to volunteer and set up the initial meeting at HotRescues."

As I left, I felt as if I'd really accomplished something important that day, although I still had work to do during the next week, to check on the affected dogs and make sure all who weren't put back into my possession were now in good home situations. I'd also need to confirm that all of the conspirators followed through and became supervised volunteers at HotRescues to atone for their misconduct.

Yes, a lot of work, but at least I'd no sense that any

animals were in danger. Plus, my figuring this out and dealing with it gave me confidence.

But I was no closer to determining what was going on with the HotPets Bling collars . . . and solving Teresa Kantrim's murder.

Chapter 32

The next week was one of the busiest ever at HotRescues.

True to his word, Marshall provided me with the information about where the four teacups he had adopted out had found new homes. First thing I did was to contact the supposed new owners and arrange to visit them.

Fortunately—and amazingly, considering his underhandedness with HotRescues—Marshall had in fact discovered good fits between dogs and adopters. Although I explained to each of them what had happened—with the idea that they could claim their exorbitant adoption fees back from Marshall if they wanted to—they all chose to keep their new babies. As far as I knew none regretted the payments they'd made.

I also let everyone at HotRescues know what had happened, and I scheduled a meeting upstairs in our conference room on Tuesday night with Marshall, Janice, and the other college students who'd come here to adopt our teacups and turn them over to Marshall for rehoming and cash.

They all looked familiar, of course. And each one appeared embarrassed and sorry. Or at least they gave that impression, even if they only assumed it because Marshall had told them to.

"Here's what we're going to do, gang," I said to all the sad faces over our upstairs conference table. "For one thing, you're each going to become HotRescues volunteers. That way, I won't pursue any further action against you, like turning you over to the police for animal endangerment or worse, suing you for fraud and breach of contract." I told them we would hold a volunteer orientation, and we agreed on the following Saturday, which fortunately worked for all of them.

Also fortunately, I was aiming for my next teacup rescue, with all its other attached baggage, for Sunday.

Next, I got them all to agree to their minimum volunteer obligations. "I'll have one of our volunteers who's here today show you around when we're through and give you a rundown of all that being a volunteer can entail." Like not only socializing dogs and cats and feeding them, but also cleaning up after them. "And you'll be subject to strict supervision while you're here."

I asked if this was, in fact, the entire group of kids who were involved in this conspiracy to make money from our little rescue dogs. They claimed they were—but I knew I'd continue really scrutinizing all the applications we'd gotten in for our current group of teacup dogs, as well as questioning all those people and any more to come.

I turned Onyx and Sapphire back over to Marshall and Janice, who made it clear that they each intended not to sell these little guys but to keep them themselves.

I didn't let them take Garnet back, though. The poor little poodle would be returned to our kennels in the small-dog building—but I knew it wouldn't take long to find her a new, real home.

I eventually sent them off with Bev, who would set them straight about the ethical, diligent, and, most important, caring obligations of volunteers here. She'd been one of those I'd explained the current situation to, and she had expressed as much outrage and disgust as I'd felt. She would be perfect for this task.

I found, to my relief, that there were still plenty of people who wanted to adopt our little teacups besides the ones who'd conspired with Marshall to achieve ill-gotten gains by reselling them. By the time the weekend rolled around, all the dogs we'd named after jewels, and nearly all of the ones we'd given tea names to, were either adopted or ready to go to new homes.

With applicants, and homes, that I'd studied even more carefully than usual.

All was well.

And I was ready for our next Airborne Adoptions flight.

I only hoped it would give me not just more little dogs to rescue and rehome—but all the results I was looking for.

This time, I planned in advance for my trip with the Faylers as part of the Airborne Adoptions rescue. Not just the part that involved the dogs. I was already quite organized about that.

But I also spent some time figuring out how to handle the other aspect of the trip: dealing with the HotPets Bling collars.

I confirmed with Tom Fayler that he would once again be meeting with some of the Las Vegas store managers and would hand over samples.

Samples I would ride with in the back of the plane.

Samples that just might not be what they purported to

be: attractive dog collars whose designs incorporated look-alike jewels. No, some might be the real thing—or at least there might be some unknown people who'd believe so.

Happily, despite my near-revelation about my knowledge of real jewels at the last HotRescues party, no one had confronted me. Matt had been royally peeved when I'd told him after the fact what I'd intended by what I had said—getting a guilty reaction from someone. I'd promised him I'd be careful, and I had. I hadn't gone anywhere or done anything on my own since then—or at least not much beyond confronting Marshall Droven about his teacup plot. And Matt had spent several evenings with me.

My ploy had been for naught. I'd suffered no attacks—a good thing, of course. No attempted poisonings, either. But neither had anyone admitted that at least some of the collars used real gems in their patterns.

Now, I was going to push even more for answers.

I also realized that my verbal digs at the party could have made whoever was guilty back down. Or give up. Or change tactics.

I, for one, readily admitted that I couldn't tell costume jewels from the real thing—although the ones I'd seen had apparently all been set within the one pattern: tiaras and dog noses. I could watch for them, at least.

And I had a plan. One that might not work, of course, but I was going to try it.

First, though, I had to reveal it to Brooke's guy, Detective Antonio Bautrel.

And Matt.

Here I was yet again. I helped Tom and Naya load a bunch of small-dog crates into the back of the plane, along with three cartons of HotPets Bling collars. One was even sealed with red duct tape.

I held on to the arms of my seat as we took off, even though I was now a lot more used to flying in a small plane. My nerves were much better than the first time, but they remained somewhat on edge.

The noise as we flew was still loud and annoying, keeping me from having much of a conversation with the two in the front seat. They both appeared relaxed, which felt good, since they'd be tense or worse if we were in trouble. They looked alert, too, which was also good. They were in charge and would know what to do if we ran into trouble. I hoped.

This time, as we flew, partly to distract me but even more to prepare for what was to come after we landed in Vegas, I once again sorted through the cartons of HotPets Bling collars.

The assortment of designs seemed to have increased. Now, in addition to the ones I'd come to understand as the costume Bling that were blue leather with dog bone and dog ear jewel designs, and black ones possibly containing real gems with designs of tiaras and dog noses, there were also some red ones with ring shapes and balls; dark brown ones in a larger size, decorated with dumbbell and splayed-out-chicken shapes, like some stuffed toys for dogs; and lighter-brown leather ones that were inset with designs of cat heads and disks like those thrown for dogs to chase.

All were done attractively, the shapes artistic yet well set, the collars themselves functional.

And I had no idea which ones had real jewels set into their designs. If any. Or all.

I still wanted to—had to—trust the Faylers. I leaned forward so my mouth wasn't too far from Tom's right ear.

"I assume you know all about these latest HotPets Bling designs, don't you, Tom?" I asked.

He turned his head a bit, and I saw his proud smile. "Of course. Chris stepped up his artistry, didn't he? We love them and want to introduce them to the Vegas managers, since we're about to do our initial rollout there."

"I've seen them, too, Lauren," Naya said, also raising her voice to be heard. "They're cute and unique in the industry the way they're done, and I've been told the ads will be just as much fun as the ones in L.A.—which means teacup-sized dogs will become popular in Vegas soon, then all over the country. This could be your last rescue like this."

"I'd hoped that anyway," I told them. I leaned back in my seat for just a short while, pondering what to say next. And then I again moved toward them. "I know you both heard what I said at our last HotRescues party about the paste jewels in the collars—or at least the possibly faux gems."

"You suggested they're real, or at least some of them," Naya said. "All of the HotPets people there discussed that before we left."

"But we didn't tell you," said Tom. He moved forward to push a button or two on the console in front of him. I had no idea why, but the plane seemed a bit more level afterward, and I could hear him better. "Maybe we should have, but what you said . . . well, it seemed so off base. We of course only use the pretty-but-cheap stuff."

"Of course, that's what you *think*," I contradicted. "But what if some of it is real?"

Tom shrugged his shoulders. "All of us in the Bling subsidiary have traded some laughs about that. But where would we get real stuff? And why would we use it in the collars, especially at the prices we charge for them? We'd have to develop a whole new pricing structure."

"Maybe you'd better," I said. "There's something I maybe should have told you before, too. Or Dante should have. But even though we trusted you, we—or at least I—couldn't be certain." Was I doing what Matt would chew me out for later—endangering myself knowingly?

But I really did believe in the Faylers.

Besides, if something happened to me on this trip, everyone knew who my pilots were.

"What's that?" Naya asked. Since she was the copilot and didn't have to keep everything under control all the time, she turned so she could look me in the eye.

"Before I tell you, you need to swear to me that you really are legit and want to know the truth, too."

"Of course we are." That was Tom, who turned enough that my stomach lurched. Was he still in control of the plane? But we still moved forward just fine, and he looked ahead immediately.

"Yes, of course," Naya agreed.

"And you don't know anything about real jewels being used in the collars?" I said.

"I've a feeling you're going to try to convince us that they're genuine," Naya said, her voice, still loud, sounding full of irony.

"You're right," I said. "Then—"

"The first we thought about the possibility was when Dante came around to the factory and asked to take a peek at the jewels, and offhandedly asked questions about their origin. Which is a paste jewelry manufacturer somewhere in China."

"Did you check?" I asked.

"After Dante left, I did," Tom said. "The place is staffed

twenty-four/seven, so I was never all by myself there, but I checked the boxes that were unpacked to create the designs and didn't see anything out of order. All of them looked pretty much the same."

"Even so . . ." I told them about Carlie's cameraman's assessment. "I'm no expert, but I gather he is." I hesitated. "I've told Dante, of course, and he has confirmed that some of them are real jewels. I understood that of the collar designs you've taken to Las Vegas before, some contained the standard attractive costume-jewelry collars and some were the real thing." I didn't tell them which. "Now, though, there are more designs, plus, since I said something that could have worried whoever is playing games with your collars, there may be some kind of switching or mixing that only the perpetrator knows about."

"If any at all," Naya said.

"If any at all," I agreed. I paused to think about the situation a little more. "I've got a suggestion, though. One you're not going to like."

"What's that?"

"I'd like to take this entire shipment of collars back with me and have it checked out by Carlie's cameraman before handing them over to Dante, so I'll know what to tell him."

They exchanged a brief glance before Tom again looked out through the front windows. "That makes sense, at least this time," he allowed.

"Good." I started to sit back in my seat.

That's when Naya's body seemed to freeze, her shoulders hiked up as if she expected a blow. What? Were we about to hit something? Nosedive? I felt myself begin to quiver.

But when she spoke, it was something else altogether that made me tense up.

"If what you're saying about real jewels is true—or even if someone is claiming it is . . ."

"What, honey?" Tom asked as she tapered off.

"Yeah, what?" I demanded.

"What if that was what Teresa was talking about, as if she was aware of it and thought we were, too?"

Chapter 33

So I wasn't the only one on the plane now wondering if the two things could be related.

But we were getting ready to land, so that was pretty much the end of the discussion. For now, at least.

When we were on the ground, the scenario began as it had the last couple of times. Some ground crew guys came over to unload the plane.

This time, Tom and Naya had already agreed to bring the collars back to L.A. The only things to be taken out were the crates for the little dogs.

We exited the plane down the steps after the crates were on the tarmac. Another similar plane was, once more, also sitting there. The pups had arrived before us again. Dwayne and Nelson Hannover came over to say hi.

"How are all our little passengers doing?" Naya asked after we'd all greeted one another.

"Great!" said Nelson. The bald father and son again

wore flight jackets with their jeans. They grinned in unison and I was again struck by how much they resembled each other.

"So what are you going to name these dogs after?" Nelson asked me. "You've already done gems, you told me. And, oh yeah, what were the last bunch named after?"

"Teas," I said. "And we haven't decided yet about this group. I told my staff and volunteers to come up with a good theme. Any ideas?"

"Why not types of small planes?" Dwayne asked.

"Like what?"

They all brainstormed then, the Faylers and the Hannovers, pilots all. Some names were fun, but I wasn't sure I liked each they came up with. I nevertheless dutifully jotted every one of them down in a notebook I pulled out of my purse as they spewed out eight, the same number as our latest group of rescue dogs: Beech, Cessna, Challenger, Dash, Falcon, Gulfstream, Lear, and Piper.

"Those may work just great," I said. "Thanks for the idea."

The Faylers were met then by several people I recognized, local HotPets managers. "Excuse us," Naya said.

"We'll get the dogs out, then be on our way," Nelson said.

I assured Tom and Naya that I'd see to the dogs getting onto their plane, and then they walked off with the others. Were they going to get an earful for not leaving some Bling collars with these managers? I hoped not. We'd already decided that, once this latest batch had been cleared—or the ones with true gems had been sorted out—Dante would have no concern about paying to get them shipped back here. Besides, the rollout in Las Vegas was scheduled for a couple of weeks from now, so their showing more to their customers and the media wasn't currently urgent.

I went to the Hannovers' plane and helped to get the little dogs' crates out. Then we removed the dogs from the crates and began walking them.

That's when I saw what appeared to be an argument going on by one of the hangars—not the nearest, but one not particularly far, either. The ground crew guys were in a heated discussion with some other men.

Could this have something to do with their failure to unload the collars?

"Excuse me," I told Dwayne. "Could you take these two guys for a few minutes? I need to go find the little girls' room. They have some in the hangars, don't they?"

"Sure." He kindly took the leashes and poop bags from me, and I headed not toward the hangar where the ground crew men were, but toward the one closest to me.

I went inside the hangar. One end also held a huge metal door that could open to allow planes inside.

It was a vast building that held a single plane just now but appeared to have room for several more. Tools and machinery lined the walls, the uses of which I could only guess. The air was drafty, the floor was concrete, and it was empty of other people just now, which was a good thing. I saw where the restrooms were located at the end.

Fortunately, there was another door there, too, which would be near the guys arguing outside. I was able to crack it open just a little.

I wasn't able to hear the apparently heated discussion near the next hangar, especially since the air was filled with the sound of another plane taking off or landing—I couldn't tell which from here. That meant I didn't know what they were arguing about. It could have had nothing to do with the Bling collars.

Or it could have had everything to do with them. Especially since I did happen to hear just a few words. If I interpreted them correctly, they included "L.A."—and one of them did, in fact, sound like "collar."

Another thought drove itself into my mind: Teresa Kantrim had had to wait for the Faylers' plane on her journey from Missouri to L.A. Had she wandered around this area? If so, maybe she had overheard a discussion better than I did.

Then, there had probably been no issue about the ground crew unloading every box of collars. And someone taking out the ones they wanted to keep.

As they might have done on my last trip here. I hadn't suspected anything then, and hadn't double-checked the box we flew back to L.A., but the only collars I remembered seeing from any of the crates, after those boxes were first removed from the plane, were of the ordinary designs that I now believed hadn't had actual jewels in them.

So what if Teresa had overheard something that then led to her digs at Tom and Naya on the flight back to L.A.? Ones she had repeated in front of other people later.

Okay, I realized I was making this up as I went along, in the hopes of joining the two mysteries and finding solutions. But what if Teresa had heard about some of the collars holding real, valuable jewels that were being transported to the Las Vegas airport that way and assumed the Faylers were aware of it—logical, considering Tom's position in the HotPets Bling subsidiary?

I stepped back and slowly pulled the door closed as I considered this. And also considered forgetting the whole idea.

Why would Teresa have cared? What good would it

have done her to gibe at people she thought were doing something underhanded, possibly illegal? She could have told Dante. Turned them over to the police. Whatever.

But pushing that way . . . I still believed in the Faylers' innocence, but what if whoever had been involved with attaching the real gems had heard her taunts and worried that she would begin aiming them at someone else—like the real culprit?

That could have been a motive to kill her. I wasn't convinced, though. It didn't seem enough—did it?

And even if it was, I still didn't know *who* it was.

"So how do you want us to handle this, Lauren?" Naya asked. Our flight back to Van Nuys Airport had been fairly uneventful—if you didn't count a couple of rounds of barking from the eight little dogs we were transporting to L.A.

Such a din in such close quarters, even when the plane itself was noisy, still made my ears ring despite the fact we had just landed and the engine was now off.

"Similarly to last time," I told her. "Let's put all the dogs in the back of my car and I'll drive them to Carlie's vet clinic." I'd brought my Venza today instead of the shelter van, since there were fewer dogs to transport.

"Naya means the boxes of collars," Tom said. Both Faylers were peering between the front seats at me. And I'd of course known what she meant.

"We'll also put them into my car," I said. "I'm going to leave them at Carlie's overnight, too. I'll ask her to have her jewel-expert cameraman take a look at them, see if any have real jewels or not before I hand them over to Dante to confirm it. In either case, I'll pick the collars up tomorrow, even though the dogs won't be ready to take to HotRescues that soon. I'll keep them at HotRescues for now."

"And if some of them are decorated with real jewels?" Naya bit her lower lip, clearly uneasy with the situation.

"They might not be, since I hinted aloud that we know the truth—assuming it is the truth," I said. "Whoever's involved might have decided not to do it again, or at least not to send any to Las Vegas."

"But if they are real?" Naya persisted. "And in those boxes?"

I looked from her eyes into Tom's, then back again. "I'm still assuming you two are innocent, but someone at Hot-Pets must know the truth behind the real bling-encrusted collars. Once I get them back to HotRescues, we'll put out the word that, on Dante's okay, I'll be giving out one of the collars from this trip to each person who adopts a dog from HotRescues, whether or not they're the teacups. If there are real jewels involved, whoever set them is going to be pretty upset."

"He or she may come to HotRescues and break in." Naya sounded horrified.

"That's true," I said. "And it won't be the first time there's been a problem at my shelter—including Teresa's murder."

"But—" Naya said.

I interrupted her. "I think you both know me well enough to realize I'm not the victim type. And I won't do anything that'll result in any danger to our resident pets."

"Then what are you going to do?" Tom's wide cheeks looked a little shrunken in concern now, and there wasn't a smile on his usually pleased-looking face.

"I can't tell you. Not now. But I'm going to ask for your cooperation soon, if all goes well. Can I count on you?"

When they both assured me I could, I just hoped that neither was lying about their involvement or about whether I could rely on their help when the time came.

As I'd told the Faylers, the dogs, the collars, and I headed to Carlie's.

If there really were genuine jewels in those dog adornments, I had no doubt that those guys I saw arguing with the baggage handlers in Las Vegas knew about it, or were at least under some kind of orders to make sure the collars were taken off the plane and secured somewhere.

Which they hadn't been.

And someone here in L.A. had probably been told that.

As a result, I swore Tom and Naya to absolute secrecy—for now. Plus, I told them to be extremely cautious, since whoever was involved with putting real jewels in the necklaces might be concerned about the disappearance of this batch, and the Faylers were the obvious people to be hiding them. They could be in danger.

For my own little scheme, I also got Tom and Naya to promise that they would tell everyone at HotPets about it when I let them know that the collars were finally brought to HotRescues.

Chapter 34

I phoned Carlie on my way to The Fittest Pet. I told her about the dogs and asked, without going into detail, if she might be able to get Darius to the pet hospital that afternoon.

"I'll check and see," she told me. "I think it's pretty likely."

And in fact, when I reached the pet hospital, she already had some of her staff on call once more to help unload the dogs.

As well as the boxes of collars.

"Darius said he'd be here within the hour," she told me after I'd made sure the cute little dogs were all settled and ready to be checked over by Carlie or one of her staff vets.

While I was waiting, I spent more time with those little dogs when they weren't on the examination tables or otherwise being checked for any medical issues.

Juliet Ansiger had previously assured me that everyone in this group, too, had been looked at by a vet before leaving

Missouri, and all had been fine. Even so, I trusted Carlie and her gang a lot more than some doctors I hadn't met half a country away.

While I was with them, I considered the names of small airplanes that the Faylers had suggested. Once they were adopted out, their new families could, of course, rename them. I supposed those names were as good as any others.

But I'd let my staff and volunteers assign who would be called what. This time, we had two poodles—a white one and a black one—two Chihuahuas, three Yorkies, and a Pomeranian.

All, of course, were adorable, and I had a wonderful time vegging out, not worrying—for a short while, at least—and hugging one after another.

Until Carlie came back into the large exam room where she'd left us. "Darius is here."

"How long will it take him to check out the collars?" I asked.

"He's already working on them."

I knelt and gave a poodle and the Pomeranian a last hug for now—enjoying that both of them licked me on the cheek—and followed Carlie out of the room, which was filled with veterinary equipment I didn't attempt to identify and a bunch of small dogs I'd eventually pick up once more and take to HotRescues.

I followed her into her office, which was where we had piled the boxes filled with collars.

I recognized the cameraman, even though, rather than a high-tech camera, he had what I figured was a jeweler's loupe in his hand, holding it up to his eye as he examined one of the collars. He sat on one of the chairs facing Carlie's desk.

"What do you think?" I asked without preamble. I figured he knew who I was, too.

"Just give me a few minutes," he said.

I'm not a very patient person, but I nevertheless sat down on the chair next to him, while Carlie went around and took her own seat behind the desk, facing us. She and I chatted for a while about the situation with the kids who'd adopted some of our teacups to resell, and what I was doing about it. I tried not to allow myself to get into as angry a state of mind as I could have in discussing this. After all, that was all nearly resolved.

But if Carlie asked if she could feature the situation on one of her *Pet Fitness* TV shows, I'd probably lose my cool and yell. Not a good idea.

I could tell her no calmly—yet really firmly. She knew me well enough that she wouldn't argue with me.

Darius, who'd seemed oblivious to our conversation as he pulled collars from each of the four boxes and studied them, eventually looked up, pulling the loupe away from his face. There was a squint to his dark eyes that I had noticed before, and I'd assumed it was from concentrating his stare on his camera. Maybe it was more than that. He was a short fellow, maybe in his forties, with thinning blond hair. "Let me start by saying that what I can tell here is not absolute, any more than it was with the earlier stones I looked at in those other collars."

"Why is that?" I asked.

"There are chemical and other ways of testing gems and their quality," he said in a formal tone, as if he were hold-ing a class. Maybe he had taught some in his past, when he'd made his living as a jeweler. "Keeping them mounted in these collars, where they're set really deeply and firmly so they won't fall out and get swallowed by the dogs, makes it even harder to tell for sure. We always look for clarity and evenness of color, among other qualities, but the glue holding them in can mess that up, too. That was the same with the earlier collars I looked at as well."

"Then why did you think some of them had real gems mounted in them?" I asked, trying not to sound impatient. What if this was all a big mistake, on the word of a guy who only wanted his supposed prowess in telling real from fake jewels to impress the star of the TV show he helped to film? But, no. Dante had had at least some of the jewels confirmed as real, and I felt certain he had checked with experts.

"Experience," Darius said simply. "I studied them a lot more carefully than I'm doing now. Over time, I've looked at gemstones mounted in expensive and cheap settings. I've looked at paste and other manufactured stones also mounted in a variety of settings. Before I dumped that whole career and went into film, where I find the larger venues and the work with people a lot more gratifying, I was a jeweler for fifteen years. I came to trust my own judgment, and so did the people I worked for." He shrugged. "Before, I'd tell you that the collar designs that depicted canine noses and tiaras contained a lot of the real thing. Not so, this time. Someone either knew they'd been found out, or they decided to change for other reasons. But now it appears that the ones with those silly splayed-out chicken shapes and dumbbells have at least a few real jewels within their designs. Am I positive? Pretty much. But to be absolutely sure, you'd want to have someone who's still in the jewelry business and designated an expert take them off the collars and test them."

"But you're relatively certain?" I asked, half standing. I'd expected the possibility, but now I was jazzed.

"Yes," he said, nodding.

Good. I now could follow up on the plans I'd been formulating, and I was excited about what other results they might have.

"So what will you do about it, Lauren?" Carlie's tone was quiet, as if she were the voice of reason in this room. She looked as if she was, in her white veterinary jacket, her violet eyes calm as she watched me.

I didn't want to tell her in front of Darius. I didn't necessarily want to tell her at all. I had a feeling she would be like Matt in this case and order me not to do what I had in mind.

But I wasn't stupid or careless. I'd factor in all the negative possibilities and make sure I was prepared for the worst.

And not do it alone.

"I'm still thinking about it," I told Carlie.

The suddenly stern expression on her TV-star-attractive face told me she wasn't buying what I'd said. "You won't do anything foolish," she ordered, not making it a question.

"Do I ever do anything foolish?" I responded. And when she opened her mouth to answer—clearly about to remind me of situations where I hadn't been exactly careful, I added, "You don't need to respond to that. But don't worry. I've thought this through carefully but still want to consider some of the angles before I do anything. In any event, don't worry. I promise I—"

She repeated right along with me: "—won't do anything foolish."

I hoped.

Chapter 35

I pondered for a while how to deal with this best, most safely, and—of the greatest importance—most effectively.

On my drive back to HotRescues on surface streets that were much too crowded, especially considering that today was Sunday, I considered a long detour to the HotPets offices. I figured Dante would be there despite it being a late weekend afternoon.

I realized, though, that the conversation I needed to have with him would go better by phone. What if some members of his staff happened to be there, too? My presence at his business right now would only complicate matters further, especially if he bought into the plan I was now finalizing in my mind.

Since this ride was taking longer than I'd hoped, I considered phoning Dante right then. But though I'd be using my hands-free system in the car, I would want to concentrate on what I was saying, not to mention to his reaction.

No, better that I be sitting at my desk at HotRescues, listening to the tone in Dante's voice and considering nuances of what he said—and didn't say.

That, of course, didn't happen as quickly as I'd hoped, even when I finally reached my shelter. First, there was a family with teenage kids who were interested in adopting a medium-to-large-sized dog. Only the mother was there, and she'd been shown around by one of our newer volunteers. She seemed taken with Wellington, an English sheepdog mix. She'd been told that her whole family would need to meet Wellington, and she was just about to dash off and pick up her kids at home. Her husband would meet them here later.

But she was full of questions about our adoption process and what we knew about Wellington's background—which was really only which public shelter we'd rescued him from—and more.

I was the person there with the most answers, so I got caught up for a while helping her. Which I didn't mind doing, since she seemed nice and, depending on her family and the contents of her application, might in fact become Wellington's new mama.

I had to swallow my impatience, though. What I really wanted was to call Dante.

Once the woman had left, Nina allowed Zoey out from behind our welcome desk, and my dog rushed at me like she hadn't seen me in ages.

It had been a long time—since early this morning. I gave her hugs while she kissed my face.

I didn't take the time to go visit our residents. Not now. Instead, I thanked Nina for handling everything in my absence, and then Zoey and I went to my office.

There, at last, I called Dante. I told him what had transpired so far that day, including my holding on to the boxes of collars originally destined to be left in Las Vegas.

"Yes, I know," he said. "Tom phoned me before. He told me a bit about what you had in mind, but I didn't quite follow it."

"It's gotten even more complicated," I told him. I let him know about my meeting with Darius, the gem-recognizing cameraman.

"No!" he growled in such an angry tone that I bent over in my chair and hugged Zoey. Even though his mood was not directed at me, I somehow felt it. "Now, that surprises me. Why would whoever's involved send more collars with real jewels to Vegas now that word's out about our suspicions? Don't they realize they'll get caught?"

"They're obviously pretty brazen—or they somehow don't think they'll be identified. Or they don't think they have a choice." I described the little I'd made out of the argument I'd heard between the ground crew and others at the Las Vegas airport. "Maybe they're committed to bringing the real jewels there, no matter how they do it. Or maybe it's simpler than that—they just figure that giving away real jewels that look like the paste ones isn't a crime."

"Depends on whose jewels they are—and where they came from. Somehow I don't think this is just some kind of altruistic prank."

It hit me then. "Do you recall the news a few months ago about some jewels being stolen from L.A.'s downtown jewelry district?"

"The thought crossed my mind," Dante said drolly. "I've a feeling that, when we catch whoever it is, they'll have some fun explaining the jewels' background to the cops.

And me. Definitely me." Dante's low, determined voice
made me shudder. "I put out the word before that some
questions about the stones' authenticity had been raised, but
that of course the ones being used were the manufactured
kind we'd imported. Period. I did it in a way that should
have left no doubt that anyone doing otherwise wouldn't
have a job here any longer. And that would be the least of
their worries."

"But who is that 'anyone'?" I asked him gently, my right
hand still splayed in the warmth of Zoey's long fur. Her
tongue was out as if she were laughing in pleasure, which
made me smile despite the gravity of the conversation.
"Until we know who they are—assuming we can figure it
out—they're safe." Before he could say anything, I added,
"But I do have an idea how to identify them."

I explained it to him. All of it. Tomorrow he would let
everyone at HotPets know that I'd brought the collars back
because I'd been so upset about the way some adopters had
acted with our little teacup dogs. While I was dealing with
that situation, I wanted everyone who even had a thought
about visiting HotRescues to know I would be giving out
HotPets Bling collars not only to all our adopters this
week—whom I'd check out even more carefully than
before—but also for their other dogs they brought in, to
make sure those they were interested in adopting got along
with existing family pets. Some of the smaller Bling collars would even go home with cats, even though they hadn't
been designed for them.

But because of the events recently, and before, that had
been problems at HotRescues—such as Teresa's murder,
not to mention the break-ins that had occurred when I was
looking into another murder not long ago—I was locking

those Bling collars in my office, since, with all the ads, they might be susceptible to theft. Not that anyone but my HotRescues "family" was going to be told that, but Dante and others who cared about the Bling collars and their reputations should know.

"Which means, I take it," Dante said, "that you're expecting someone from here, whoever's messing with the collars, to break in and steal these back."

"I expect someone to try," I acknowledged. "And when they do—"

"We'll have our culprits."

I told all of this to Antonio Bautrel when he came to stay over with Brooke that night.

Zoey and I walked through HotRescues with Cheyenne and them as they did their initial check of the evening, and then accompanied them upstairs to the security apartment.

I was pleased at how well Brooke appeared, especially when she shared smiles with Antonio. I thought she grew even prettier over time, just as her health continued to improve. Antonio looked like . . . well, a cop, with his usual jagged features outlined in the apartment lights and the expression on his face intense when I started to speak.

As we all sat in the small living room and each drank one bottle of beer, I gave them a rundown of all the day's happenings. The dogs lay together in a small pack on the area rug on the hardwood floor.

"Do you happen to have any contacts in Las Vegas who can check things out from that end?" I asked Antonio when I was done.

"I don't personally, but all police departments cooperate with one another, at least somewhat. I'll get that started."

"And will you be able to make sure someone's here watching the security cameras downstairs?" Brooke asked. We have a really nice setup with monitors there, in a room on the first floor. We don't use them every night, but they'd helped in an earlier incident where there'd been break-ins at HotRescues relating to a killing that hadn't happened here, but which I'd helped to solve. And tomorrow, after Dante made his pronouncements at Hot-Pets, would be a really good time to use those monitors again.

"You and I can do that," Antonio told Brooke. "And I'll alert some of the guys at the Devonshire station that I might need backup." That was the closest LAPD station to HotRescues.

"Great," I said, and thanked him in advance.

"Will you really lock the collars in your office?" Brooke asked. She leaned forward from where she sat on the couch beside Antonio, holding his arm as she picked up her beer mug and took a swig.

The dogs stirred and looked up at us, then both settled back down on the rugs, obviously realizing we weren't going anywhere yet.

"No. Maybe I shouldn't even tell *you* where they'll be." I grinned.

"Maybe not. I like the idea of real jewels in a collar. Don't you, Cheyenne?"

Her beautiful golden retriever looked up at the sound of his name and appeared to smile. Zoey stood, as if she felt left out of the conversation. I held out my hand, and she came over to me.

"Get a good night's sleep," I told the two humans. "Tomorrow may be a busy night."

But it wasn't. Brooke and Antonio took turns watching the security monitors from dusk till dawn, or so they informed me on Tuesday morning. I'd also warned EverySecurity management to be on alert and to monitor the cameras, too.

That Monday night, though, nothing at all out of the ordinary happened at HotRescues.

I had told Matt what was going on. He told me to go home and stay out of the way if someone happened to appear, then scolded me over the phone when I said I was staying at HotRescues for the night. I felt a little bent out of shape when he told me he had plans that night and couldn't stay there, too, to be with me.

He told me about a nighttime animal rescue exercise that had been on his schedule for a while. He needed to be there to observe. I wasn't thrilled, but I understood.

But I didn't obey his command to leave and allow the security people and cops to deal with whatever happened.

I took pleasure in telling him, the next day, that nothing at all had occurred. But that was the only pleasure I derived from our exercise in futility.

I'd slept curled somewhat on the little couch I used for meetings in my office, with Zoey on the floor to start with, but a couple of times when I woke up—since I'd told myself to awaken at any kind of noise—I discovered her sleeping on top of my feet.

I didn't mind. I appreciated her company.

I'd thought about taking a walk through the shelter to check for any unwanted visitors, but at that moment any visitor would have been wanted—because there'd be only one motive for him or her to be here, looking for the collars.

Besides, with the word out that the collars were in my office, I was in the ideal locale to catch the suspects.

But no one even attempted to sneak in.

We had another busy day on Tuesday, showing off cats and dogs who were available for adoption. The third group of teacup dogs was ready to be picked up from Carlie's, but only for the dogs to start their quarantine here. I was tired, but I brought Pete along to help me take the little guys to their new temporary home.

Even though it was Tuesday, public school apparently hadn't started yet, since the family who wanted to adopt Wellington—both parents and kids—all came in and bonded with him.

I went over their application with them in great detail. Wellington wasn't one of the little teacup dogs, but I felt as if I'd been burned by those kids adopting for profit, so I was even more careful than usual.

Eventually, I allowed this family, the Agustins, to take Wellington home with them—with the usual proviso that I could visit at any time.

Which I definitely would.

I also made good on the promise that was getting publicized a bit more. I gave them one of the HotPets Bling collars for Wellington—one of the original designs that Darius hadn't found any actual jewels on.

The day went quickly.

Evening arrived. So did Brooke, Cheyenne, and Antonio once more.

Matt did, too, along with Rex.

We ordered in pizza. Brooke and her crew retired early to the building with all the security monitors.

I told Matt that he didn't have to stay here with me—but of course he thought he did. There were no training exercises that night.

Rather than staying in my office with its compact sofa, we went upstairs to Dr. Mona's office. The shrink's couch we had there was much roomier.

I only hoped we'd hear it if someone came in looking for the Bling collars.

It turned out we did, thanks to the dogs.

Both Zoey and Rex woke at maybe two in the morning. Both growled first, then started barking. We both shushed them quickly, although someone visiting a pet shelter, legitimately or not, should expect to hear dogs around.

"Stay here," Matt ordered me as he untangled himself from my arms and stood, straightening his clothes.

I just gave him a look intended to say "Yeah, right," and got up, too.

We both leashed our dogs. I let Matt precede me down the stairway, since he did have a weapon—a gun that wasn't supposed to be used on people, only on severely injured animals suffering too much to be transported to a vet, but if he needed to use it, it would obviously be for self-defense.

When we got down the steps and turned down the hall toward my office, we saw that it was unnecessary to use any kind of weapon. Antonio had someone in custody, and the EverySecurity people also helped to surround whoever it was.

I wasn't happy that I couldn't see the person. At least I couldn't at first.

But as Matt and I, and our dogs, got closer, Brooke touched Antonio on the shoulder and nodded in our direction.

He glanced our way, then grabbed whoever it was by the shoulder and swung him around.

Really? I supposed I should have guessed, since he had more opportunity than anyone else to play games with the collars—he was their chief designer.

The person who'd broken into HotRescues, presumably to steal back those collars, because some of them had real jewels in them?

It was Chris Mandrea, the main HotPets Bling designer.

Chapter 36

I'm not a law enforcement professional. I recognize that, and I have no interest in becoming one.

I was nevertheless a little miffed that I wasn't allowed to listen in on the initial interrogation of Chris. After all, this was my shelter. And it was my plan that had resulted in his being apprehended.

Plus, I'd helped the cops before in solving murders. And as I'd learned over the past weeks, I wasn't the only one who thought that the oddity about the HotPets Bling collars could somehow be connected to yet another murder, Teresa Kantrim's.

But I wasn't even permitted to hang out in the next room when the detectives who'd come at Antonio's behest started to question Chris.

The only thing that made me feel a little better about it was that the EverySecurity guys who'd shown up to help were also exiled from the interrogation.

At least they let Antonio sit in. He was law enforcement, one of their own. And I knew him well enough to feel certain he'd tell me anything he legitimately could.

Which, of course, might be nothing.

I sat in the welcome area with Matt and Brooke and our dogs and waited. And waited.

Eventually, after over an hour, Antonio joined us. "Mandrea is being taken into custody. We'll have a team stay here to check the shelter out as a crime scene, at least for his breaking and entering."

"Is it okay if I go look in on our residents?" I asked. This wasn't the same horrible situation as a murder, so surely we wouldn't be entirely on lockdown.

"Yes, although I'll come with you," Antonio said.

Both Matt and Brooke said they would, too. We left Zoey, Rex, and Cheyenne in my office and headed out the door to the kennel area. Some cops milled around under the lights that were still on at full blast rather than dimmed for the night. I noticed with interest that a bunch of the officers were leaning toward the glass kennel doors, looking over the dogs inside.

The dogs, in turn, were all fairly quiet now, mostly standing and wagging their tails at the attention.

I wondered if any of the officers would return to meet any of the dogs up close and personal, maybe even look into adoption.

But that was premature, and not the reason I was here. I looked over the men's and women's shoulders toward the kennel inhabitants, assuring myself that all was well.

I had to excuse myself to go around a couple of the police so I could clean out those kennels, but they were all nice, and in fact one woman helped me use rag towels to scrub down a couple of the floors with disinfectant. Not just her, though. I really appreciated how Matt chipped in to help, and Brooke and Antonio, too.

I continuously looked around, but the police had apparently taken Chris out the back door. It was unlocked, and some crime scene tape had been stuck to its frame, but the cops still used it for coming in and out.

We stopped outside the building containing the small dogs, and despite my exhaustion, I went inside. The eight newbies from our latest rescue hurried to the fronts of the kennel runs they shared, but their lack of energy suggested they were as tired as I was.

For the moment, there weren't any cops around except for Antonio, so I could ask questions without attracting glares.

I leaned against the mesh gate of the nearest enclosure, Matt standing close to me, and asked Antonio, "I know you're not supposed to say much, but I'm going to ask anyway. Did Chris admit to anything—even the break-in here tonight?"

"No." Antonio crossed his muscular arms as he smiled at me. That looked like a mixed message—holding me back with his off-putting gesture but expressing amusement at what I'd said.

"Then he didn't get into how the gem exchange was done, or why?" I pressed.

"Lauren, I don't think you'd better—" Brooke began. She took her place beside her boyfriend. She'd been here long enough, and we were good enough friends, that she knew I would listen to her warning, even if I didn't like it.

"I know," I broke in. "But you've got to understand how curious I am."

"I get it," Antonio said. "And I'd tell you more if I could, but I honestly don't know much else. Not yet. But what I can tell you is that it sounds as if Chris is hoping to negotiate some kind of plea deal already."

"What do you mean?" That was Brooke, stating exactly what I'd been about to ask.

"He keeps saying he could tell us something we'd be a lot more interested in, and who's involved, but he won't do it until he can be sure that he'll be treated fairly and released. He's asked for a lawyer to help him negotiate it, and that's the way he's phrased it, too."

"Does that mean Teresa's murder is somehow related to the jewelry situation, and he knows who killed her?" Matt asked. "Assuming, of course, it wasn't him, and it doesn't sound like he's admitting that."

"That's our speculation," Antonio said. "I'll keep you all informed about how things go, at least as much as I can."

Matt had an early morning meeting the next day—or actually today, since it was already past midnight. He was taking Rex and going home for whatever sleep he could manage.

I drove Zoey back to our home. I parked in the garage, pushed the button to close the garage door, then approached the door into the kitchen.

Before I could use my key to get in, Zoey stopped and growled.

"What's wrong, girl?" I kept my voice low. She didn't act this way. Not usually.

There could be a simple, if nasty, explanation, like a mouse or bird in the kitchen. But I doubted it.

Just in case, I reached for my phone in my pocket and pushed the button that went automatically to Matt's line.

I gasped as the door opened, and shoved the phone back where it had been—but I didn't end the call.

Whatever was going on, I hoped that Matt heard it. And figured something out if I wound up needing help.

Which I immediately figured I did.

"Hello, Lauren." The woman facing me had a gun, and she aimed it at my chest.

It was someone I really hadn't expected to be involved, although as my mind raced to figure out what was happening, some things suddenly appeared to make sense. Maybe.

"Hello, Sheila," I said to Dante's assistant, the obedient, good-natured little woman who undoubtedly knew everything there was to know about HotPets and how to manipulate anything to her advantage. This was the first time I'd seen her out of her work uniform—a nice suit or dress, befitting the person who backed up the CEO and did everything he needed done behind the scenes. Instead, she wore a HotPets T-shirt, jeans, and tennis shoes, looking like any ordinary woman around my age. Her short brown hair was a little messy, and she didn't wear any makeup, either. Definitely playing a role I hadn't seen her in before.

Maybe this was the real her.

"Come on in. Please." She laughed. "Although you should be saying that to me, since this is your house. Oh, and by the way, I know Zoey is sweet and very well trained, so I'd like you to tell her to sit and stop growling."

My girl was definitely sweet—usually. Right now her growls were an undercurrent to what passed for a conversation here, and she bared her teeth as if ready to attack. By reflex, I'd put my hand down on her collar to keep her by my side.

I would have let her go do what she would have done naturally if there hadn't been a gun involved.

Instead, I said, "Zoey, sit." Which she did. I tilted enough to pat her head. "Good girl."

"Now both of you come inside. Unless, of course, the collars with real gems that you saved are in your car. If so, you and I will go get them now."

I frowned in confusion. Yes, this had to be about the real bling collars, but why would she think I still had possession of any?

"No, there aren't any in the car or anywhere else around here. I assume they're all with the police now, at least any that I brought back on the Las Vegas trip, if those are the collars you're talking about." Or they might still be at HotRescues, where I'd hidden them. But I wasn't about to mention that now.

Her innocent smile turned into an angry glare. "Of course they're what I'm talking about. And I've heard about Chris and what happened at your damn shelter. There's something—well, never mind. I just need those jewels. The real ones."

"I'm sorry," I lied, "but I can't help you."

"Sit down," she snarled, waving her gun toward my small, round kitchen table with its chairs pushed under it. Still holding Zoey's collar, I complied.

I hoped Matt was listening, or at least aware that something was wrong. Just in case, I wanted to learn all I could.

"I know I'm just speculating, but here's what I think could be going on," I said. "I'm not aware of your relationship with Chris Mandrea, but I heard an unsubstantiated rumor"—just in case Antonio had said more than he should have to me—"that he's making some kind of deal so things will go easier for him, which means he'll turn you, or whoever else is involved, over to the authorities with whatever information he has. Did you kill Teresa Kantrim?"

I doubted she'd admit it, but I watched her face. "Of course I did," she spat. She took the chair facing me at the table, without lowering the gun. "And I'll kill you, too, if you don't help me."

"Why don't you tell me what's going on, and I'll see what I can do." And delay things as much as I could, till Matt and backup arrived. I hoped.

"If you don't have the jewels, do you have any money around here that you can give me? I have to get away."

"From being arrested?"

"That, and more." She sucked in her lips for a moment. "There are things . . . Hell, you want to hear what's going on? I'll describe to you how bad it is, so maybe you'll understand. And do just what I tell you." She stared hard into my eyes, holding the gun so it was now aimed at my forehead.

I hoped she didn't get some kind of twitch. Or just decide for the fun of it to pull the trigger . . .

I tightened my grip on Zoey's warm, furry back as she sat there, as much to bolster my own strength as to try to keep her safe.

"Please tell me," I said quietly.

"There's no time to tell you much," she said. "I'm in trouble with my boyfriend, Vince, because I didn't get the real jewels to the right people in Las Vegas, like I promised. That bitch Teresa interfered first, threatened to blackmail me. I took care of her. Vince helped. He just happened to have some cyanide for me to add to her drink that night at the party—had brought it along in case the opportunity arose to use it, which it did. Teresa was so blitzed already that she didn't know what she was drinking." Her smile made me shudder. "And now you've gotten in my way, too. He gave me one more chance, and it's also gone wrong. So you owe me. Especially since I'd already heard that Chris Mandrea is now being questioned about the jewels. He knows . . . enough. And I have to get out of here. So, give me some money. Fast."

"But I don't keep cash around here," I said. I was becoming really frightened now. She had admitted to having murdered Teresa, and I figured she'd have no compunction about killing me, too. "I'll be glad to give you what I have."

But what I'd said initially was true. Oh, if I scrounged in my purse, my kitchen drawers, and my kids' rooms, I might come up with a hundred dollars, maybe two hundred if I was lucky.

Nothing like the value of real gems, as she was looking for. And not enough for her to escape and go live in some other country that didn't have an extradition treaty with the United States. I figured that was what she was hoping for.

I reached down to where I'd laid my purse on the floor near Zoey.

"Let me have it," she insisted.

"Sure." I handed it over to her. "I don't have any weapons in it, if that's what you think."

"Yeah, that's what I think." Still keeping the gun trained on me, she began to root through the contents, pulling out my wallet. I had about fifty dollars in it, which she extracted. She also took my credit card. That didn't worry me much. I'd be able to stop payment on it—assuming she didn't kill me first.

And then I almost gasped aloud. She'd probably see my phone. What if she realized I'd made a call and hadn't hung up?

"I think I have some more in a hidden compartment," I said hastily. "Not sure, though. Can I take a look?"

Fortunately she didn't question that. She just handed my purse back to me and I dug in it.

I didn't see the light on the phone. That was a good

thing, because Sheila wouldn't have seen it, either. But was it off because of the light's timer, or because the call had ended?

I couldn't check.

Matt was right. I shouldn't be putting myself into dangerous situations. I didn't look for them, but sometimes they found me.

Even if he was sending help, I could be shot before—

The door from my kitchen into my backyard suddenly burst open, as did the nearby window.

"Police!" came the shout from several sources. "Put down your weapon."

"You damned—" Sheila raised the gun to aim it again at my chest.

"Put it down." The shout was closer now—from a guy all dressed up like the SWAT team members I'd seen on TV. He had an even more vicious-looking weapon trained on Sheila.

If glares could kill, the one she aimed at me would have done it.

Fortunately, they don't.

She put the gun down on the floor and raised her hands in the air.

Chapter 37

I still had questions. Lots of them.

One was how all the cops got into my gated community so easily—but they were cops, after all. And it seemed to me I'd once heard there was a special code that could be used by emergency vehicles.

It didn't matter now. They'd done it, and they'd rescued me.

More important for future safety in this area was how Sheila had gotten inside the fence, but I might never learn that.

Both Antonio and Matt appeared almost immediately. They must have followed the uniformed guys inside. I rushed up to Matt, and he took me into his arms. "You heard," I said roughly.

"I heard," he acknowledged, talking directly into my ear. "And did a three-way call with Antonio, so he could hear, too."

I pulled away a little. "Thank you both." I stooped next to give Zoey a hug. She'd tried to protect me and done a good job, but I was just relieved she hadn't been hurt, either. Then I rose again and asked Antonio, "Does Brooke know?"

He nodded. "I called her while I was on my way here. I just hung up after assuring her that I got here and you're okay."

I realized how late it was, but I was wide-awake. I assumed both these men were, too. "Would you like me to brew some coffee? I'd like to talk a little about what just happened."

But there were crime scene investigators all over my kitchen. Antonio recognized this, and said gently, "Probably not a good idea. In fact, I'll stay with you while you're questioned, and then I'd suggest that you and Zoey go stay with Matt for the rest of the night."

"Oh. Right." I'd been so glad to see these guys, and to watch Sheila being taken into custody, that my mind had tuned out how busy my small kitchen remained. "Besides, it'll be better to talk tomorrow." I leaned upward so I could whisper to Antonio, "You'll know more then and will have some answers."

The incisive-looking cop aimed a brief, lopsided grin at me. "And as long as you're discreet, I may even be able to share a few with you."

A woman dressed in a suit came up to us and was introduced as Detective Janvers, the detective in charge. She wanted to ask me a few questions.

At least Antonio was permitted to remain with me during the interrogation, which was conducted in my living room, since the kitchen was still being examined by crime scene techs.

I told all I knew. I was told nothing in return. But I wasn't surprised.

I'd gone through this before.

When I was finally allowed to leave, it was only after I'd agreed to accompany some investigators to HotRescues so they could take the boxes of HotPets Bling collars along to examine—since they had apparently left them for the crime scene techs to check out on site first and hadn't picked them up when they'd arrested Chris. We formed a small caravan on the way there, although Matt was sweet enough to drive Zoey and me. Not that I'd admit it, but I was a bit shaky.

I showed the cops into the office where I'd stored the crates. Because the stuff wasn't really mine, I did have them sign receipts.

I'd be interested to hear their analysis of which stones were real and which were manufactured. Which I hoped Antonio would tell me.

Brooke had stayed at HotRescues along with some guys from EverySecurity. Even though I yearned to perform my usual routine and go see the dogs and cats before I left, I was exhausted, and Brooke assured me they were all just fine.

Once more, Matt was there for me. He waited in the welcome room with Zoey. He had gotten all the way to his house before receiving my call, and he had left Rex there.

The three of us set off in Matt's car so Zoey and I could spend the rest of the night at his place. Matt promised to drive us back here in the morning.

And as pleasant as it was to spend another night with Matt, I was much too exhausted to do anything but sleep.

Matt let us sleep in a little, even though he had work to do, too. And, true to his word, he did drive Zoey and me to HotRescues before heading off to his own job.

The day was busy, which was both a good thing and a bad thing. First, I called Dante at his office and let him know what had happened—and why his assistant wouldn't be reporting to work today.

"Sheila?" His disbelief reverberated through the phone. "And after Chris, too? You've got to be kidding."

"I wish." But when I described what had happened at my home, his sigh was audible.

"You're okay, I take it." I assured him I was. "Well, at least something's good in this mess. You don't have any details about why?"

"No, but I'm hoping to hear from Antonio later." I promised to call him and tell him everything—or at least all that Antonio said I could—as soon as I heard.

I handled three adoptions that day, a couple of which were for our latest teacups. In my office, sitting in the conversation areas with each group, I pored over the applications of all of the potential adopters. They might have thought I was interrogating them about a crime they'd thought about committing rather than just wanting to take a sweet dog home with them.

I reminded them all of the parts of the contract they had to sign that allowed me to visit anytime, to make sure all was going well.

And then I let them take their new family members home with them, with one proviso: "You'll need to bring him"—or her, with one of them—"back in about a week. I owe you a HotPets Bling collar, but right now I'm out of them." I didn't explain why to any of them.

I suspected they'd wind up hearing something about it on the news eventually, though.

Between the adoptions, I roved the kennel area, mostly with Zoey keeping me company. The place was busy with people who'd come to check out our temporary residents, even though it was a Thursday, not a weekend.

I watched Bev accompanying three new volunteers around, instructing them: Marshall Droven, Janice Crift, and Sissy Silver.

Although we hadn't yet held an orientation for new volunteers, they were complying with my demands to start helping out here—in exchange for my not following up in some scary way for their having adopted some of the teacups under false pretenses.

I went over to say hello, and Bev met my eye and winked. I supposed all was going well.

Just to make sure, I told Marshall, "Why don't you go into Ruff's kennel, there, and show me how you'd work on socializing him."

"I'll do it," Janice said right away, and I recalled that she had seemed quite taken with the adorable bearded collie mix when she'd come here to "adopt" Sapphire. She still had Sapphire, which was fine with me, but I wondered if, under other circumstances, Ruff might have had a new home instead.

On the other hand, I wasn't worried. He hadn't been here long, and I was sure he would be adopted by the perfect family soon.

Zoey and I eventually headed back to the main building, where, in between visitors arriving, phone calls coming in, and everything else that occurred on this busy day, I brought Nina up to date on all that had happened yesterday.

Our busy day was soon at an end. And I hadn't yet heard from Antonio.

I retreated to my office to call him in private—and that's when my phone rang. It was him.

"If you're available in about an hour, let's all meet for a quick dinner—Brooke, Matt, you, and me. I'll fill you in on what's happened so far with Sheila. You might want to call your EverySecurity guys and tell them no one will be at HotRescues for an hour or so while we eat."

"Will do," I said.

With Sheila and Chris in custody, I doubted any more murders would occur at my shelter.

It was a warm late-summer evening, and we sat outside in a corner formed by the fencing around the patio in a family restaurant not far from HotRescues. Fortunately, they sold wine. They also provided water for Zoey, Rex, and Cheyenne.

After we ordered, I'd waited long enough. I looked at Antonio, who sat at my left side. "Tell us."

"This is all still a moving target," he cautioned. "And some of it's speculation. But I'll tell you what I know or suspect so far, as long as it goes no farther."

"I'd like to tell Dante," I cautioned.

"And he'll tell his Kendra," Antonio said in resignation. "Fine, but make sure he knows the two of them can't say anything to anyone else."

The glare from his stern brown eyes made me raise my brows and nod vehemently. "You got it."

Sheila had apparently started talking, at least some, even though she had lawyered up. It turned out that her boyfriend, Vince, the guy she had brought to one of our HotRescues parties, had—as I'd come to suspect—been involved in the heist in the downtown jewelry district that had made the news a few weeks ago.

The cops were on to him and his abettors. They couldn't easily get the gems to their fences. They were under observation and didn't even know who was undercover, watching them, so even mailing the stuff or sending it by a delivery company wouldn't work.

They'd promised to deliver the jewels fast and were getting desperate—until Sheila had come up with the idea of transporting them out of the area on the HotPets Bling collars.

She didn't live with Vince, and as far as the police could tell, she wasn't one of those under surveillance. She had visited the factory and seen how the false jewels were mounted. Realizing it would be too easy to lose the real jewels among them, she appealed to Chris Mandrea to create some other designs without telling him why.

She merely went to work, and sometimes to the factory, as she usually did. Even if she was being watched, she was just fulfilling her daily routine. No one apparently suspected anything out of the ordinary. No one stopped her. No one questioned her—not even when she got some of the workers at the factory to mount the real jewels into those designs—without, of course, alerting them to what they actually were doing.

In retrospect, it might have seemed obvious, but she got away with it. At first.

Chris figured it out, though. He demanded a cut, and Vince agreed. Not happily, of course.

When things really started going wrong was with the first trip to Las Vegas. It had seemed a godsend to them, a way to get the collars away subtly, without alerting anyone.

Only Teresa had gotten to Las Vegas early on the plane before the leg to L.A. She'd apparently overheard the people who were there to meet the Faylers' plane and sneak the real gem-encrusted collars away.

That was when she had started with the verbal jabs against the Faylers, who'd been innocent, and justifiably baffled.

Sheila had tried using tact to shut her up, to no avail. Teresa wanted money, and, now knowing who was really implicated, was ready to blackmail Sheila to get what she wanted. Sheila had to shut Teresa up or get in big trouble with Vince, who would have been sent to prison if he was caught for the original heist.

Tact hadn't worked. Neither had threats.

Murder, via the cyanide Vince provided, had.

Of course Chris, by then involved with the real jeweled collars, suspected what had happened.

In fact, one of the reasons Sheila wound up confessing was because she didn't want Chris to get off free for all he'd done by testifying against her.

She'd pay. She knew that. But she wanted him to, as well.

"That's it in a nutshell," Antonio finished. Our meals had been served, and my bacon cheeseburger now tasted even better than it would have before.

Brooke had ordered a salad. It looked good, too, but I'd decided to splurge. "You do get yourself into some interesting situations, Lauren," she said, taking a bite.

"Not by choice," I responded, meeting Matt's gaze. His expression looked amused, at least, and not angry. Which was right. I had kept him informed about what I was up to this time. In fact, I'd kept him so informed that he'd helped to save my life.

Our conversation remained on the bling and the murder and the arrests for a while, and then segued into a discussion about the teacup dogs.

And what had happened with the young conspirators who'd hoped to make a fortune from them.

"They're all handled now," I assured my friends. "And the dogs will find great new homes soon, I'm sure. The Hot-Pets Bling ads are continuing, and so, according to Dante, is the manufacture of the collars with faux jewels. The roll-out in Vegas will start in a week, and it'll be followed soon nationally. That means more people will want little dogs, even though other shelters are getting into the act and perhaps even having teacup-sized dogs brought here from other locations. I've already started contacting some of the shelters in Vegas to warn them."

We finished eventually. Brooke and Antonio said they were hurrying back to HotRescues for the night and would let EverySecurity know they were there.

Matt and I headed for his car, since he'd driven us here.

"You okay with going home?" he asked me.

"Sure. It's free of the crime scene guys and their stuff, and the memories of Sheila's confrontation are watered down a lot with all that's happened since." I looked up at him, straight into his gorgeous, sexy, toast-colored eyes. "Besides, I'm going to have some really special company tonight, aren't I?"

He grinned. "Count on it."

"Gutsy Lauren Vancouver easily wins over the hearts of
animals in need—as well as readers."
—Rebecca M. Hale, *New York Times* bestselling author

FROM
LINDA O. JOHNSTON

The More the Terrier

A PET RESCUE MYSTERY

When shelter manager Lauren Vancouver finds out that
her old mentor, Mamie Spelling, is an animal hoarder,
no one is more shocked, and she jumps in to help
rehome the cramped critters. But Mamie's troubles
don't end there. She's accused of murder when the
CEO of a pet shelter network is found dead. And Lauren's dogged determination to clear her former friend
of murder may put a killer on her tail.

PRAISE FOR THE PET RESCUE MYSTERIES

"Animal lovers will delight in a new series filled
with rescued dogs and cats needing loving homes.
Lauren Vancouver is a determined heroine."
—Leann Sweeney

facebook.com/TheCrimeSceneBooks
LindaOJohnston.com
penguin.com

M998T1011

The first book in a new series from

LINDA O. JOHNSTON

Beaglemania

A PET RESCUE MYSTERY

At a particularly nasty puppy mill, Lauren helps rescue four adorable beagle puppies that were dumped down a drainpipe, and she's pretty sure she knows who is responsible. Efram Kiley, one of the mill's employees, has a history of dog abuse. And it seems he has a bone to pick with Lauren, because he soon shows up at HotRescues and stirs up trouble by threatening her. When Efram is found dead at the shelter, Lauren becomes the prime suspect, and she'll have to sniff out the real killer to keep herself out of a cage—for life . . .

penguin.com

M898T0511